The Singular Passion

MATT MINOR

dead tree

"No Poets verses yet did ever move,
Whose Readers did not thinke he was in love."
- Ben Jonson

"The death of a beautiful woman,
is unquestionably the most poetical topic in the world."
- Poe

"Each of us is all the sums he has counted; subtract us into nakedness
and night again and you shall see begin in Crete four thousand years
ago the love that ended yesterday in Texas."
- Thomas Wolfe

*"The singular passion
Abides its object and consumes desire,
In the circling shadow of its appetite."*

- Allen Tate

One

All cities are provincial, no matter how big or small. No matter how worldly or removed, they are each isolated planets in the solar system of the infinite body politic.

The August sun, though ninety-three million miles away, felt like it was right overhead when John David Dothan returned to district after a tumultuous legislative session in Austin. He was homeless and alone and recently divorced from his pregnant wife, Tryphena. He had witnessed more ignorance than injustice and had endured great heartache as a victim to the folly of his own nature.

The ultraviolet rays of self-doubt were exacerbated by the seemingly endless highway construction that barricaded his destination. Through of a sea of mortar and rebar, bent and twisted like some perverse imitation of post-modern sculpture, his frustration mounted. He finally pulled into the Ft. Bryan Cultural District, parked, and exited his green '74 short-bed Ford pickup. Though his boots were firmly planted, he felt like a man without a country, or rather, a man without a planet.

The slim, graying representative, who still walked with the need of a cane some years after suffering a stroke, was coming to collect the keys to his new district office. He climbed the handicap incline to the sidewalk and hobbled hurriedly toward the desired real estate office. He buzzed and stood sweating as he awaited entry. The glass door clicked and he entered.

"Can I help you, sir?" a young lady in her twenties asked from behind a counter.

"Yes, I'm Representative Dothan. I've come to collect my keys. The State of Texas is leasing the office just across the street."

"Oh, yes, I was told you'd come by today." The young woman went to a large cabinet behind her, located the keys, turned, and placed them in Dothan's palm.

"Thank you," he said.

"Thank you, sir. It's been a few years since the building's been occupied."

"Yes, I am aware of that."

"So you know that some big-shot politician got shot in there?"

"I do."

"Really? Can you fill me in? Like everyone here is so hush-hush. I know the building was previously owned by some drug cartel folks…but that's it."

"I wouldn't know anything about that, but I am aware that some bad things have happened there in the past."

"All I know is our company purchased it not too long ago. Got the building pretty cheap, but it's a mess—needs a lot of work."

"It will do fine."

"What do you represent, Mr. Dothan?"

"This area…in the state legislature."

"What's that?"

"It's the lawmaking body of the State of Texas."

"Oh?"

"Yes, we meet every two years in Austin."

"You mean that old building in downtown, ATX? I've never been inside it. I go up to Austin to see friends, you know."

"No, I didn't know, but if you are referring to the Texas State Capitol, yes, that's where we meet."

"Kind of old, isn't it? Why don't they tear it down and build a new one?"

"That's a very good question."

"It's like down here. Everything's, like, a hundred-plus years old. I mean… Why? I don't like old things, by the way." She smiled.

"I've gathered that."

"You what?"

"Nothing. Look, it's been enlightening. Thank you for the keys. Before I go, what is your name?"

"Anne."

"Just…'Anne?'"

"Oh, you mean my last name? It's Spencer. Anne Spencer. I'm the admin here."

"It was very nice to meet you, Anne Spencer. You have a great day."

As Dothan made his way to the door, he noticed the local paper sitting on a table.

"Will anyone mind if I take this?" he asked, holding up the newspaper.

"Oh, I think it will be fine. It's Friday, and everyone's out. I don't read newspapers, anyway, and when we get back on Monday, it'll be old news."

"And we know how you feel about that."

"What?" Anne asked, confused.

"Nothing, thank you very much. Good day to you, Miss."

"Oh, wait!" Anne called out as Dothan was opening the front entry. He paused.

"What is it?" he asked.

"We're about to get the plumbing up and running in the loft upstairs from the offices. If you know anyone looking to rent a space for living purposes, let us know. I was told to tell that to everyone who comes in…"

"Well, Anne Spencer, let me check it out. I think I might just know someone."

"Great! Enjoy your paper!"

The Legislative Council was to arrange for installation of a computer and printer in Dothan's district office. He took a seat behind the large oak desk that had been left behind in the main office. He took a sip from a bottle of water and then unfolded the *Ft. Bryan County Courier*. A headline caught his eye…

Woman Reports an Alleged Stalker to Police

The article went on to describe how a woman named Kathrine Page had recently reported to officers that a man had repeatedly appeared nearly everywhere she went. This went on for days, then the alleged stalker eventually loitered outside her residence where she lives alone.

A spokesperson for the Fort Bryan City PD stated, "The department takes Ms. Page's report seriously and will provide her neighborhood with an added police presence."

Dothan flipped through the rest of the local paper, but nothing else juicy caught his eye, so he cast it aside. He also took note that Mitch Stevens, an old friend of his in the publishing business, had apparently purchased the rag. The Stevens Publishing moniker was stamped on the corner of the newsprint. *Hmm, I should give Mitch a call at some point,* he thought.

He stared at the stately wooden paneling that lined the spacious office. To stave off boredom, he got his phone out and called his headquarters in Austin.

Meredith, his admin at the Texas State Capitol answered. Her elation knocked him out of his malaise.

"Yes. Why are you so excited?"

"Well, I literally just got off the phone with the state cemetery, they've installed her grave marker!"

"Really?"

"Yes, it's there. I was just about to call you. I know how much it means to you."

"Do you?"

"Mason said some things. Maybe he shouldn't have?"

"It's fine, and it's about time. Rachael died last spring."

"Well, it's been installed, JD."

"Thank you for keeping on top of this, Meredith. I really am grateful."

"I know you are, JD. I know you are."

"By the way, when is Mason returning from his honeymoon?"

"Hang on, let me look at the calendar. Ah, the first week of September. Why? Do you need to talk to him?"

"No, not really—just wondering. Leave him alone. Let the man enjoy himself for once, if that's possible."

"Are you at your new office yet?"

"Yes, I'm sitting in the main office. Mason was right, it's perfect."

"Isn't that the same building where he shot his former boss?"

"It is, but we have the front offices. Halliburton Cranes' office was in the back."

"That's creepy. I still don't know why you went for it."

"Well, it's in the beating heart of the district. Besides, it's cheap, and it has nice furniture, so I don't have to use that crap House Property sent over. Oh, I've just found out… There may be living quarters upstairs."

"What? I don't understand."

"There's a loft upstairs that the real estate company says is for rent. I think I may take them up on it…for the time being."

"Short commute," Meredith joked.

"Very short."

After Dothan and Meredith ended their call, he decided to check out the loft. The hallway from the main office was some thirty yards, with offices on each side of its stretch. Through a pair of slated French doors lurked a narrow flight of stairs. He climbed them to a spacious loft that had all the accoutrements of a hip, downtown studio. He stepped into the bathroom and noticed that the toilet was empty of water and the sink faucet delivered nothing when turned on.

He started making plans.

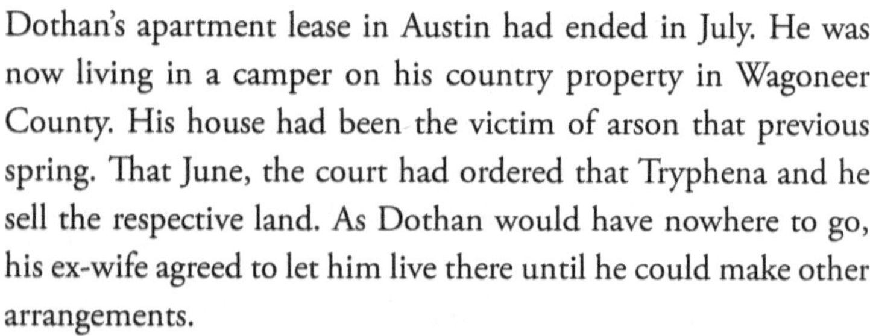

Dothan's apartment lease in Austin had ended in July. He was now living in a camper on his country property in Wagoneer County. His house had been the victim of arson that previous spring. That June, the court had ordered that Tryphena and he sell the respective land. As Dothan would have nowhere to go, his ex-wife agreed to let him live there until he could make other arrangements.

It was mid-afternoon the next day when Dothan made his way to Austin up Highway 71. He slipped The Cult's *Love* album into the CD player and listened repeatedly to the final track, "Black Angel." Over scorched earth, he pondered his past, present, and future. Somehow, they all co-mingled and bled into one another. *Was there ever a time my life was not a mess?* he wondered as he gazed out at the rolling landscape while pumping gas in La Grange. He concluded that women had been at the core of all his messes. *Maybe I need a break?* he mused. Yet he could not remember a time when women were not the core of his life. First, his mother, then numerous girlfriends, his first wife, Jessica Langhorne, and his second wife, Tryphena Taylor. Of all these women, one woman stood apart from all the others, though they'd never married. The one woman he had resigned to love forever—alive or dead—was Rachael Logan. She would always be The Rose of my Memory.

When he was back on the road, he made a pact with his heart, soul, blood, and flesh to just give it a rest. He philosophized as he navigated the highway. *Relationships are like the core of civilization—hunting and gathering or the cultivation of crops.* The former rendered one a nomad, with no time for the time necessary to cultivate the things that require leisure, particularly art. The latter did. Seeking companionship meant he was a slave to survival. He must learn to live alone, but time and again, he jittered recalcitrant. *Is it not love that has been the great inspiration for art?*

For John David Dothan, this pact would be difficult to honor.

Austin was the expected logjam, particularly I-35. Dothan exited the highway, drove up 7th Street, turned onto Navasota, and parked his car outside the venerable Texas State Cemetery gates. He wandered onto the grounds like a trespasser. The royalty of Texas had been laid to rest here (and those with the money to have themselves interned posthumously, title aside). As for Racheal, he had missed the burial due to the fact that it would cause too much scandal. This had hurt him deeply, but he knew it was the mature, responsible decision. He had yet to visit her grave.

He hobbled through the heat down a common sidewalk and came upon a sea of Confederate dead. In this instance, sentiment usurped guilt. He knew he would find it imperative to keep his pride close to the vest forever forward. He was not a racist, far from it. He had loved and married an African American woman, who would soon bear him a child. But the world had changed, and now knew nothing of the gray area of things. *We are living in world of absolutes,* he concluded. The remains under his feet had not only passed but were in the past, a criminal past: *Anachronisms all!* His affinity for the southern dead concurred with the reason for his visit.

He must find Rachael's grave.

Dothan could have flagged an attendant to help him locate her, but he was taking his time. Eventually, he found it. Her pink granite gravestone marked the ground under a sprawling oak. It matched the stone of the Texas State Capitol she so cherished. For Dothan, this spot was the capital of his heart. Its inscription was banal, as was the font, *obviously chosen by her husband*, he thought. It didn't matter. Below his feet lay the one thing left in the world he believed in. He thought of Heathcliff and Cathy. His eyes scrutinized the grounds for an available shovel, though none was to be seen. *NO*, he thought. How foolish she would find it, laughing from above. Musing on the fact that he had never believed in a God, perhaps until this instant, his thoughts found another literary reference, Graham Greene's Sarah and Maurice.

The longer he stood, the further the sun descended. His shirt and slacks were by now patched with sweat; his slow tears were in fierce competition with the stains that spotted his clothing. "Black Angel" repeated in his head again and again.

"Sir, I'm sorry to interrupt, but the cemetery will be closing in few minutes." A passing attendant interrupted the music in his ear.

"Thank you."

"Yes, sir." It seemed he recognized Dothan's tear-stained face. The man left as quickly as he had appeared.

"I'm almost done," Dothan called after him, getting himself together. He reached into his suit coat pocket and took out a red rose, its stem cut to the length of a pen. Though ready to open, it was ragged from travel. He placed it at the head of the stone where Rachael's name was etched. He bent over and kissed the ground that now consumed her. He stood, sighed, and started back.

Again, he took his time. He had been a man who had hurried his whole life—rushing to and fro, often never savoring the moment. His stroke, which had significantly affected the right side of his body, had curbed this to some degree. Today, it was cured altogether. Dothan knew he would remember this afternoon until his final breath.

The attendant was kind and respectful as he unlocked the front gate. Dothan simply flashed a humble smile coupled with a nod.

"Nice cane, Sir," the attendant commented as Dothan negotiated the cobblestone front lot.

"It's a sea monster, not a dragon!" Dothan snapped.

"Oh, I see," the man responded to the unexpected outburst.

Dothan turned the key and fired the engine. "Black Angel" immediately resumed. Dothan's thoughts were on Rachael, Tryphena, and even Jessica as he made his way back to district. Heavy sunlight gave way to heavy twilight. Soon, darkness enveloped the winding highway.

Behind the wheel, Dothan ruminated on the horror that love was not only a lost cause, but a strict impossibility.

Two

Anne Spencer was a pretty, amicable, generally nice person. She was a Generation Z clock watcher. The instant the hand of Father Time hit five p.m. she grabbed her things and exited the real estate office. She jumped into her Chevy truck and zoomed out of the Cultural District toward the gym. A green Ford pickup parked across the street followed behind.

The gym was only a few miles away. The twenty-year-old, part-time college student had changed her clothes before leaving work. Through his front windshield the bearded driver of the green pickup watched her eager, yoga-panted bottom as she bobbed into the fitness club.

The driver's cell phone rang from the passenger's seat. When he answered, he spoke softly in a thick, southern accent. "What is it? Uh-huh… Oh is he? Interesting, very interesting… Well, he's in trouble for sure… He can't think that sitting in the middle of things is gonna save him… Look I have to go; I'm in the middle of something… I'll catch up with you tomorrow… No, I'm being good, I promise… I'm signing documents…a heap of them… All right, bye-bye."

Anne Spencer was oblivious to the world as she worked out to the generic pop music blaring through her earbuds. Her thoughts were mainly concentrated on several young men but occasionally wandered to the paper she still had to write for school. She emerged an hour later, sweaty and relaxed. The driver in the green pickup knew the details of how to allot his time. He had studied her routine for weeks. He knew Anne's next destination by rote.

Anne bolted out of the gym parking lot and headed to the grocery store. The green pickup had preceded her by several minutes. He had parked a safe distance away, and when he saw her emerge from her truck, he followed her into the store, careful to remain unmemorable. A casual roll of thunder could be heard from the south as the doors automatically opened. His blue jeans, green golf shirt (which cradled a paunch), white tennis shoes, and black ball cap rendered him indistinctive from the sea of shopping suburbanites.

◆

Early that morning Dothan signed a lease on the loft above his new district office. He had loaded into the bed of his truck what little he still owned post-fire. It was the easiest move of his life. He plopped down on the king-sized mattress on the floor and stared up at the rotating ceiling fan. He scratched his newly grown beard, a look that he donned more out of laziness than style. He felt alone and wondered what Tryphena might be up to. September had arrived, and the sun was setting earlier with each night. In the twilight, rain pattered on the leaded windows encased in glazing. He decided to call Mason Dixon, his chief of staff.

"Hey man, you got a minute?"

"Always for you, JD, you're the boss."

"You can stop saying that at some point, you know."

"Whatcha got?"

"Well, I've moved into your old digs, is what."

"Seems to be a pattern of yours, doesn't it?"

"Shit, I guess you're right. First, I bought your country property, and now I'm leasing your old DO."

"I'm glad you took my advice. It's cheap as hell."

"Yeah, both the State of Texas and I are getting quite a good deal, let me tell ya."

"Let's hope no one sets this one alight."

"It's built like a fuckin' brick shithouse. I doubt anything but me could actually catch fire—just don't shoot me!"

"Ha, ha. Why would I wanna shoot you, JD?"

"Give it time, Mason, give it time."

"Naw, man, we're good. My former boss Haliburton Crane was a sociopath in business with the Gulf drug cartel. You're just a poet-legislator—no harm in that."

"Boy, that sounds anachronistic."

"That's a compliment, actually. It's not always so bad to be a remnant of the past. Remember W.B. Yeats? I know he's an idol of yours."

"Minus the fascism."

"We're all victims of circumstance, JD. All of us."

"Speaking of the past, I checked out the Confederate graves while visiting Racheal a few weeks ago."

"You know I'm a big Civil War buff."

"That's why I mentioned it."

"So, what about it?"

"Well, professor…"

"I was a high school history teacher. There are no letters after my name."

"You don't need them. The reason I mention it is I'm surprised they're still there."

"Oh, they won't be for long…along with everything else."

"You mean statues?"

"I mean history, JD. You can't have a cultural revolution without confiscating the existing culture. Hence, Mao."

"Yeah, maybe you're right. I guess we'll be left with nothing but dilapidated shopping malls."

"Dilapidated for sure…online shopping, JD."

"God, what am I doing?"

"What do you mean?"

"Just what the fuck am I doing with my life? Wasting my time fucking with bills and arguments associated with bills, lobbyists and PACs, corrupt politicians… I mean, what the fuck am I doing? I should be on a beach somewhere chillin' with a beautiful lady who loves me."

"Well, I taught history, not psychology, but, yes, you should be on a beach somewhere with a beautiful lady who loves you."

"But there isn't one."

"Have you talked to Tryphena lately?"

"No, not since she let me stay out on your old property until I could make other arrangements."

"So y'all are going to sell the place, I guess?"

"Looks like it."

"That's a shame, JD. Couldn't the two of you just cut it in half?"

"She ain't no country girl, Mason."

"I know. So, when's the due date?"

"In a few weeks."

"Damn, are you nervous?"

"What do you think?"

"Well, at least we know it's going to be a girl."

"Yep."

"You don't want to talk about it, do you?"

"Not really, the whole thing has me upside down."

"I imagine, and frankly, JD, it's bad political optics. A state rep divorced from his pregnant wife. Republicans could have a field day with that one."

"I don't care what they think. It wasn't my choice, so they can go fuck themselves."

"Tell me how you really feel, dude."

"So, what's going on this week? I haven't even checked the damned calendar."

"Let me look on my phone…looks like Meredith scheduled a meeting with you and the Mayor of Ft. Bryan City for… Shit! Tomorrow!"

"What? Why?"

"No notes on the entry, but I imagine just to stop by and say hi…for a welcome you to the neighborhood kind of thing."

"What time?"

"Ten a.m."

"I guess I can't get drunk tonight."

"Not a good idea in any case, JD. Isn't your condition acting up again?"

"Yeah, fuck me. I don't want to talk about it, Mason."

"You're the boss, JD. By the way, you haven't even asked me about my and Brenna's honeymoon."

"Ah, hell, dude. I'm sorry."

"It's okay. You've had a lot going on. We had a blast. Cabo was everything I expected and more."

"Well, good. I'm glad someone is enjoying himself."

"Now I'm back and ready to get to work. What about you?"

"Frankly, I don't know. Actually, I could use the money from the property. This independently wealthy thing ain't going as planned."

"Isn't there some firm or company you could score a gig with? Being a state rep is like having four PhDs."

"Probably, but then I would be a slave to their agenda. At this point, I have no idea where I'm at. I'm making it up as I go along." Dothan was thirsty, but he didn't have any beer. A day of moving had parched him and his isolation was eating at him. "Look, man, I need to hit the store."

"It's five o'clock somewhere, JD."

"Actually, it's after seven and I need to unwind."

"Do you at least have a TV set up?"

"Yeah, but nothing other than movies to watch until the satellite guy comes later in the week. I think I'll throw in *Solaris*. I hooked up my stereo today as well."

"Good job on the stereo. About the movie, you mean the one with Clooney and that dark-headed, tan gal?"

"She's olive-skinned not tan. That's the one. I haven't seen the original French version. It's based on a book by Stanisław Lem."

"I just know you prefer your women with a bit of tint."

"Yes, I do."

"Good film, if I recall…sci-fi."

"Yep, haven't seen it in a while. I picked it up at Half Price Books the other day."

"Well, enjoy."

"Thanks, Mason…"

"Oh, JD!" Mason blurted into the phone.

"Damn, dude, you almost burst my eardrum."

"Sorry, man. I almost forgot…"

"Forgot what?"

"Commissioner Cook…"

"Yes?"

"He's been indicted for his part in the water conspiracy over in Wagoneer."

"It took long enough. What about the others on the Wagoneer Water District Board?"

"Not sure. I think they're like the Nazis…they fled to South America."

"Or Costa Rica."

"Same difference in the end…for everyone who goes down, a dozen get away."

"I know. Well, I feel for Karl Cook, but he fucked up. He'll get what's coming to him."

"Or not."

"What do you mean?"

"Just something an old state trooper said to me after I shot your predecessor, Haliburton Crane."

"A cynical cop is almost a proverb. I guess he would know."

Anne had yet to remove her headphones. Music continued to blare into her ears. The man shook loose a shopping cart and trailed behind her. Occasionally, Anne would let slip a word or phrase from the song pounding in her head as she half-walked, half-danced her way through the aisles. Her stalker carefully tossed miscellaneous items into his cart. This went on for almost thirty minutes until Anne entered the checkout line.

The wine aisle was directly across from her line, and the stalker loitered, pretending to peruse the array of bottles. The checkout girl spoke, so Anne removed one of her earbuds. "Credit!" she shouted, then immediately reinserted the earbud. The stalker leered at her from underneath his sunglasses in a predacious fashion. Anne grabbed the receipt from the clerk and moved toward the exit, shaking her butt as she left the store.

The stalker saw her move to the door, then gently put the bottle he was holding into his cart and slithered into action. He turned abruptly and almost ran into another shopper. "Excuse me," he said, obviously irritated.

"No problem," the trespassing party replied, startled. For an instant the two men were face to face. "Hey, do I know you?" the shopper asked. Without replying, the stalker abandoned his cart and hurried toward the exit. It was raining, and Anne was not in the parking lot. It didn't matter because the man knew her address. Lucky for him, it was not a gated community.

The green pickup pulled casually into Anne's apartment complex near the deconstructed highway. The stalker stopped the engine and waited for nightfall.

When it became sufficiently dark, he removed a pair of leather gloves from the glovebox. As patient as a serpent waiting to devour an unsuspecting rodent, the driver methodically opened his door and exited his pickup. The recent rainstorm would ensure that few if any would be walking their dogs or lounging in the apartment courtyard. He had not checked the weather report, but somehow, he instinctively knew tonight was the night. White tennis shoes stepped casually from the pavement, over a curb, and onto a freshly cut green lawn. Blades of damp grass stuck to the treads. Moving with ease, the stalker walked confidently toward Anne's first-story balcony which faced the parking lot. The back porch light was not on. When he got close, he kneeled down and pretended to tie his shoes as he spied through the sliding glass door where Anne danced in and out of his vision. When she was out of sight, the stalker darted into motion. He checked his flanks with a quick one-hundred-eighty-degree glance, and slid one leg, then the other, over the banister. He stood upright on her patio.

Her figure strutted into view. She was singing and waving her arms. She grew bigger in the glass. Something was in her right hand.

The stalker swiftly pressed his back to the wall. His gloved palms were flush against the cheap siding. Anne grabbed a lighter from the small end table not more than two feet from where he stood. With a flick, she lit a small pipe and began puffing. The exhaled smoke bounced off the glass. He knew that once she was high, sleep would soon follow.

Patience…

The stalker was gambling. Through several weeks of observation, both morning and night, he had identified a particular habit: Anne was vigilant when locking her front door, but not so much with the patio entry. Instinct told him that tonight was the night.

He waited for the lights to go out.

The sliding glass door pulled open with ease…

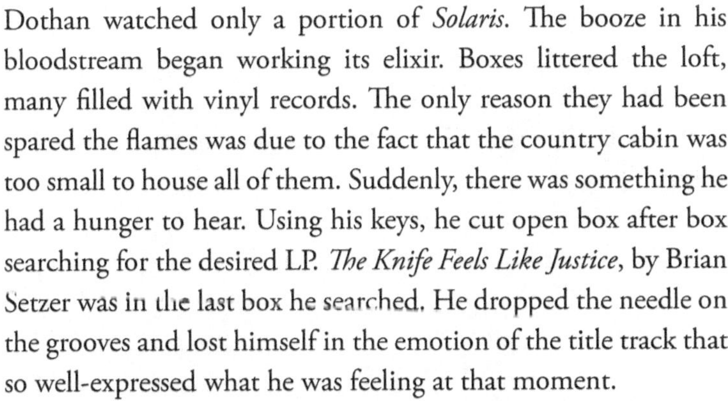

Dothan watched only a portion of *Solaris*. The booze in his bloodstream began working its elixir. Boxes littered the loft, many filled with vinyl records. The only reason they had been spared the flames was due to the fact that the country cabin was too small to house all of them. Suddenly, there was something he had a hunger to hear. Using his keys, he cut open box after box searching for the desired LP. *The Knife Feels Like Justice*, by Brian Setzer was in the last box he searched. He dropped the needle on the grooves and lost himself in the emotion of the title track that so well-expressed what he was feeling at that moment.

The song would prove a companion going forward.

Three

en a.m. arrived too soon for Dothan. He had barely showered and was dressing when the table bell in the office downstairs rang. *I must remember to lock the front door,* he thought as he combed his wet hair straight back and hopped awkwardly into a pair of jeans. Tucking his beige, Alarm T-shirt in, he limped the hallway that led to the front office.

"Anybody here?" a voice asked through the door. Dothan recognized the tall, slightly pudgy, dark-haired man from his profile on the city website.

"Right here, sir. Mayor Adams, I presume?"

"Call me Andy, Representative Dothan. Just gettin' goin' today, huh?"

"Call me JD…and yes, sir, it would appear that way."

"Never been an early riser myself, JD."

Dothan led the full-suited mayor to his personal office just off the entry of the hallway.

"Take a seat May—Andy."

"Don't mind if I do. Damn, it's hot, JD. Let's hope fall gets here soon." The mayor took a seat in front of Dothan's desk. Dothan seated himself behind it. "This is some office you got here, JD."

"Yeah, it belonged to a fella that ran an oil and gas company out of here for years. He's retired now."

"Well, this place has quite a history around these parts. In fact, the man that preceded you was shot, I believe, in this very office."

"No, that was in one of the office's down the hall."

"Is that right? What would possess one to rent out a place after all that?"

"My previous district office was in a strip center not too far from here. The commercial real estate company sold the building and the buyers didn't renew the lease. My chief of staff was the guy who shot my predecessor. He suggested this place…thought it might come at a good price. He was right. In fact, I'm presently renting the upstairs loft."

"Your chief of staff shot your predecessor? Hmm... You were living next door in Wagoneer County, as I recall."

"You recall correct, Andy. Place burned to the ground last spring."

"You're just a mess of drama, JD!" Mayor Andy laughed.

"You can say that again, Andy."

"Well, JD, I didn't come by to rehash the past. The reason I'm here is to say hello. As I'm sure you know, I was elected last May, while you were in Austin. We haven't had a chance to meet."

"I appreciate that, Andy. That's very kind of you."

An odd silence came between the two. Mayor Andy and JD were mutually uncomfortable. The mayor looked around the office. "You got quite a few books on that shelf, JD."

"Yes, I'm an avid reader, particularly of literature."

"Literature…where did you go to school?"

"Southwest."

"What's your degree in, if you don't mind me asking?"

"Not at all. I have no degree. I left to pursue a music career."

"Music? Well, that's different."

"Yes, it is. Unorthodox, to say the least."

"Well, I'm unorthodox, too, JD. Believe it or not, I studied acting."

"No shit!" Dothan let slip. "Excuse my language, Andy."

"'No shit' is right, and it's cool, JD," Andy jovially replied. "Pissed my dad off to no end. He said I wouldn't add up to a hill of beans."

"Well, I suppose he was wrong on that end. No disrespect to him, of course."

"None taken…none at all."

Given this mutual brotherhood, the two politicians relaxed. Dothan was about to offer Mayor Andy a beer, but it struck him that it was still morning. Then he figured he'd ask anyway.

"Say, I know it's early, but would you like a beer?"

"Sure. Why the hell not, JD?"

Dothan excused himself to the kitchen and returned with two cold brews. "So, tell me, Andy, out of curiosity, who's your favorite actor?" He handed the mayor a beer and returned to his prior position behind the desk.

"Ya know…I'd have to say Humphrey Bogart. Yours?"

"I'd have to say Steve McQueen."

"Good choice. To Bogart and McQueen!" Andy declared, raising his beer in a toast. Dothan reciprocated.

"Got an actress in mind?" Andy asked.

"That's a hard one…"

"I know! I go back and forth between Elizabeth Taylor and Eve Marie Saint."

"Hard to top either… You've got quite the taste, there, Andy. Let's see…how about Jane Seymour?"

"Interesting choice, and not expected."

"*Somewhere in Time* is one of my favorite films, actually."

"I saw it. It's a bit soft for me, personally, but one of my ex-wives probably loves it."

"Natascha McElhone!" Dothan declared.

"Who?"

"She's the woman in *Solaris*. Beautiful! She's a dark-haired, dark-eyed beauty with olive skin. She's kind of the classic damsel in distress-femme fatale from old-school film noir but in a modern sense."

"Well, I'll have to check her out. My hobby these days is actually politics."

"Really? Never had an eye for that…my politics has always sucked."

"It's all about the twisting of words."

"Right, but I prefer honest words."

"As evidenced from all these damn books!" Andy chided.

The conversation was going well. Still, Dothan felt an undercurrent of unfinished business. He felt comfortable enough to just ask.

"So, tell me, Andy, what's on your mind? You didn't just stop by to say hello, did you?"

"Not entirely, JD."

"So, what is it?"

The mayor leaned forward in his chair and asked, "What can we do about all this highway construction?"

"Honestly? Pray that it's completed as soon as possible."

"Nothing against prayer, but that's all? It's too much, and you can't get anywhere!"

"I'm not going to argue with you about that. Look, I think the highway department bit off more than it can chew; it's an unmitigated disaster."

"You can say that again."

"I will. It's an unmitigated disaster! But the reality is, it's already underway, and the best we can hope for is that it's completed as soon as possible."

"Hmm…" Mayor Andy grunted and fell back into his seat.

"I know, it's frustrating."

"Well, JD, I hope you can find an answer. The constituents are getting hot."

"I understand, sir."

Dothan rose, took Mayor Andy's empty bottle, and discarded it along with his in the office trashcan. Then he took him on a tour of the building. He followed the mayor out into the bright day where they chatted about old movies until the heat dictated that the two part. JD took a moment to observe the sun and shadows coming off the century-old buildings that surrounded him before going back in.

JD's afternoon was open, and the weary representative thought he might spend the rest of his day snooping bookshops in Houston—what few availed themselves—but as he searched for his wallet up in the loft, he heard the table bell chime once again.

"Anyone here?" It was a voice he recognized.

"Mitch?" Dothan called as he struggled quickly down the stairs. He was beginning to reevaluate his choice of lodging.

"JD?" The voice echoed.

"Well, hell, Mitch, it *is* you!" Dothan announced with tempered excitement.

Dothan made it down the stairs and welcomed the blonde, athletic looking man into his side office. "To tell you the truth, Mitch, I've begun to reconsider my living arrangements. I mean,

I'm just up the stairs in the back…"

"That's the equivalent of having a mattress at the capitol, JD. I'm sorry I just popped in unannounced."

The two shook hands and took their respective chairs. "To tell you the truth, if it was anyone but you, I'd of hid."

"Nice office, by the way."

"Thanks. So, yesterday I saw you've bought the local paper."

"Yes, I did," Mitch said. "Sealed the deal about a month ago. It was failing, and I got it for a good price. I figure I'll make a go at it."

"Kind of like this place here—I also got it for next to nothing."

"No surprise, given its history."

"So, what's up, Mitch?"

"Just out and about and I thought I'd see how you're doing."

"Not well, to tell you the truth."

"I understand."

"So, I guess you've heard that my wife and I are divorced?"

"Of course. It's quite the talk, actually. I have to hand it to you, JD…you know how to stay in the headlines. Trouble seems to find you."

"I'm certainly not trying to be found."

"How are you holding up, with your wife gone and you about to be an estranged father?"

"Damn, that's quite a way to put it, Mitch. This ain't some impromptu interview, is it?"

"Of course not, JD. I'm not trying to be insensitive. I'm sure the whole thing sucks."

"You can say that again. That was not my decision, if that has any significance in the scheme of things."

"Of course it does…for fair-minded people, at least."

"What do you mean by that?"

"Look, JD. I came by today because I wanted to give you a heads up and a few words of advice."

"Oh?" Dothan adjusted himself defensively in his chair.

"Yes. I strongly suspect that your seat in the House is in serious jeopardy."

"How do you mean?"

"Frankly, you've made a lot of enemies—for all the right reasons, no doubt—but in my experience, no good deed goes unpunished."

"I'm listening."

"I'm telling you this because I like you and respect the work you've done as an elected official…"

"You don't have to preface it, Mitch, just tell me what the fuck you're thinking."

"I'm not finished with my preface. By the way, I'm violating every journalistic principle I have by telling you what I'm about to tell you."

"Damn, Mitch. You're scaring me now."

"You should be scared."

"Of being picked off?"

"Yes."

"That's the reality of being an elected official, Mitch."

"Of course it is, but this is as bad as I've seen it in a long time."

"Can you elaborate?"

"Given what happened over in Wagoneer last spring, by busting the water district, you've alienated yourself from that county."

"It won't help that I'm living in Ft. Bryan now?"

"No, it won't. And your divorce will only fuel the alienation further, both in Wagoneer and over here. It just looks bad, JD."

"So I've heard."

"What?"

"Nothing, please continue."

"Not only are the elected officials next door out for your hide, but I believe they are in Ft. Bryan, as well. In fact, I've heard from reliable sources that the bulk of the Ft. Bryan City Council is actively trying to recruit someone to run against you."

"Funny you say that, because Mayor Andy Adams preceded your visit today."

"Really? What did he want?"

"Just to say hi…and to bitch about the highway department."

"Don't trust him, JD."

"We got along well, I think. Not a bad guy…"

"Be careful, I'm serious."

"Actually, we hardly discussed the issues. Mainly, we talked about films."

"Yeah, that guy sends the paper reviews of films made before we were born."

"Are they any good?"

"Are you kidding me?"

"I guess not."

Mitch asked where the bathroom was then excused himself. Sitting alone in the vacuum of his office, a tremendous unease overtook Dothan. The weight of isolation, a feeling he had always known but had labored his whole life to keep at bay, seemed heavier with each breath. Mitch returned from the bathroom but remained in the doorway.

"Before I go, JD, the real reason I came by was to tell you something you don't want to hear."

"Well, hell, Mitch. If you're going to do it again at least take a fuckin' seat!"

Mitch obliged. "I think you need to think really hard about changing parties," he said.

"What? You mean run as a Republican?"

"Yes, absolutely."

"Why?"

"Because I think it's a smart move."

"I have to disagree, Mitch. First of all, you know how loyalist the two parties are. No one would buy it. Although I have to confess, I understand your inclination. I'm the only blue motherfucker in a sea of blood red. My former father-in-law had a problem with it from the beginning."

"You're not really a Democrat, are you? You're not a progressive socialist. That's what they've become, by the way. Jesus, not only are they going for statues, but now they want to change the name of the capital city from 'Austin!'"

"You have a point. I'm not into the whole cultural-revolution thing, but I'm not a Republican, either. Frankly, I feel like a goddamned remote planet unto itself at this point. I mean, whatever happened to being a statesman?"

"I think a lot of people are starting to feel that way, JD."

"And what about a primary opponent? You know there will be someone running as a Republican. As a Democrat I'm safe, I think."

"So defect now. Beat everyone to the punch. It'll show your sincerity."

Dothan hung his head and began shaking it in confusion and consternation. His drying, straggly long hair curled like wacky snakes from his scalp. After a moment, he rose and looked Mitch sternly in the eyes.

"You know what they did to Rachael Logan, those…those fucking Republicans? She was their greatest advocate and they destroyed her. I believe all of that is what killed her, Mitch."

"She died of Lupus, JD, plain and simple. But I can understand your anger. Too often the Republican party can be its own worst enemy. They're harder on their own than on the actual opposition—cannibals, to tell you the truth. I fear you'll lose if you run as a Democrat, though."

"I think I have a better chance running blue. I think we have the wind to our backs."

"I've told you what I think, JD. You need to re-cultivate your constituency. If there is a blue legislative wave, you might lose just because you don't fire that base."

"Could I ever fire a Republican base?"

Mitch could only shrug in response. Dothan stared at the stained-wood paneling that comprised the four walls. The perfect geometric patterns belied his sense of inner chaos. "On a lighter note…"

"Sure, JD. I didn't mean to throw your day, man."

"It's all right, Mitch."

"So, on a lighter note?" Mitch asked, sensing the situation was untenable.

"I'm publishing a book of poems in the next few months."

"Poetry? That won't win over any constituents, JD. I'm not trying to be cruel, just honest."

"I don't care about that. That's not why I'm doing it."

"I'll tell you what. When it comes out, get me a copy and I'll give you a review."

"It should be out in the next couple of months—before the end of the year."

"I'm looking forward to it. Knowing you, it will be really good. Oh, before I go, there's a leak in your bathroom. Water's coming down the wall."

"Great!"

Mitch Stevens shook Dothan's hand and left. The beleaguered poet-legislator was left to ponder alone. He felt as if the poles of his life were wobbling out of control, and that at any moment, he would be hurled out of orbit. At his core, he knew Mitch was right. The proverbial wolves that he had managed to keep at bay smelled the blood of his misfortunes.

He rose to inspect the leak coming from the upstairs bathroom.

◇

The impetuous sun roared down upon Dothan as he made his way across the baking street and down the sidewalk. A cool waft of air slapped him in the face as he entered the real estate office. The front desk was empty.

"Can I help you, sir?" A tall, distinguished woman made her way from the back office.

"Yes, my name is Dothan, I rent the spaces across the street," he said, pointing over his shoulder.

"I know who you are," she replied coldly.

"Yeah, well, I just wanted to let y'all know that I have a leak in my upstairs bathroom, and it's coming down the wall into the downstairs bathroom."

"Okay, we'll send someone to look at it this afternoon."

Dothan turned to leave then paused. "Is Anne not in today?" he asked, noting her absence from the front desk.

"She didn't come into work today; didn't even call." The woman turned and walked away, shaking her bushy head as she made her way down the long hallway. "These young people today…"

Four

"Today is the day," Dothan said to himself when he rose around nine a.m. The mid-September light through the loft's leaded glass widows washed out the room and left it stale. He had plans to meet Tryphena mid-afternoon in Austin. She had recently relocated there after landing a job with a lobby firm. He languidly got his act together then got on the road.

He was to meet his ex-wife at a hipster taco establishment called Fresca's on 1st Street. The traffic in Austin was uncharacteristically negotiable, but parking was an issue. Pride had kept Dothan from applying for a handicap tag, and as he was debating whether he should pay the hijacker valet or park across the street at his own risk, a spot opened up.

Dothan struggled through the sea of young patrons with the aid of his cane. In district, he was beginning to think the sea creature grip was too much. If he knew anything about conservatives and Republicans, it was that they were born squares and devoted to convention. Was his eccentric cane too dynamic for them? Here in Austin, he fit right in—another non-conformist conforming to non-conformity. The humor of the whole thing inspired an ironic smile as he approached the woman bearing the sole heir of his DNA. She was so consumed with her laptop she had yet to notice his arrival. Even with her vibrant purple dress, she looked as if she would pop any minute. "Hi," Dothan greeted.

"Well, hello, John David. Take a seat. You're late."

"Parking was an issue. What are you reading?"

"Oh, nothing, just Texas politics. You look like shit."

"Thank you, you look incredible. Pregnancy agrees with you."

"Yuck. I know I look awful, too. I feel like a blimp. I'm ready for this to be over."

"The due date is about a week away?"

"It can't get here soon enough."

"Well, I think you look lovely…as always."

"Thank you, John David. I didn't mean to be cruel. You just look so gaunt…and those circles under your eyes. You need to dye your hair. The gray suit looks nice, though."

"So, what's up?" Dothan asked hesitantly, his palms clenching the grip of his cane. "What couldn't be conferred through a phone call?"

"I wanted to see you. Aren't you glad to see me, too?"

"You know the answer to that."

"Before I go into why I asked you here, my God, what's going on in Ft. Bryan?"

"What do you mean?"

"I mean the murdered young woman found just a stone's throw from your new district office!"

"How do you know about that?"

"I still read the local paper, John David. Believe it or not, I still care about your district."

"I thought you hated it."

"That's not why I left."

"Then why did you leave?"

"Do we have to go into this again? I'm trying to have a good lunch with you."

"Speaking of that, does anyone actually work here?" Dothan asked, looking around. He began scouring the menu for something edible.

"You know how these hipster places work. It takes forever."

"Right, they're too cool to take your order. We should have gone to Conan's."

"I'm fat enough! I can't eat pizza, John David."

"Okay."

Tryphena took a deep breath and touched her belly with both hands. "Back to what I was asking…"

"The murdered girl?"

"Yes, that's insane!"

"I'm not going to argue that one. I talked to Mitch Stevens about that the other day."

"You mean the paper guy?"

"Yeah, he owns the local paper now. He said that the whole thing is being handled poorly by the local police."

"How so?"

"They're just not releasing any information. They still haven't disclosed what exactly happened—how she was killed, I mean. Mitch said he interviewed an apartment maintenance guy who told him there was fucking blood everywhere. Of course the maintenance guy didn't see the body, so…"

"Oh, my God! Why isn't Mitch reporting that?"

"I imagine he's trying to be responsible and not freak everyone out."

"I can see that, but what freaks me out is the calling card the killer left."

"You mean the feather?"

"Yes! What the fuck was that?"

"The cops haven't even revealed what kind of feather it is or what kind of bird it came from."

"Does Mitch think that's important?"

"He doesn't know, but it clearly demonstrates some sort of potential clue. You know, another woman reported a couple of weeks prior that she was being hard-core stalked."

"That's creepy, John David."

"Mitch has been trying to get an interview with her, but she's been unresponsive."

"She's afraid, John David!"

A young waitress laden with piercings and tattoos appeared. She took their orders with an air of contempt.

"Wow, I guess she's not looking for a tip," Dothan commented. "I guess she's too cool for that."

"The food's good, John David. That's why I come here."

"So, why am I here?"

"I was thinking about our little girl's name. I know we've discussed some options, but I had an idea."

"I'm listening."

"I know how much you loved your mother. I never had the chance to meet her, but I believe the best part of you was imparted from her—"

"By what I've told you."

"Yes, by what you've told me. So, I was thinking that we'd name her after your mother."

"*Delilah?*"

"Yes, Delilah, and you don't have to say it like that. My God, it's out of respect for your late mother."

"You're right, Tryphena. That's very kind and thoughtful of you. I have to say I'm really surprised, though."

"Why?"

"I just am. I never would have expected something like this. Okay, Delilah Dothan, it is. I just hope she doesn't get picked on by the other girls."

"Why would she be picked on?"

"It's a nineteenth century name, and, frankly, a bit Old South."

"I think it's beautiful, and I'm sure she'll be as lovely as her name."

"I'm certain she will be. Are we still sticking with Madeline for the middle name?"

"Yes."

"Delilah Madeline Dothan. Wow! With a name like that, she'd better be a senator, or the first woman on Mars."

"She will probably be both, John David," Tryphena replied with a giggle.

"That's the first time I've seen you smile, let alone laugh, in a long time."

"There hasn't been much to smile about lately," Tryphena retorted sadly.

This struck Dothan's heart, and the feelings he had tried to suppress were resurfacing. "It wasn't all so bad, was it?" he asked, half dreading the answer.

"Of course not. You were the first man I ever truly loved. A part of me thinks that you'll be the love of my life forever."

"Then why don't you come back to me? Let me raise our child at your side."

"John David, I know I will never be the love of *your* life, and that is unacceptable to me."

"She's dead, for Christ's sake! Can't you let that go?"

"Can you?"

The terse silence that overtook their table was a stark contrast to the raucous hipsters parading around them.

Dothan spoke first. "So have you talked to Mia lately?"

"Only once since I relocated to Austin. I know you blame her for me leaving you, John David."

"Can you blame me?"

"She helped me out when I was in a bad place."

"She also made it clear that she thinks I'm an asshole."

"She doesn't think you're an asshole, John David."

"No? What was it I heard her say to you when we were on the phone that time? 'Just hang up on that narcissist!'"

"I'm sorry about that, John David."

"What did you do? You fucking hung up!"

"Please, we're in a public place."

"Okay, but I want to give it a second chance, Tryphena. Despite what you might believe, I do love you."

Tryphena hung her head and began to tear up.

"What is it, baby? Please…"

Tryphena slowly raised her head, and Dothan saw her eyeliner was compromised. The pained look in her eyes betrayed the faux smile her soft face fought to portray. Dothan got the picture. "You always clam up when I need you to communicate the most. All right. I'm out of here!" He threw a fifty-dollar bill on the table and lifted himself from his seat with the aid of his cane. He faltered.

"Baby, please!" Tryphena pleaded. "Please, you don't have to go."

He got his balance and towered above her.

The waitress arrived with their food. "Here ya go," she said, placing the two plates on the table. "Will that be all?" she asked.

"Yes, that will be all, thank you." Dothan said. Then he turned and left.

Having lost her appetite, Tryphena gave the money to the startled waitress and asked for two to-go boxes. With the uneaten lunches in a knotted bag, the very pregnant Tryphena waddled out the same door her ex-husband had just hobbled through. She just made it to her car before breaking down in profuse sobs.

◇

Back in Ft. Bryan, another woman with child struggled through a troubled birth. Jane Sellers, an unwed, twenty-two-year-old meth addict with ties to a respected local family, had been found that morning by the constable. The man had come to evict her from her apartment for failure to pay rent. Now, she lay struggling for her life in Ft. Bryan County Hospital. Though her child would be born, due to her final wishes, Jane would not survive the night. No family or friends were present as she expired. Only a bearded man in a green Ford pickup paid her any notice. On this particular morning, he had forgone the hat. Instead, long, bushy black hair hung wildly about his shoulders, but was tempered by a black suit.

The man had been made aware of her circumstances through a mutual friend. Though the family had tried to keep the situation of their wayward daughter hush-hush, inevitably, people talk. For some weeks he had shadowed the woman, which was not hard. She rarely left her apartment. He had been present in the parking lot the morning the constable arrived to remove her. He followed from apartment parking lot to hospital parking lot. He loitered in his truck for some time as he waited for the constable to leave the hospital. It was nearing dark.

The man patted an odd bulge in his coat pocket, as if to assure himself of its presence. With concerned confidence, he approached the front desk of the ER.

"Ma'am, could you tell me where I might find Jane Sellers' room? I believe she was admitted some hours ago."

"May ask who you are, sir?" The preoccupied nurse at the desk inquired.

"My name is JD Dothan. John David."

"Mr. Dothan, I'm sorry to inform you, but Ms. Sellers has passed. She was in bad shape when they rushed her in, and she died giving birth. The child survived."

"Oh my God…" the man feigned with excessive charm.

"Yes, sir, I'm terribly sorry. It's a tragic situation, I have to say, and not something we deal with too often here in Ft. Bryan."

"This may sound odd, but have they transferred her to wherever one goes once they've passed?"

"That's not an odd question," the nurse replied. "People ask that frequently. No they haven't. We're still trying to negotiate arrangements. Unless you're family, I can't allow you in to see her, Mr. Dothan."

"Is there a window to the room that perhaps I could just look through to see her one last time? You see, I've known her since she was a young girl. I'm not supposed to tell you this, but I've come on behalf of the Sellers family."

"At this point, I don't see a problem with that, Mr. Dothan. Her room number is 425. That's the fourth floor and it's ICU. I'll call upstairs and let the staff know to let you through; please sign in."

The man took the elevator to the fourth floor. He wondered if his desires could be fulfilled; if his art could be realized. Again, his instincts were correct. Permission was granted and the ICU doors opened as if by black magic. The white hall where

Jane Sellers laid in state was as quiet as an unloved person's grave.

Room 425 was some twenty-five yards from the entrance. The germs of doubt infiltrated his mental designs again, but luck or dark providence was on his side. Room 425 appeared to his left. What appeared through the long, rectangular window was merely a ghost—nothing more than a relief on the bed covered by a white sheet. The doorknob turned, and the man entered. He pulled two latex gloves from a dispenser that hung on the wall and slipped them over his hands. He drew back the sheet to reveal a pale, naked, emaciated woman. He removed a mason jar from his pocket. The lid gave way under a measured clockwise motion. He methodically traced the image of a bird in stick figure with ashes. The figure began at her sternum, wove downward between her breasts, and ended just above her belly button. The horizontal wings were applied across her nipples. The man did not return the sheet. He left her uncovered to the waist.

His exit from the hospital was even more liquid than his entrance.

Hubris overtook him as the green Ford pulled onto the feeder road that straddled the interstate.

Delilah Madeline Dothan was born in Austin, Texas the evening of September 21, the last day of summer before the Autmn Equinox. She was a healthy eight pounds. Dothan had suppressed the anxiety of fatherhood until the instant he held his newborn daughter in his arms. Dothan stayed with Tryphena until she and Delilah were released from the hospital.

He would later come to regret traveling back to his district for several reasons.

Five

othan awoke to an apartment in disarray. Nearly a month had passed since his move, and he had yet to unpack the few belongings he had. The walls of the loft were barren, and the crooked mattress was still sitting non-congruent to the wall and flat on the floor. Unopened boxes sat in the corners. Only his toiletries and clothes were in any order.

A week had passed since he'd left Tryphena and Delilah. First guilt and then a stark depression overcame Dothan. Fatherhood had thrown him. He wasn't sure what to do. What he did know, however, was that he believed it imperative that he have a significant presence in his daughter's life. Due to the fact that Delilah was an infant, the divorce decree gave him visitation rights only. It also didn't help that the district judge was a political enemy. Politics aside, Dothan harbored hope that he and his ex-wife would at some point reconcile and remarry. This hope occupied most of his waking thoughts.

After washing up and dressing, Dothan made his way down to the district office. He unlocked the front door and got busy in his stately business quarters. He listened to phone messages, which consisted largely of constituent complaints, most particularly concerning highway construction. He struggled with indifference as his pencil jotted random comments on a yellow legal pad. *It's time to hire an assistant*, he mused. He still had the phone up to his ear when he heard the mammoth glass front door of the DO swing open. He listened… A message from an angry constituent was still buzzing in his ear, but nary the bell in the foyer. In his gut, he knew something was wrong. He carefully hung up on the voice still proselytizing from the receiver. He gingerly rose from his chair, grabbed his cane, which rested in the ninety-degree angle of the enormous desk that nearly surrounded him, and slowly maneuvered around the desk.

Dothan entered the foyer. Two men stood staring out the glass entry with their backs turned.

"Can I help you?" Dothan asked.

In the time it took for his greeting to travel to the ears of the recipients, Dothan knew he had trouble. Both men turned. One was dressed in a standard, cheap suit, and the other was a police officer.

"Ah, yes, sir. Hello," the suited one greeted him. "I'm Detective Alan Garza from the Ft. Bryan PD, and this is Lieutenant Jimmy Young. Are you Representative John David Dothan?"

"Name's right there on the door above the state seal," Dothan answered in a cavalier tone.

"May we speak with you, Representative?"

"Of course, gentlemen…my office," Dothan signaled the way, allowing the two men to precede him. Once seated, Dothan placed his cane against the desk's right angle.

"That's some cane you've got there, sir." The detective observed. The lieutenant sat quietly without expression.

"Thank you, it's a sea monster, not a dragon," No sooner had he uttered that truth than he regretted it. In fact, he regretted revealing the creature at all. In his experience, cops had no sense of aesthetics. "So, what's on your mind, gentlemen?"

"First of all, thank you for taking the time to visit with us off the cuff like this." Again, the detective spoke as the lieutenant sat stiff as a stone. His body language confirmed what was in Dothan's gut. Something was not right.

"Of course," Dothan's breathing heaved suddenly. He struggled to relax in his chair.

"Are you aware of the brutal murder that occurred at the Grove View apartment complex the first of September?"

"Uh, yes, I am. Awful."

"That's an understatement, Representative. It was insane, and methodical."

"Methodical, what do you mean?"

"This murder was premeditated. In fact, the evidence suggests it may be linked to several instances of stalking, both before and after the murder of Anne Sellers."

"Anne Spencer, Detective Garza," Lieutenant Young corrected. It was the first time he'd uttered a sound.

"Anne Spencer, excuse me," the detective confirmed with a degree of superior contempt toward his colleague.

"I believe I read about the stalking in the local paper some time back. If I recall correctly, it was reported that only one woman had made this accusation."

"You seem to be well-informed and with very good recall, Representative," Garza said.

Dothan was no dummy. The detective's statement let him know that he was in a mousetrap and had just made a significant lurch at the incriminating cheese. His brainpower kicked in.

"I'm an elected state official, and it's my business to be up to speed on occurrences in my district. I read several thousand bills each session, as well as a ton of books recreationally. I have a very good memory for the written word…sir."

"You don't need to get defensive, Representative Dothan. I'm merely stating what we have surmised, or rather are in the process of surmising, with regard to this investigation."

"So who was the other woman that reported being stalked?" Dothan demanded.

"Your tone is not necessary, sir." Garza responded. "The other woman is actually the reason we are here."

"Really?"

"In what fashion were you acquainted with a young woman named Jane Sellers?"

"I never heard of her in my life. You're speaking in the past tense, by the way, Detective."

"I am, Representative."

"Would you like to enlighten me?"

"Ms. Sellers died a tragic death on the morning of the fourteenth of this month while giving birth to a son who survived her."

"That's terrible. How the hell does that happen in this country?" he demanded.

"She was a drug addict, and, frankly, she's lucky she didn't die beforehand."

"But you knew that already, didn't you?" Lieutenant Young asked definitively.

"What? I told you I never met the poor woman!"

"Then why did you go to see her post-mortem at Ft. Bryan County Hospital early the evening of September 14th?" Young asked.

"What? Whoa. I don't know what the hell are you're talking about!" Dothan bellowed.

"I suggest you calm down, Representative." Young demanded.

"Calm down? No! You're in my office, by the way, bud. Interrogation concluded. Either arrest me, or get the hell out of here!"

"No one's arresting you, sir." Garza said. "Let's just calm down…everyone."

"So, I'm not a suspect?"

"A person of interest," Garza corrected.

"Well, I ain't interested. I never went to the hospital on the fourteenth. I'm certain I have an alibi. I'd like you two to please leave. Now!" They rose to exit. Dothan pulled a stack of unopened mail that sat to his left on the vast desk. He started sifting through it.

"Are you going to be going out of town anytime soon?" Detective Garza asked.

"Yes, I have a newborn child in Austin, and that's also where the State Capitol is—where I work!" Dothan answered without looking up.

"Any other travel plans?" Garza asked.

"No, but I wouldn't worry about me going to the capitol, that's probably got the highest concentration of law enforcement between here and D.C.," Dothan stated, looking Garza straight in the eyes.

"Good day, Representative," Garza said before turning back. "Oh, and one last question."

"What?" Dothan asked with muted hostility.

"You do drive a green Ford pickup, correct?"

"Yes, a '74 short bed. Beautiful," Dothan answered, returning his focus to the mail.

"Nice. I've always been a fan of the classic cars, myself."

"Wonderful."

Detective Garza and Lieutenant Young stepped out into the sunlight and returned to their unmarked black Ford Taurus.

Young drove while Garza sat starring out the window. The Taurus wove through a series of shaded streets filled with churches, schools, and residences.

"Why didn't you ask him back to the station like we discussed, sir?" Young asked.

"I was feeling him out."

"Feeling him out? I don't understand, the man signed in at the hospital. We've got it on video!"

"Yes, a video of someone from behind the whole time. The camera was to the right side of the front desk, yet we never got the view of his profile. Don't you think that's strange?"

"Yes, it is. Doesn't that answer it for you?"

"Answer what?"

"It looks like him doesn't it?"

"I'm not convinced."

"Not convinced?"

"Look, I'm not going to take a state official down to the station to be interrogated until I'm at least fifty-one percent sure he's guilty. Let's let him get us an alibi for the fourteenth. We'll go from there. I want to keep this investigation close to the vest as long as I can. The minute we move in on Dothan, the Texas Rangers will get involved."

"What about the truck?"

"What about it?"

"It's green and it's a Ford!"

"We have nothing but that. Remember, that fella that gave us a statement about witnessing an alien-green truck pulling out of the complex at the approximate time of the murder was stoned out of his freaking mind. So what if the killer drives a green Ford pickup? We have no year, and Dothan's truck stands out. It's not just green. Plus, it has SO plates."

"I'm not familiar with the acronym, sir."

"State official plates."

"The average citizen doesn't notice license plates."

"Apparently, neither does law enforcement."

"What does that mean?"

"It means nothing—most of all where Dothan is concerned."

"Why didn't you ask anything about the calling cards?"

"You mean the falcon feather and the ashes in the shape of a bird?"

"Yes, and the other calling card, the first one. What about matching signatures from the hospital?"

"I was feeling him out, Young. You obviously haven't learned patience."

"What if he strikes again?"

"If he's the killer, he won't for some time."

"How do you know this?"

"Our man may be verbose, but he's methodical. He's up to something. I suspect everything he's done, if the three instances are related, has been well plotted."

"I don't know. That guy Dothan is an asshole."

"Have you ever met an elected official who isn't?"

"No." Lieutenant Young parked the Taurus.

The two entered police headquarters.

The man in question sat in his living room drinking vodka straight up. Outside, the sun had just set. He toasted the air while listening to an album from his extensive record collection. "Kate, Anne, Jane! I loved you all, but you all failed me in your own ways!"

Instrumental music filled the dark room as he repeatedly refilled his cup. From his antique chair, he reached for his humidor that sat on a small rococo-style table to his right. He carefully lit a Connecticut wrap and puffed. Smoke coiled upward from the healthy cherry like parallel, turning time.

To know the insane mind, one would have to be insane as well. What demons lurk within the labyrinthine halls of a demented brain? What process plants them there? Is it nature or nurture?

Instrumental keyboards swirled as the madman picked up his phone and began scanning social media.

People give everything away on social media, he reflected. *In their desire to look important or live the glamorous life they always dreamed of, they reveal their secrets and insecurities. If social media reveals anything about human nature, it is that far too many spend their lives gazing at their reflections in the proverbial pool. The methodical and patient need only wait for the movement of a thumb.*

While he sifted through innumerable profiles, his phone rang. With his stereo remote control, he muted the spinning Rick Wakeman album that took him further and further back in time.

"What is it? Okay, well keep me abreast of the situation. I appreciate your diligence in this matter. Okay. Yes, sir, goodbye." The conversation was brief but telling.

The madman continued with his search. Something nagged at him, however. He had yet to hear from a certain someone since he unveiled the barbarity of his craft at the Grove View apartments. *She must know it was me.* The madman knew she would not tattle.

He was looking for a specific profile. *She must live nearby.* She must have recently moved to a rural area.

After Detective Garza and Lieutenant Young's departure, Dothan sat in his office, both perplexed and infuriated. The office phone rang. He did not answer. Instead, he repeatedly checked his cell to see if Tryphena had texted. She hadn't. He contemplated calling her to inform her of his recent visit—she was an attorney, after all—but he didn't. In truth, he craved her return so much that he reasoned if she knew of Garza and Young's incorrigible visit, it would only serve to push her further away. Then again, she was his alibi. Dothan could not remember the date they met in Austin for lunch precisely, but he knew it was near September 14. He scrolled through their text messages. He found his alibi.

Believing that he was absolved, his mind wandered and pondered. *Am I being set up?* He questioned. *Who would do such a thing?*

Garza seemed like an intelligible man; the Lieutenant, not so much. Dothan had recently left that proverbial Isle of Paranoia, the State Capitol, but he felt like a tugboat that had unwittingly dragged it back with him. He needed a drink. He checked the calendar. There were no meetings scheduled for later.

By mid-afternoon he was getting smashed. He had drained the beer from his fridge and needed more. Not wishing to drive, mainly because he suspected he would be tailed, he walked in the treeless heat several blocks to the store. For some reason, the bass line from The Clash's "The Magnificent Seven" pumped in his head.

Who to call? He questioned himself as he walked to the store. Traffic was starting to pick up, and he had difficulty getting across the main road that hugged the south entry of the Cultural District. A twelve-pack was too much to lug back with a cane in the other hand, so he opted for a sixer. On the journey back, the nagging question of what to do and who to call returned.

MASON!

Back at the DO, he didn't even bother with state business. He shut the office down and went upstairs to the loft. He needed the catharsis of music. The only song he hungered to hear was "Jail Guitar Doors" by The Clash. Dothan had thumbed past the puke-green cover of their first album (the American release) while searching for something else to listen to on a previous drunken music craving. He remembered the storage box.

"Gotcha!" he exclaimed when he located the album. Before he put it on, he called his chief of staff.

"Mason!"

"JD, what's up? You sound alarmed."

"Why didn't Meredith answer?"

"Uh, she's away at the hurricane preparedness briefing… like you instructed."

"That's today?"

"Yeah, man…what's up?"

"What are you doing this weekend?"

"I'm supposed to go with Brenna and Will to my mother-in-law's new timeshare in Canyon Lake."

"Oh," he muttered disappointedly.

"Why, what's up, JD?"

"Look, I hate to break you away from your wife and step-son, but I've got a situation, man."

"Can you expound?"

"No, but it's big-time fucked up."

"Okay, now I really want you to explain."

"Not over the phone, Mason."

"You sound paranoid, JD."

"If you can get out of the sojourn to the Hill Country I need you here—at least Friday night."

"Let me see what I can do, boss."

"I'll make it up to you, Mason, I promise. I will make it up to you."

Six

ason met Dothan Friday night at an art bar called BR Vino, just a stone's throw from the district office. Dothan arrived prior to his chief. He sat sipping a beer in solitude on the rear Bourbon Street-style patio. Pacing the sidewalk toward the bar Mason discovered a litter of kittens and an emaciated mamma cat slurping from a paper bowl. The sound of his boots on the loose gravel of the alleyway scattered the felines in spurious flight. He entered the long, slim, canvas-lined bar and headed toward the back.

"I just frightened a bunch of cats in the alleyway on my way in," Mason said. "They were sipping from a bowl. You wouldn't have anything to do with that, would you, JD?"

"Yeah, I've been feeding that mama and her litter the last few days. I think I might catch one and bring it to Tryphena as an overture."

"I see. What will you do with the rest of them?"

"Take them to the shelter, maybe. You know I can't stand to see animals suffer."

"Nor I, but you know what they say about herding cats…"

"I work in the state legislature, dude."

"Ha ha, I understand."

"You know Galveston died after I rescued him after the fire at our old house."

"What happened there?"

"He wandered into the wild and caught feline HIV. Tryphena had neglected updating his shots."

"So, she blames herself?"

"Yeah." Dothan changed the subject to the predicament that called for the summoning of his chief. "Look, I'm sorry that I took you away from your family, but I really needed to talk to you, Mason."

"It's cool, JD. I'm going to split after we're done and head back to ATX. I'll head up to Canyon Lake tomorrow morning. You don't mind if I straggle in late Monday do you?"

"Of course not. Hell, take the day off if you need to."

"To tell you the truth, I'm really interested in what the hell you have to tell me."

Beers flowed for a couple of hours, during which time Dothan relayed to Mason the encounter from earlier in the week, as well as everything else that was troubling him.

"Wow, is all I can say, JD. Fucking wow!" Mason sat back in his chair. "What the hell are you going to do now? If this gets out, you'll not only have to deal with a Republican in the general election…you'll have a Democrat challenger in the primary."

"Like I said earlier, I have my alibi."

"But you don't want to tell Tryphena?"

"You know how she is…she'll just judge me, and it will push her further away."

"Dude, if it's going to hold, she's gonna have to vouch for you, period."

"I know. It's fucked. I can go to the scaffold or lose my lady."

"If you go to the scaffold you'll lose your lady for sure."

"I know, but don't you see the sick irony in all of this?"

"I do, my friend. But you're just going to have to accept the fact that you're in a pickle."

"I fucking hate pickles."

"But you drink straight vinegar."

"Yeah, so?"

"Not to diminish your potential execution, but what really intrigues me is the mystery of it all. I mean, this is high-rent shit, JD. You've got a real sick motherfucker at work here, but I find this really interesting."

"That's because you're demented in a benign way. That's also why I called you and wanted to meet. It intrigues me, too."

"I have to say, you and I must have a magnet sticking out of our asses to attract the kind of shit we do."

"So, where do we start?" Dothan asked after killing the backwash of his beer.

"Well, the problem here is, we don't know what the cops know. If we did, we might—and I stress 'might'—have some kind of handle on this." Mason drank the last of his beer just as the waiter appeared.

"You want another one?" Dothan asked him.

"Naw, man, I'm good. I'm kind of tight on money right now, after the wedding and all."

"It's on me."

"If I were you, I'd hold on to my money at this point, JD."

Dothan asked the waitress for the check. "After I get this settled, let's head back to the DO."

"Have you got any alcohol?"

"You shittin' me?"

The night had set firmly in as the two made their brief journey back to the office. Dothan paused in the alleyway to examine the paper bowl. It was dry. He discarded it in one of the numerous trash cans that hugged the old brick buildings. "You know what's been on my mind since moving in here, Mason?" he asked as he made his way across unsteady gravel toward the sidewalk.

"Staying out of jail, the birth of Delilah, getting back with Tryphena, staying the fuck out of jail… I imagine a lot."

"You're right about all of that; however, I wonder why you never told me that BR Vino was next door to your old district office when you worked for Haliburton Crane."

"You mean when you, me, Brenna, and Tryphena came here during the last legislative session?"

"Correct."

"I didn't want to talk about it because of what happened to Brenna. She kind of blacked a lot of that out."

Dothan removed his keys to open the back door of his building when he spotted a young woman nervously pacing on the sidewalk near the cross street up ahead.

"What's up, dude, are we going in?" Mason asked.

"Who's that woman?"

"What woman?"

"She's pacing back and forth. Wait, there she is."

"Okay, what about her?"

"From here, she looks kind of hot." The woman stepped down from the sidewalk and opened the passenger door of her small red KIA. After rummaging through the console, her head reappeared and she vanished around the front of the building. "Let's go see what she's up to; what do you say?"

"JD, you've got too much on your plate at this point to be thinking about pussy."

"Never. Come on."

When the two men turned the corner, they found a young woman with dark hair, dressed in yoga pants and t-shirt. She leaned against the thick exterior of the DO, scribbling on a small piece of paper, which looked to be a receipt of some kind.

"Miss, can I help you with something?" Dothan asked as Mason hung back.

"What?" She turned, startled.

"Can I help you with something?"

"You're that representative, aren't you?"

"Name's right there on the door. Can I help you?"

"I don't know." It was obvious she was frazzled. Dothan, always a sucker for a damsel in distress, was smitten. "I know you're closed, sir…but I really need to talk to someone."

"Of course, please come in," Dothan approached the shimmering front doors and unlocked them. The woman stood still. Mason took the door from Dothan as he entered and began switching on the lights. "My name's Mason. I'm Representative Dothan's Chief of Staff, please come in. Your name is…?"

"Katherine Page," she replied. Her name sounded familiar to Dothan.

"Ms. Page, please…please come in. It's okay," Dothan said.

With her arms folded and her head down, Ms. Page quickly crossed the threshold past Mason, where he remained holding the door open.

"Thank you. Y'all are very kind," she muttered meekly.

Mason took a seat behind Dothan's vast desk as Dothan and Ms. Page sat down in the two chairs set before it.

"Wow, this is a nice office," she said. "A little messy…and a fireplace, too. Does it work?"

"To tell you the truth, I've no idea," Dothan replied. "I guess I'll find out if it ever cools off. What can I help you with Ms. Page?"

"Call me Kate, please, and thank you again for seeing me like this."

"No problem. Would you like something to drink? Water, wine?"

"A glass of wine would be wonderful, thank you."

Mason was dispatched to grab the bottle of merlot from the lower kitchen.

Dothan crossed his legs and tried looking relaxed. "So, what's troubling you?" he asked.

"As I said, my name is Katherine Page. I'm not sure if you read the papers, but I reported a stalking to the police about a month and a half ago."

"Of course, I knew I recognized your name. I read about it in the local paper."

"I wish they wouldn't have run that story. Now, I'm terrified."

Mason returned with the bottle of wine and sat behind Dothan's desk again. He began wrestling with the cork.

"Why are you terrified, Kate?" Dothan asked.

"I feel my life might be in danger."

"What? Why?" Dothan and Mason asked in unison.

"Because of the murder of that young woman, Anne Spencer."

"You think it may be the same man who stalked you?" Dothan asked, unfolding his legs and leaning toward Kate.

"Yes, I do. I do believe it was the same man."

"Have you told the police this?"

"They're idiots. Excuse me for saying that, but they are. They have no idea who they're dealing with."

"Who are they dealing with?" Mason asked as he poured Kate a glass of wine.

"A nut job of the highest order," she answered. She grasped the glass in both hands and gulped the wine.

"Whoa, slow down there, Kate. Obviously we're dealing with a crazed madman, if it is indeed the same guy," Dothan added.

"I'm sorry. I can't sleep; my stomach is always upset; I'm afraid to go out and about. I go to work and come home in fear."

"Why don't you tell me what your stalker looks like? Let's start there," Dothan said.

Kate wiped the purple stain from her lips with her wrist. "Well, he looks a lot like you, actually," she began.

"Why does that not surprise me?" Dothan opined, looking at Mason.

"What do you mean?" Kate asked innocently.

"Nothing. Continue, please."

"Well, he looks a lot like you, but now that I see you in person, not really."

"What do you mean 'not really?'"

"He had a beard—like you—and long black hair, but there wasn't as much gray in it, and he wasn't as thin as you are. I wouldn't say he was chubby, but healthy."

"I see. What else?"

"At first, I didn't think much of it. I just thought it was a coincidence. I'd run into him at the store or the gas station. Then, one night, he was at a bar not far from here. I acknowledged him and he just kind of ignored me. At the time, I thought maybe he thought I was hitting on him. Then…" Kate took another large gulp of her merlot.

"Then what?" Dothan pleaded.

"I went jogging one night around my neighborhood. I didn't know it was that man, but I remember passing a man, from behind, on my way back. I was jogging and had head-phones on. I really didn't notice him as I went around him on the sidewalk. I thought it rude that he just kept in the middle and didn't let me by. I looked back with a bit of disgust, and even though he was wearing a ball cap, I recognized him. I tried to keep my cool, but I hauled ass back to my house. I rushed inside and immediately started peeking out of the front windows. After about fifteen minutes of doing this, I relaxed a bit and started making my dinner. After I ate, I looked out again, and there he was…standing there!"

"Jesus, did you call the police?"

"Yes! But he was gone. The weird thing is what he left on my doorstep."

"What was it?" Mason asked.

Kate picked up her small purse that was resting in her lap and removed an odd-looking fruit along with a dead, dried flower. The stem was cut to the size of a ballpoint pen.

"What the hell is this?" Dothan asked as she placed the two items in his hand.

"A pomegranate and a rose."

"A what?" Mason asked, confused.

"A pomegranate and a rose?" Dothan asked. He held the two wrinkled articles up so Mason could see them clearly.

"What did the police say about this?" Mason asked.

"Nothing, really. In fact, one of the cops thought the man was a disgruntled ex or something…like it was my fault!"

"Something like what Representative Dothan is holding in his hands is obviously way over their heads," Mason said.

"I have a question, Kate," Dothan said.

"I have a lot of questions, Representative."

"We all do, but if I looked like this man, why were you inclined to come seek me out?"

"First of all, I didn't know what you looked like, or even who or what you are. I don't know anything about politics. I didn't even know what a state representative was, but a friend of mine told me you helped with an issue she had and that you were someone who seemed honest and trustworthy."

Dothan smiled at Mason, knowing that it was Mason who most likely handled her friend's constituent issue himself. "She told me that when no one else in government could or would help her, you did."

"Well, tell your friend I appreciate her confidence. However, just to clarify, it was Mason here who most likely aided her in whatever situation or issue she had."

Mason smiled sarcastically at his boss.

"Please, let me continue," Kate interjected impatiently.

"Yes, please," Dothan said.

"Representative Dothan, my friend told me to find your contact info. When I looked you up on the Texas Legislature website, in your picture, you don't have a beard like you do now." Kate polished off her wine and set the glass on the table. Mason refilled it. Kate took another drink and looked right at Dothan. "Frankly, sir, I thought you were really good looking. I think you should shave the beard. Just saying," Kate looked away, grabbed the wine glass, and took two large gulps. Blushing, Dothan turned to Mason, who was obviously amused.

"Thank you for that compliment, Kate."

"No problem," she said, her eyes still turned away.

"Do you have a gun?" Dothan asked.

"A gun? No."

"I see. Have you ever handled a gun?"

"Never."

"That's unfortunate. It's my belief that all women should be proficient with, and carry, a handgun. In fact, that should be a bill," he declared, addressing Mason.

"You file something like that, and you'll definitely have to change parties, JD," Mason countered.

"I'll tell you what. Short of giving you a security detail, what I can offer you, Kate, is this office. If you feel threatened in anyway, just come here. I actually live here, upstairs. So someone is usually around. I'll give you my cell phone number. If I'm out, just call me. If I'm in Austin or wherever, I'll put in a call to the police on your behalf. How does that sound?"

Kate seemed to appreciate the offer. She finished off her wine and let JD escort her out to her car. Mason remained in the office. Her departure took some time.

"So, did you kiss her goodnight, JD?" Mason asked when Dothan returned.

"Fuck you. Is that what you think that was?"

"Uh…yeah."

"Well it wasn't. She is pretty, though."

"If she were ugly, would you have offered your office, house, and personal number?"

"Of course."

"Whatever, dude. Sit down. I will tell you this, JD, dating a girl who is involved in a murder investigation that you may or may not be a suspect in… That ain't smart."

"I know. I'm just so eaten up with loneliness. It's contrary to my nature. It's eating at me like a tumor."

"I know it is, but you need to lay low, at least until the candidate sign-up deadline."

"When is that, exactly?"

"December 10th, dumbass,"

"Lord, that's suspenseful, to say the least."

"So, back to our murder mystery, what do you think of all this?"

"What do you think?"

"The pomegranate and rose was a calling card…and what about that feather? I'd be interested to know what kind of feather it was. There's a pattern here, JD."

"Do you think that might predict where he strikes next?"

"I would think so. Here's what's wacky: if it's the same guy, which appears to be the case, why did he just stalk Kate but kill the other woman?"

"What about the poor pregnant girl who died?"

"I'm willing to bet he left something with her body…a clue as to what he's doing."

"You're probably right, but regarding our recently departed damsel in distress, how is it we always get these kinds of constituent cases? I mean, do I have 'Oskar Schindler' printed on the door, or what?"

"That's politically incorrect, JD."

"I know, you're right, Mason."

"By the way, this office is a mess. I mean, look at this place."

"I know it is. I need to hire an assistant."

"Yes, you do."

CODA – Act I

Dothan spent the fall trying desperately to court Tryphena. Every attempt failed. His visits with her and his newborn daughter left him increasingly with the notion of absolute dislocation. He was unable to capture a kitten to replace Galveston.

Detective Garza was correct in his belief that the serial madman would hide dormant. There were no reported incidents. Nothing.

Dothan had yet to speak with Tryphena regarding his alibi for that bizarre night in September. Garza had yet to follow up.

As news regarding the serial madman subsided, the day-to-day routine of life took its course, and Mason's and Dothan's interest in the case subsided.

Dothan found himself alone on Thanksgiving. Though Mason and his wife Brenna had invited him to their home in Austin, Dothan declined. Tryphena only contacted him to inform him that she and their daughter would be spending the extended weekend in East Texas with her late father's family.

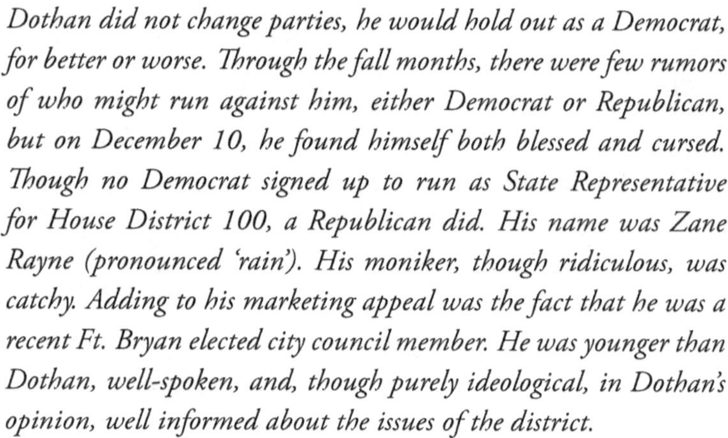

Dothan did not change parties, he would hold out as a Democrat, for better or worse. Through the fall months, there were few rumors of who might run against him, either Democrat or Republican, but on December 10, he found himself both blessed and cursed. Though no Democrat signed up to run as State Representative for House District 100, a Republican did. His name was Zane Rayne (pronounced 'rain'). His moniker, though ridiculous, was catchy. Adding to his marketing appeal was the fact that he was a recent Ft. Bryan elected city council member. He was younger than Dothan, well-spoken, and, though purely ideological, in Dothan's opinion, well informed about the issues of the district.

Dothan had never met the man. Rayne had never come to introduce himself, and Dothan had never made the effort on his end, either. He kicked himself in the ass for not doing so. Were his feelings of isolation due to his lack of involvement? Dothan rarely attended events, and his nagging isolation often manifested ubiquitous depression within him.

What hurt him the most was the lack of comradery he felt from his fellow Democrats, particularly the grassroots activists. Most were much younger than him, and they either were not aware of his past exploits or they regarded them with indifference. Dothan suspected they felt they had little to learn from him.

Kathrine Page never sought out Dothan's assistance. Through the abnormally warm autumn months, he neither sought out, nor was sought by, female admirers.

Christmas was the dagger to his soul, as Tryphena replicated her Thanksgiving trip. Dothan spent Christmas Day at Rachael Logan's grave.

At the forefront of many minds, save all but the born wealthy, was the issue of money. Dothan was not immune to this. The country property finally found a willing buyer, and he and Tryphena divided nearly three-hundred grand. This, coupled with the insurance on his destroyed dwelling, would buy the representative much-needed time. It would also help with child support.

Autumn had scarcely made its presence known, but as the new year approached, winter arrived with all the modesty that can be expected on the Texas Coastal Plains. Stepping out of his office on New Year's Eve, the strong, cool breeze breathed new life into Dothan.

Seven

January is the antithesis of renewal. Sequestered in the shadowed half of the tilted globe, its gray-bearded frown belies our resolutions; but not altogether in Texas. Though the nights were long and the days were short, which suited Dothan, they served to awaken his innate rebellious nature. Even if the world was gray, he shouldn't be.

"Time to shave this fuckin' beard," he said, speaking to his reflection in the mirror. Indeed, he resembled Jim Morrison circa *L.A. Woman*, minus the gut. He cut the scraggly tendrils that jutted from his chin with a pair of scissors. Jason Isbell, an artist Mason recently had turned him on to, played in the background. Once the length had been trimmed down, Dothan lathered. It was the longest shave of his life, but it revealed a man who looked at least a decade younger. The sharp, angled jawline dropped itself like a block of marble. Next was his hair. He'd never been good at instructions, and he feared he might burn his locks off completely. In a stroke of responsible genius, he decided to have it professionally colored. Fortunately, there was a salon across the street. That afternoon, Dothan stepped out onto the sidewalk with freshly trimmed, jet-black hair.

His next step was to join a gym.

All of this physical reinvention was not just to remake his

appearance and confidence; there was something on the horizon he was preparing for.

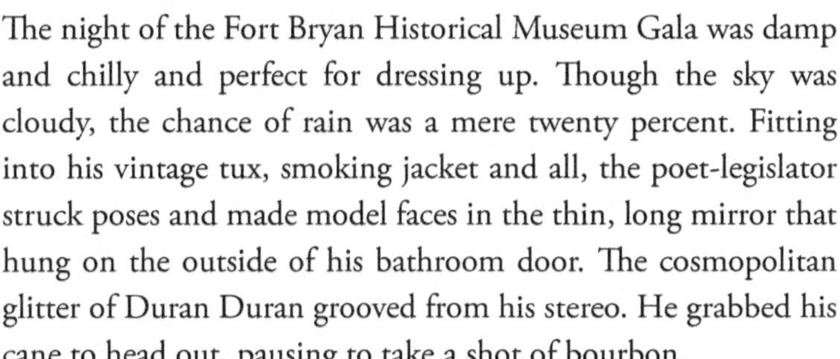

The night of the Fort Bryan Historical Museum Gala was damp and chilly and perfect for dressing up. Though the sky was cloudy, the chance of rain was a mere twenty percent. Fitting into his vintage tux, smoking jacket and all, the poet-legislator struck poses and made model faces in the thin, long mirror that hung on the outside of his bathroom door. The cosmopolitan glitter of Duran Duran grooved from his stereo. He grabbed his cane to head out, pausing to take a shot of bourbon.

The gala was located at Zoo Ranchero, an odd colonial barn situated in the midst of an exotic animal menagerie. Peacocks wandered the grounds as he entered the vastness of the building. Dothan collected his name badge from the front desk and then went straight to the bar. Various thoughts raced through his head as he stood in line. He knew without a doubt that tonight he would meet his opponent. Everyone of any political account in the entire county was there. In fact, numerous statewide officials were to be present as well. The vast majority were Republicans. He wasn't about to let this fact blemish his swagger. He was out for romance, not blood.

Mayor Andy was the emcee for the night, and in a fateful stroke of luck, Dothan was a guest at his table. He had his beer poured into an elegant tall glass and strutted—as much as possible with his limp into the immense dining room. He was stopped by guests who wished to say hello, but not too many.

Mayor Andy's large, round table was front and center. Dothan pulled out a cloth-draped chair and took a seat. The night's festivities were just commencing, and there was only one woman at the table. She was of average build and her dark hair was teased, as if she were stuck in the 1980s. Her dress was of the softest pink satin. The play of light on the fabric nearly rendered the shade invisible.

"You must be Representative Dothan," the woman said. "I don't think we've met, I'm Janet Morgan. I'm on the Ft. Bryan City Council."

"You are correct, ma'am, I don't believe we have met," Dothan replied. "Yes, I'm JD Dothan. Very pleased to meet you."

"I have to tell you…you stick out like a sore thumb in that tux with that cane."

"A sea monster not a dragon…"

"A sea monster?"

"Yes, I call it The Kraken."

"Oh, my. Well, I heard that you were different."

"You're looking spectacular tonight, by the way, ma'am."

"If you keep calling me 'ma'am,' I'm going to throw what's left of my pinot in your face, Representative Dothan. You make me feel so old. I can't be much older than you are."

"I'm terribly sorry, Councilor Morgan. I in no way meant offense. Please, call me JD."

"Do you talk like this for effect? Has it got something to do with your getup?"

"I'm not sure what you mean, ma'am…Councilor Morgan."

"I'm sure you don't, Representative."

Mayor Andy arrived and stood above the two nervously. "Ah, JD! I'm glad you made it. You're looking very nice this evening, Janet."

"Thank you, Andy. I was just introducing myself to our state representative."

"JD, she says what's on her mind to everyone, so don't take it personally," Andy joked.

"She been nothing but kind, Andy," Dothan said.

Janet sat smugly with her legs crossed.

"Go easy on him, Janet. The man's a published poet. I think that's pretty cool, by the way, JD. Congrats on the new book." Mayor Andy excused himself. The room was beginning to fill up, but still the table was vacant with the exception of Dothan and Janet.

"Yes, your book. I read a glowing piece about it in the paper."

"Oh, by Mitch Stevens? He was very kind."

"A poet, huh? That's an odd profession, now isn't it?"

"It's about as arcane as any of the arts at this point, I'd say, but it is something I enjoy," Dothan mused. "I was grateful that The University of Texas Press found it within them to put out something so esoteric—and in two volumes. A second edition is slated for release at the end of the year."

"It probably didn't hurt that you are an elected official who works down the street from them in Austin."

"I'm sure you're right, ma'am…Janet…I mean, Councilor Morgan."

"You seem as nervous as Andy, Representative. Relax. By the way, you're drink is empty."

"It can wait."

"So, tell me, do you think that having a book of poems will help you with the electorate?"

"Absolutely not. I quite expect to lose votes over it."

"Do you? Are you saying that the average voter is too unsophisticated to appreciate it?"

Dothan laughed and reached for his glass.

"It's still empty, Representative."

"Councilwoman, I have no idea what the average voter thinks about a book of poems by me or anyone else, but if a respective voter chooses not to vote for me based on that, then let the proverbial chips fall where they may."

"Okay, fair enough. I guess we'll see."

Dothan excused himself to get another drink—something stronger. Once back at Mayor Andy's table, he was disappointed to find that, though the table was filling up, Councilwoman Morgan wasn't quite done with her interrogation. Out of spite, he was going to give her what she wanted, come what may.

"So, JD…" she began.

"I'm back at last. Yes. Continue, please."

"If you're so passionate about being a poet, I assume you're well-read in that area?"

"I would say so, yes."

"I have to tell you, I'm not very knowledgeable about poetry, but will you quote me something you admire?"

"Hmm…let me think…"

"Of course, take your time."

"I've got it! It's something I read just the other day, actually." Dothan leered at her.

"The suspense is killing me." Janet smiled devilishly.

"'Though the day of my destiny's over, and the star of my fate hath declined… Thy soft heart refused to discover…The faults which so many could find…'"

"Well, I'm impressed. Who exactly are you quoting? Are you sure it's not one of yours?"

"I wish, Janet. Actually, it's from Lord Byron. It's a piece written to his half-sister, who he loved and had an affair with."

"What? You're kidding me, right?"

"Not at all; they consummated the relationship repeatedly."

"That's disgusting. This is something you admire?"

"If only for the fact that it causes the same reaction today as it did two-hundred years ago."

"So you admire this…Lord?"

"Yes, I do. Lord Byron is, or was, a genius of the highest order."

"Well, I have to say, I'm shocked at something so perverse. I'll also add that the fact that you seem so regarding of this Lord Byron is…"

"Is what, ma'am?" Dothan interrupted defiantly.

"Is…actually, sick."

"I'm sorry you feel that way."

"I not only feel that way, but I think that way—as I'm sure the bulk of your voters will, too. Of course, these days, I have no idea what the average Democrat voter thinks is immoral or not."

"And what are implying?"

"What am I implying? Today it's transgenders, tomorrow bigamy, and then, what? Incest and pedophiles?"

"No…bestiality. My staff is working on the bill as we speak."

"Your humor is not in the least bit funny," Janet said. She turned her head away to ignore him.

Lord, this woman is a bitch. Please get me the fuck away from her! Dothan's brain screamed in agony.

Thankfully, rescue was on the way.

The call was made from the stage for guests to find their seats. The ceremony was about to begin. Bodies filtered into the vast dining hall like waters rushing through a crack in a dam. Mayor Andy's table filled up entirely.

A young woman who worked for the Historical Museum Society was the first to take the stage. As she welcomed everyone,

Mayor Andy stood just off to the left, wiping sweat from his forehead. His tuxedo jacket was too tight and his collar too taut. Dothan felt embarrassed for him. The young woman began with the usual welcoming litany, going over the night's agenda, making reference to the silent auction and the actual auction. Then, she introduced the emcee for the evening.

"Ladies and Gentlemen, Fort Bryan City's native son, Mayor Andy Adams!"

Dothan was distracted as Mayor Andy commenced. He was regretting having ever taken a seat as early as he had. *I should have played the room*, he scolded himself. Tossing back his freshly trimmed shock of curls, he surveyed the surrounding tables. Each one was like a constellation to his sight; the bodies seated in circular formations were like stars littered everywhere.

Several times throughout the program—a program he never took the time to review—he lifted himself from his narrow seat and ventured out to the bar. On his way out, and on the way back in, he scanned the room for someone who might ignite his passion. Etiquette dictated that his due diligence was less than thorough.

The worst part was the auction. Dothan had coyly neglected the silent auction, but the regular auction was in his face. As the auctioneer bellowed rapid-fire, repeated phrases, Janet would turn to him with judgmental facial expressions when he didn't participate in the bidding. So of course, he felt obligated. *Who wouldn't want to support the youth club?* Thoughts rattled around in his head like the auctioneer's appeals. Fortunately, he was repeatedly outbid.

Drink was the only antidote to anxiety. As the night's frivolities waned toward conclusion, Representative Dothan was fucked up.

"Are you all right, Representative?" the wife of one of Mayor Andy's mutual colleagues asked as Dothan staggered getting up from his chair.

"It's my condition. I'm fine." Dothan's response was more harsh than he intended, and her puffy face crinkled. Dothan might have been drunk, but his perception was sober. "Thank you, ma'am, for your concern," he said, placing his free hand on her bare shoulder. "You are very kind, but I assure you, I will be fine."

The woman smiled, smitten by his sincerity and his good looks. *But is it sincere?* Dothan understood that older women of status, appreciated, if not longed for, the reverence of younger men. He was brought up as a Southern Gentleman. Aggrandizing matrons was something he had done since Sunday school. Rather than stay and make polite conversation, he excused himself. Her face quickly reverted to its initial expression.

Well-dressed bodies stood up throughout the room as guests prepared to leave. The pathways between tables began filling with people. Dothan was distraught. At the night's outset, he had endured the reproaches of Councilwoman Morgan. Though he'd given her what she was looking for out of spite, he was now regretting it. Also, there had been no females who'd sparked his interest.

The oddly dressed representative, who walked with the aid of an odder cane, was stopped on his way out by the usual fare of sycophants. There is a slight, nearly undetectable delineation between eccentric and weird. Dothan possessed artistry and notoriety, but the former was dependent on the latter. Lord Byron was an eccentric. The poet Clare was a weirdo who was later confined to a mental institution. *Is everything slipping?* Dothan worried.

His worries would soon be realized.

The foyer was stuffed with sycophants seeking affirmation. Dothan had made it halfway to Zoo Ranchero's official exit when he was stopped by a gentleman he had met on numerous occasions, but whose name he failed to recall. They stood under the large stairwell that dominated the center of the foyer.

"Ah, JD. How are you doin' tonight? Great event, don't you think?"

"Fine, yes," Dothan replied, bewildered. Someone bumped into him from behind. Dothan turned, and the offending party turned around as well. Dothan recognized him.

"Ah, JD, this is Councilman Rayne," the lobbyist informed him awkwardly.

"Hey, man, nice to finally meet you," Dothan said. He was struck by how much Rayne resembled him, though he was clean-cut and slightly heavier.

"Yes, sir, likewise." As Councilman Rayne spoke, a woman obscured by the hoard of people surrounding him maneuvered to introduce herself to the poet-legislator.

"Looking forward to a nice clean race, Rayne," Dothan remarked.

"Wouldn't have it any other way, Dothan."

"Great, I'll see you on the campaign trail this fall."

"See you there." Rayne felt a tug on his shoulder and turned to Dothan as Dothan turned away. "Representative, I'd like to introduce you to…" The chatter of the room deafened Dothan as he made his way to the exit.

Eight

South of Ft. Bryan City, a vast agrarian and small-town culture still existed in the growing county of the city's namesake, although developers had for some time been buying up ranch and farmland to be sold as acreage plots.

Annie Casey was recently divorced from her husband of nearly twenty years. This move proved to be the best business decision of her life. The settlement had left her with upwards of ten million dollars. She was not quite forty-five and would spend the rest of her life in comfort. Though this had been the course of her life for the past decade, now she could enjoy it without the irritating man she was previously betrothed to.

February is usually a nasty month along the coastal plains of Texas, but not so much this day. The night's rain reflected a forgiving sun as numerous moving vans rumbled their way down the rocky drive that led to her home. Annie excitedly stood at the front doorway of her freshly constructed, spacious, divorce settlement house. If money couldn't buy love, it most definitely could buy out any unhappiness associated with it.

Movers lifted immense pieces of furniture from the respective vans and delivered them to one of ten rooms. A separate van arrived later that afternoon. It was stuffed entirely with boxes.

The house sat on a gracious twenty acres. Though there were few trees in the immediate vicinity of the dwelling, healthy woods surrounded the lot.

To the south, some fifty yards from Annie's property line, a green pickup sat in the area wilderness. The engine grew cold like the approaching night.

Exterior lights illuminated in unison around the home. Annie thanked the movers as they departed.

A face appeared from the peripheral foliage.

Annie loved animals. Her plans were to build stables and purchase horses. Though she loved all animals, she loved cats the most and had no dogs.

A pair of legs started moving toward the large home. The feet quickened with each muddy step.

On the night of the museum gala, Kat Morgan returned to her apartment perturbed. She was only half-buzzed, and when she arrived, she popped a fresh bottle of wine. She plopped down on her substantial blue sofa, and her conflict morphed into blues. With each glass, her blues turned to burning anger.

"How dare that motherfucker snub me?" Kat protested to the loneliness of her den. "What a douchebag!"

Contrary to her usual behavior, Kat did not dial one of her numerous beta-orbiters to spew the bile increasing in her spleen. Instead, she fortified her pride by pouring out a glass too many. She got up, went to the bathroom, and looked in the mirror. As she removed her makeup, she resolved herself to a plot of seduction and conquest.

Late winter sunlight streamed into her bedroom, where she woke alone. It was Sunday, and she had time on her hands. Kat was thirty-five and adroit at research. Research was, in fact, crucial to her political campaign consultant career. Though she was unaware of Dothan's recent lyric opus, it took all of five seconds to discover it, and another ten to order a copy. Her sense of rejection had subsided enough for her to refrain from expediting shipment, which she would regret.

The madman had little cover, as there was sparse landscaping around Annie's house at this point. He did have one advantage: the house was built on the edge of a floodplain. The builder had constructed a considerable slab, and the foundation rose some four feet from terra firma. Ducking was an asset.

Lights and lamps spotted the interior. Annie could be spied going from room to room, at least on the first floor. The madman watched as she strutted with pride about her prize with a glass in hand. As there were no homes completed in the vicinity, he was as unobserved as a tree falling in the forest bereft of an available ear. Something of a pro at this point, his every glance through an available window was coupled with a scan of that window. Annie had an alarm system installed. He would have to determine if Annie's cat was an indoor-outdoor pet, and if so, he would exploit it.

Though the weather report had called for a clear evening, the sky opened up into a downpour as the green pickup navigated toward the highway. Whether by luck or curse, the madman's tracks would be washed away by morning.

Kat read everything as it pertained to local politics and goings-on. She was a provincial junkie. She also followed social media as a secular religion. Kat friended Dothan online.

Hmm, who's this? he pondered the morning her notification pinged his phone. *Kat Morgan?* He was struck by her picture. "Whoa!" Kat was quickly accepted.

Dothan was a poor planner. Women had always handled this aspect of his life. Now, there were no women in his life. The poet-legislator had yet to schedule a book signing. In truth, the idea of being a poet imparted unease, as it does with anyone who lives in the South, particularly Texas. The image of the poet to him was ingrained early on as a wimp getting sand kicked in his face by a Neanderthal jock in front of the popular girls, of course. Though he really had never cared for convention and certainly had no use for what people thought of him, in a state that continuously cuts arts programs then mortgages its soul for billion-dollar high school football cathedrals, this image was indelible and justified. At the same time, he felt that the arts had been corrupted by his brethren on the left. *Are they not censors?* Reason rarely vetoed his sentiments—he had Mason for that, but this notion troubled him profoundly. In fact, it was a lone conservative on the editorial board of UT Press that had pushed through his verse for publication. The idea of himself as a man without a country increasingly plagued him.

But artistic vanity is perhaps the greatest source of vanity in existence.

Impulsively, on Monday morning, Dothan decided he would hold an ad hoc, local signing next door at BR Vino. The art bar manager was receptive, and it was scheduled for that coming Saturday. He informed Mitch Stevens and posted it on social media that night.

WTF? Kat texted one of her most endearing male friends early Tuesday morning.

No book yet? he replied.

NO!

Sorry.

What are you doing tonight?

Being naughty. Don't ask.

LOL! Be good.

Kat was beside herself. *I can't show up to a book signing without a book! What if he blows me off again?* She considered reordering it and specifying overnight shipping this time, but money was tight. She was a strict businesswoman with a budget. *I'll send someone to spy for me,* she reconciled. Having never been to a book signing, she had failed to realize she could purchase a book at the signing. She was thinking emotionally.

The beta-male orbiter who was dispatched to do her reconnaissance was a young man named Ernesto. Ernesto was both obese and swarthy. He was defined by his own insecurities, which made him incapable of being objective when judging other men. He arrived at BR Vino promptly at seven the night of Dothan's book signing after viewing the barrage of hearts and red lights decorating the buildings along the sidewalk. Valentine's Day, a dagger to the unwanted, was right around the corner. Ernesto disliked Dothan immediately.

The establishment was filling up. The poet-legislator stood at the bar trying to look cool. He didn't need to try. Between every sip of his beer he was met with another patron present on his behalf.

"JD, are you going to read for us, buddy?" a local judge asked.

"Tried reading your work, Representative. Damn, you should be teaching at Rice." a county commissioner commented.

"I thought I'd get my copy tonight—in cash and under the table," the county treasurer joked. Even Zane Rayne made an appearance. Dothan was not aware of his presence until he tapped him on the shoulder.

"Well, well, if it isn't the man angling for my job," Dothan jested. "It doesn't pay much."

"Naw, man, just coming out to support a local author."

"Poet."

"I stand corrected, a poet. Congratulations, Representative Dothan. I don't understand poetry at all, but what the hell do I know?"

Dothan wanted to make a snide remark to put Zane in his place but caught himself. When Zane placed his foot on the bar rail, Dothan noticed his boot was sullied with mud.

"So, what have you been up to today?" he asked Zane.

"Shooting skeet."

"In a suit?"

"Fundraiser."

The room was full, and the band for the evening had set up. Ernesto stood nervously aloof, sipping a Coke and tucked safely away from the neon glow. Watching Dothan, his dislike turned to hatred.

The night wouldn't be complete without the presence of Mayor Andy. He was fashionably late.

"Andy, great to see you!" Dothan called.

"Of course, JD, I wouldn't miss this for the world!" Both parties had to shout over the obnoxious chatter, so they drew in closer to one another.

"Have you given a speech yet?" Andy asked.

"No speeches, please."

"Ah, come on, man, you've got a platform. Use what ya got!"

"People don't want a political speech, Andy; this is a book signing."

"Bullshit, JD, half the local leadership is here, including Zane. Hell, I'm going to the mic," Andy insisted. With his characteristic balance of command and deference, he marched through the crowd toward the stage, which was really just a tiny corner to the right of the bar's entry.

"Listen up, y'all!" Andy boomed. "I've been back there talkin' to JD, and he doesn't want to come up here and give a speech." Disapproving boos and hisses followed. Multiple slaps on JD's back motivated him forward. Zane snuck off to the bathroom to clean his shoes.

"All right, Andy," Dothan began reluctantly. "I have nothing prepared, by the way folks."

Ernesto began recording discreetly from his secure corner.

Dothan continued, "I've heard it said that there's nothing more terrifying or dangerous than well-intentioned lawmakers. I assure you I am neither well-intentioned nor sound of mind." Everyone looked on somewhat awkwardly. "Haven't all you rubes heard, poets are insane?" Dothan joked. It took a moment, but slowly, the attendees began to smile and chuckle. Dothan was encouraged. "In fact, anyone who would spend hundreds of thousands, if not millions on a six-hundred-dollar-a-month job is either insane or stupid! Either way, y'all are fucked!" A sea of glasses and bottles clinked, coupled with uproarious laughter and applause.

"Read something, JD!" A patron yelled from the back near the bar.

"Okay, grab me a book out of that box sitting over in the corner, if you would, please," Dothan requested from a young man who unknowingly stood guard. The box sat on a table directly behind Ernesto. The spy was confused as those around him looked at him with impatience.

"Oh, yes sir, Mr. Dothan," Ernesto grumbled.

Once the book was passed up, Dothan had to decide on what portion to read. He literally had not planned on reading anything. He flipped through the pages. Ernesto commenced filming.

"Okay, not sure what y'all are expecting, but here she goes.

TO THE LAWMAKERS

Go ahead, rage against your artlessness from the podium,
Swinging at posterity.
Angry because that, after God, only art is immortal?
For your schemes, deals, trickery, bullying and compromise
Are but a trickling hose at the trunk of a drought thirsty,
Giant tree.

Yes, you may witness a bud or two, but prematurely
The leaf will yellow.
From your artlessness nothing artful can you craft from decay.
The Eye of the world, that will not gaze on you, you have blinded.
A morass of vacancy you will impart; sucking into its vortex…
Nothingness."

The final word of the poem had hardly trailed off into the claustrophobic air when the crowd, which was there on his behalf, which he had won over with his incendiary, yet comic banter, was lost. It was not only over their heads, but it was foreign to their collective concept of public service. Truth does not set one free, it enslaves one…or worse, excommunicates one. One knows they live in a time of lies when they dwell in the presence of fear. The enthusiasm muted. Dothan, like all born performers, knew he had lost the audience, and like all born performers, fed on them like a vampire. But these veins were empty. "Thanks for coming out, everyone! I'm truly grateful! I'll be hanging out and have books for sale for anyone interested."

Ernesto in his generational acumen had shot Kat a document of the presentation in the time it would take to tie his shoes. Zane had been loitering in the back, listening and observing, his shoes wiped clean. Zane's political instincts told him Dothan may not have stuffed his head in the beast's mouth, but he had certainly offered it up. He salivated at the potential for blood.

Dothan sold a few books, and, of course, signed all of them. As much as possible, with each offering, he scribbled a certain remark or quote, coyly applicable to the buyer, but all in all, the night was a disappointment to him.

The party thinned, and the night ended too soon. Dothan was drunk when he left, and the moon had never seemed so far away as it did tonight. It was a mercifully short walk from the bar to his loft.

Kat wasted little time in watching the clip Ernesto sent. But where those present may have felt reproached by Dothan's perceived self-righteousness, she had a different reaction.

I'm going to get this guy…

Nine

Detective Garza sat in his small office in his overvalued, small, suburban home. The single-story dwelling sat on the outskirts of Ft. Bryan and was landscaped with tiny trees and flowerbeds. Though it was a modest place, he lived with a degree of comfort. He feared what little he had acquired would be lost. Garza's home office faced the front drive. The beam of headlights pierced the blinds, then he heard a tap at the front door. He rose to answer it.

"Ah, Sheriff," Garza greeted. "I appreciate you coming this late. Come in, please."

"No problem. You got an adult beverage?" Sheriff Nielson asked in his nasally accent.

"Of course," Garza answered and headed toward the kitchen. "What would you like? Beer, wine…something stronger?"

"Something stronger," Nielson answered, remaining in the entryway.

"Tequila?" Garza asked over his shoulder.

"Fine."

"I think I'll join you." Garza pulled two glasses from his cupboard. "Come on back, please."

"How are you holding up?" Nielson asked as he entered the kitchen.

"You're about to find out. Here." Garza handed him a full glass.

"That bad?" Nielson commented, observing the quantity of alcohol and the size of the glass.

"You asked for it, and you're gonna need it."

The two went back to Garza's office. The detective's computer screen partially blocked their view of one another.

"So what's up?" Neilson catechized after taking a sip of his straight tequila. His face twisted like a squeezed lime.

"I got the forensic back from the crime lab."

"Great, and…?"

"I'll start with the bad—and most of it is bad. I'll conclude with the good, of which there is little."

"I'm listening," Nielson replied, his face contorting with each sip. "This shit just gets stronger with every swig."

"It's real Mexican tequila. I get it from my grandmother."

"I'm not going to black out, am I?" Nielson half-joked.

"To tell you the truth, I haven't tried this batch."

"Forewarned."

"Okay, the bad news is, this guy is either a fucking crime fiction junkie, or he's a genius."

"How so?"

"He's checked every box. He's done everything without leaving evidence. The act itself is the only indication he was there. The calculation is amazing in the case of the beheading. There is almost nothing to suggest that he was ever present— no evidence of entry, no signs of a struggle, nothing dislodged in the apartment, and no signs of a robbery if there was one. There are no marks on the body anywhere to suggest that there was a struggle of any kind between the victim and the murder. She wasn't drugged, nor was there any alcohol in her system.

There was THC, though. Her fingernails were clipped, so I imagine that at some point she scratched him. Bleach was applied methodically afterward, so no DNA. The only thing left behind on the bed other than blood was a hair, and it turns out it was synthetic nylon like you get from a common, cheap Halloween outfit."

"This whole thing is Halloween. What about the murder weapon?"

"Well, as you know, there was nothing found at the scene; but an examination of the neck and severed head show that the blade was wide in width in the middle."

"Like a dagger."

"Exactly!"

"Anything left behind in the tissue?"

"Yes, several minute shards. I'm waiting on an analysis."

"Don't expect much. If it's really old, then you'll never track it to anyone. At least if it was something common and new, you could check inventory at area stores and associated transactions."

"This guy would have purchased it in cash, anyway."

"It appears that way."

"So what's the good news?"

"A sliver of grass."

"A sliver of grass?"

"Yes, outside on the patio. At some point, he must have slipped something over his shoes. Either that or he vacuumed before leaving."

"Because the carpet was spotless."

"Yes."

"What about a vacuum cleaner?"

"There wasn't one."

"So he may have left with a fucking vacuum cleaner?"

"Who knows?"

"Back to the sliver of grass…"

"On the back patio, there were particles of dirt and blades of recently cut grass from the apartment complex. However, this blade is slightly curved and solid, and it was molded, as if it was dislodged from the groove of a tennis shoe. It does not match the grass from the apartment complex, and there was a piece of decaying grass found within it."

"You are grasping at straws, aren't you? So what is it?"

"I'm still waiting to find out. It's still at the DPS crime lab in Houston."

"This is going to cost the city a pretty penny, and it's going to take forever to get an answer, both for the blade of grass and the murder weapon."

"It's really the only lead at this point."

"What about the other two incidents? The jogger and the woman who died giving birth?"

"So you do agree with me that Kate Page fits into this mess somehow?"

"Yes, but I staunchly disagree with the way it was handled by the local police."

"Because they believed the pomegranate and rose were from an angry ex-boyfriend?"

"Damn right. They should have collected it as evidence!"

"We did reach out to her after the hospital incident, but she said she had discarded the items."

"No point in scavenging a landfill."

"Look, I know they fucked up. They're just a bunch of amateurs, to tell you the truth."

"So what about the other two incidents?"

"Regarding Ms. Page…nothing. As for Jane Sellers, the

woman who died during labor, basically nothing. The only evidence on the body or in the room itself, including the sheets, were fragments of latex."

"From surgical gloves?"

"Yes. They match those from the dispenser in the room where she laid in state."

"And the hospital staff?"

"I interviewed everyone present that night, as well as all who signed in at the front desk."

"Including Representative Dothan, as you told me previously."

"That is correct."

"And what about his alibi?"

"Truthfully, I never followed up on it. Do you think I should?"

"Well, you and I both know he didn't do this, but I would, just to check all the boxes."

"I can do that. The reason I didn't—"

Neilson interrupted, "…is because you didn't want to deal with the Texas Rangers."

"Yes, and honestly, that's why I asked you here tonight."

"You're worried about the Feds."

"I am."

"I can tell you that if anything else happens—like another gruesome murder, God forbid—one of us is going to have to ask for their assistance. After the murder of Anne Spencer, I got a call from my contact at the FBI."

"I know. Can you keep them at bay for now?"

"I'll try, but we have an unsolved murder that seems connected to a bigger picture. Oh, and I should add, I'm up for reelection next cycle—just saying."

"I know. I don't like politics, but I understand it."

Garza switched off his computer and invited Neilson into his unlit den. Only the lights from the kitchen area provided any illumination. The homemade Mexican tequila was replaced with American light beer.

"I appreciate you sticking around for a bit, Neilson. Obviously, this whole thing is like an albatross around my neck."

"No problem. Not to fatten up the bird, but any news on the calling cards or a profile on a potential suspect?"

Garza put his beer on a coaster then rubbed his eyes. "The calling cards…"

"Fucking bizarre, I know."

"This is out of my league, and it ties into the profile."

"No doubt about that, the symbols are the clues, and clues are the key."

"This guy is obviously establishing some kind of pattern—symbols, as you called them—hint by hint. I have my staff doing all kinds of online research, but they don't have a clue themselves. What I need is someone outside of law enforcement… someone with a creative mind. My gut instinct is that this man is not malicious by nature."

"So you think it may be nature versus nurture, and nurture is the culprit?" Neilson asked.

"I can't say, but it's almost like he dwells in an alternate reality, like a schizophrenic. Maybe he has multiple personalities. The calling cards, or 'symbols'…I don't think they are meant to lead us to him. I don't think he is looking to get caught. In fact, frankly, I believe that maybe he's living in some world where he thinks he's some kind of master."

"How do you mean?"

"Maybe it's my passionate Latino background—forgive me, but you Minnesotans are all Vikings to me—I think the man is maybe..."

"Maybe what?"

"...maybe a raving fucking lunatic, but also..."

"What?" Neilson passively demanded, popping open his beer.

"...a romantic."

"A romantic?"

"Yes. He is certainly mad, but he is playing out some insane fantasy roleplay."

"What about the green truck?" Nielson asked.

"You don't want to entertain the idea, do you?"

"To tell you truth, for all I know, you're fucking right, but it's speculation at this point."

"Ah, the ever-cold Northman."

"Cold as ice."

"I ran every shade of green truck, and there are some silly-sounding colors, to tell you the truth."

"Like paint swatches?"

"Pretty much. I ran every plate on every green truck within a one-hundred-mile radius. Green is not a popular color, by the way."

"That should narrow it."

"Yes, to about four thousand."

Neilson laughed half-heartedly. "It's like trying to find a needle in a haystack, I know. Did you run background checks on the owners?"

"Every one. Only a few flagged, and get this, there was only one felon."

"So I guess I'm supposed to deduce that people who buy green trucks are overwhelmingly law-abiding?"

"Very funny."

"I have a cold sense of humor, too, Garza. How many

misdemeanors, and what classes?"

"No Class As and only a few class Bs and Cs for illegal substance possession, DWIs...nothing that would make one a suspect."

"And the felon?"

"The truck was purchased by a sex offender after he was let out on parole. The man lives with his grandmother and works as a welder."

"What was his offense?"

"He had sex with his sixteen-year-old girlfriend when he was nineteen."

"Jesus...our sex offender laws have gone overboard. Sure, some of them are truly evil but...are they still dating?"

"They're going to get married at some point."

"He'll still have to register as a sex offender forever...fuck me," Neilson commented, shaking his head in bewilderment.

"I went and spoke with the man at his grandmother's home in Pasadena. He's as docile as a mouse—nothing there. It disturbs me that he was incarcerated with the most vicious of criminals."

"We don't make the laws, Garza, we just get stuck cleaning up what those "representatives" in the legislature dump on us."

"I understand."

"I've heard it said, there's nothing more terrifying and dangerous as a well-intentioned legislator."

"Amen to that, Sheriff," Garza said, then lifted his sweating beer and toasted Neilson.

"Well, it's getting late, and I need to get back home to the boss and kids."

"I know, but before you go, I just wanted to confide something in you. We've worked closely together before, so I trust you and your judgment."

"What's up?"

"This guy, he makes me feel so mediocre. It's a terrible feeling."

"You are mediocre, Garza. So am I. That's law enforcement. If we were geniuses, we'd be the one's committing the crimes you and I try to solve."

"Interesting perspective—and not at all what I wanted to hear," Garza joked.

"You know, when I was a kid in Minnesota, I would read Sherlock Holmes. I don't know what you guys read down here as kids, maybe cowboy stuff, but up there, it was good old fashioned Conan Doyle. So when I got into law enforcement, I figured I'd meet people of that caliber—at least from time to time, but I didn't. I met a lot of regular people. You said earlier that you thought this guy is either a crime fiction junkie or a genius. He's probably both." The sheriff rose to leave.

Garza followed him out to his car. "Again, thank you, Sheriff, for coming over tonight," he said.

"Of course. One last thought… You said you need someone outside law enforcement who was creative. Well what about JD Dothan? He's some kind of poet. I went to his book signing not long ago. I don't know much about that kind of thing, but he's creative, and, he's got a pedigree. He's dealt with, and solved, some interesting situations in the past. By what I know, most of that was luck, but it can't hurt to talk to him or check out his alibi."

"I suppose," Garza said, hesitantly.

"Look, he's a state official. He's got legislative privilege. Spill the beans with the guy with the understanding that it's in confidence. It can't hurt."

"Thank you, sheriff. I'll consider it."

Garza watched as Nielson's headlights illuminated yard after suburban yard as he exited the subdivision.

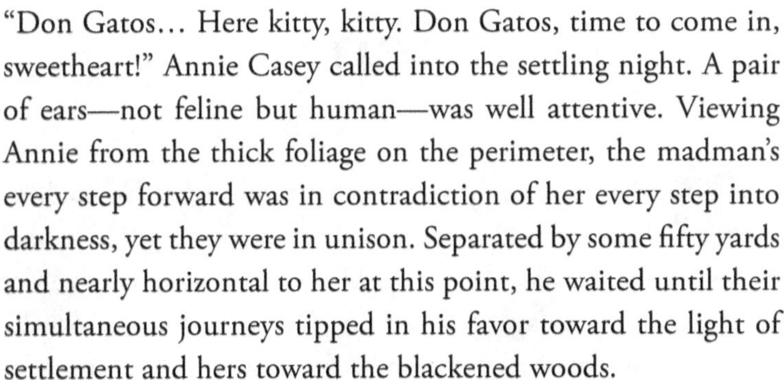

"Don Gatos… Here kitty, kitty. Don Gatos, time to come in, sweetheart!" Annie Casey called into the settling night. A pair of ears—not feline but human—was well attentive. Viewing Annie from the thick foliage on the perimeter, the madman's every step forward was in contradiction of her every step into darkness, yet they were in unison. Separated by some fifty yards and nearly horizontal to her at this point, he waited until their simultaneous journeys tipped in his favor toward the light of settlement and hers toward the blackened woods.

Her back was squarely in view. He slipped inside…

Ten

othan awoke in the middle of the night. He couldn't sleep and had tired of tossing and turning. He looked at his phone, it was three a.m. Sleep was harder and harder to come by these days. *If only I could rest and dream of her*, he thought as he splashed water on his face. *Even if it were a nightmare…but she refuses to visit me.* Switching the coffee pot on, Dothan dressed as the appliance took life.

With cup in hand, he descended the short, dark stairwell, and sauntered the long, unlit hall toward his office. Out of habit, he turned on the computer and took a seat. His desk was still a mess. In fact, its surface was a continuing mass of confusion that grew by the day. Sip after sip of the piping-hot coffee led him closer and closer to a simple conclusion he had heretofore avoided. He needed to hire an assistant.

Dothan drew his cell phone from his jean pocket. With his thumb, he scrolled social media. The feed sped by faster and faster with the usual bullshit, but a very familiar image caught his eye. Ceasing his scroll, and then backing up, he paused at a post made by a woman named Kat Morgan.

It was a picture of his book of poems leaning against a bottle of wine. The post read:

What I'm doing tonight.

Dothan immediately clicked her profile picture. She was stunningly beautiful. He had a fleeting memory that she'd friended him recently, but he had yet to visit her page. A quick scan of her profile revealed that Kat Morgan was Councilor Janet Morgan's daughter. *What the hell!* The shock of this wore off quickly as most of his social media 'friends' were of a political nature. It disappointed him slightly when he discovered that she was also 'friends' with his opponent, Zane Rayne. Yet there was something about her…she was an active volunteer for causes ranging from children with disabilities to animal rescue. *And, she is reading my book!* He decided to reply.

I hope you enjoy it. My poems are kind of dark.

The ping of Kat's reply came shortly thereafter.

I'll let you know.

What struck Dothan was that the woman was up at such an hour. This intrigued him even more. Representative John David Dothan was becoming beguiled.

Dawn arrived, and with it the shadow of the state seal across the hallway, visible from his open office door. Since the front entry was made of glass, the insignia worked its magic when the sun was at a certain point. It was usually too early for him to witness it. The oblong shadow, disfigured due to the angle along the wall, had a strange effect on Dothan. For an atheist, portents and omens held no mystery, they were absurd and coincidental. But this early March morning was different. The latent pagan was awakened. He believed he had risen early for some unexplained reason. Dothan turned in his chair to his PC and opened a blank document. He began crafting a job posting. When it was finished, he shot it out to local officials, several colleges in the area, and posted it on social media. Afterward, he felt he'd accomplished something. He left for the gym. It had been a productive day.

Not far from the state capitol, Tryphena Taylor sat on the posh couch of a fellow lobbyist. A fine dinner and film had preceded their present situation. She now found herself with a slight buzz in a cloistered high-rise apartment in downtown Austin. Nervously, she waited for her date to return from mixing drinks in the kitchen. "Avalon," by Roxy Music played softly. Fox News, bereft of sound was on the large television that hung from the wall.

Jimmy King emerged with two fancy glasses in hand. "Here's your Tito's and tonic."

Tryphena graciously took the glass and sipped. "Perfect," she said.

"I'm glad you like it."

In fact, everything Jimmy had done that night had been perfect, hence her agreeing to his request for a nightcap. Jimmy was at least a decade older than her, but younger than her ex-husband. After dating and then marrying John David, she had decided she'd rather date older men.

Jimmy sat down on the couch next to her. Their buttocks were at least a foot away from one another.

"I like this song, by the way," Tryphena commented.

"It's Roxy Music," Jimmy replied, thinking she did not know the artist.

"I know. This is the kind of music my ex-husband listens to."

"Oh, is that right?" Jimmy said. He placed his glass on the coaster of his spotless glass table, and turned slightly toward her. "I don't want to talk about your ex-husband."

"I'm sorry. I understand. It just slipped out."

"No worries, it's just kind of a buzzkill."

"I understand." Tryphena suddenly felt awkward. She had

not been with a man since John David. With his left hand Jimmy took her glass and set it on the table. Tryphena adjusted herself on the sofa. She nervously brushed her hand over her hair.

"Hey, just relax, Tryphena."

"I am relaxed, Jimmy." She reached for her drink, but Jimmy caught her arm and moved suddenly toward her with his entire body. His breath smelled of gin. He had BO! His mouth opened and his tongue protruded. Many thoughts raced through Tryphena's mind in that instant. Most of them were of John David. *Did I treat him unfairly?*

Jimmy's tongue was at the entrance of her mouth. She accepted. The two started kissing, his whole form squiggled to fit atop her, as if he were a puzzle piece. Jimmy's hands supported him at both sides of her behind. Tryphena was trying, but Jimmy had no craft for kissing.

Still she tried.

Slouching into the sofa, she raised her arms and placed her hands on Jimmy's cheeks. Several times she opened her eyes. She didn't like what she saw. Tryphena ran her fingers across Jimmy's heavily balding skull. All she could think of was John David's thick, flowing locks. Still, she tried. She sunk into the couch. Jimmy used this opportunity to place his entire form on top of hers. He abruptly broke off the kiss.

"So, how do you like it?" he grunted as his right hand moved up Tryphena's short dress. His palm and fingers felt strange as they slid under her panties and began massaging her hip. Now his thumb was near her groin. She was looking at him, but he was staring down at her dress. "Let's get this off, what do you say?" Jimmy removed his hand from her pocket of privacy, and reaching around her shoulder, unzipped her. The sound of it traveling south sent a shiver down Tryphena's spine.

Jimmy roughly yanked the dress from her shoulders to below her bosom. He shoved his face between her bra-clad breasts. Tryphena looked around the room. *Why am I here?* she questioned herself. *Nothing about this is right.*

"Are you getting wet?" Jimmy asked with a tone of insistence.

"Okay, enough!" Tryphena exclaimed.

"What?" Jimmy clamored. It was the first time their eyes had met since this scenario ensued. "What's the problem? You like it rough—I know you do…"

"No! Get off of me!" Tryphena pushed with all her strength. The clueless Jimmy finally got the picture.

"Fine," he retorted, rising off of Tryphena. She sat up and pulled her dress back over her cold shoulders. Jimmy rose, grabbed his drink off the table, and stood up, obviously pissed off. "So, what's the problem, don't you like me?"

Tryphena felt a sudden pang of guilt. "Yes, of course. I just…just…"

"Just what?"

"I'm just not ready for this, Jimmy. I'm sorry."

"Well, do you want to stay for a while? I could stream a movie, if you'd like."

"I think I should be going, Jimmy. It's getting late, and I need to get back to my daughter."

The madman sat in his regal den, puffing a cigar, sipping wine, and listening to Rick Wakefield. His mind was not on the foggy purple that comprised his outward reality, but rather, on Annie Casey. His entry into Annie's home was again providence. It could not have been easier. The labyrinth of his twisted mind began retracing its twisted maze.

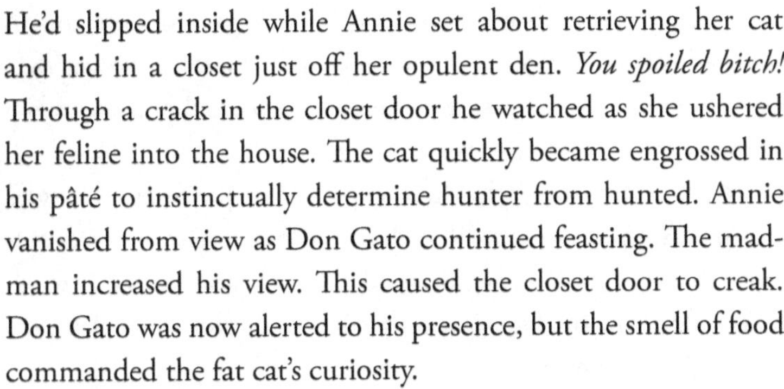

He'd slipped inside while Annie set about retrieving her cat and hid in a closet just off her opulent den. *You spoiled bitch!* Through a crack in the closet door he watched as she ushered her feline into the house. The cat quickly became engrossed in his pâté to instinctually determine hunter from hunted. Annie vanished from view as Don Gato continued feasting. The madman increased his view. This caused the closet door to creak. Don Gato was now alerted to his presence, but the smell of food commanded the fat cat's curiosity.

Then Annie appeared, dressed in a white silk night gown. *You are not beautiful, Annie, but homeliness is not a crime.*

"You really like the fishy ones don't you, sweetheart?" she'd asked Don Gato as he licked his whiskers contentedly. Annie went to the wet bar just to the side of the kitchen. The alarm on the paneling awaited instruction. She hadn't set it yet, or perhaps she had done it remotely, via her phone. It was impossible to know. But, somehow, he knew. *I always know.*

Annie flitted around the den in…*self-absorption.* And still, she had yet to set the alarm. Or had she?

She had not. She walked past him without a notion and called to Don Gato. *Should I close the closet door…certainly the cat will smell me?* But he trotted past as ignorant as a peasant's jackass.

He heard a door shut and knew it was her bedroom door from the first time he'd stalked the house. He'd seen it from the windows that he'd peered through with much dexterity.

Now the back door... Was the alarm set or wasn't it?

How beautiful!

The madman leaped up from his chair and began pontificating.

"Oh, you foolish women…how little you understand! If you remove attraction and reverence, you have no power over us men at all! You can deceive, lie, and betray all you want, but without those two traits, we will crush you!"

The room was dark when he paused at the finely wrought, bronze-trimmed mirror that hung above the furniture-style turntable. He took a long drag off the cigar and puffed into his oval reflection, his face was only slightly lit from below by the blue lights of the stereo.

"And if you can be merry, then I'll say…a man may weep upon his wedding day!" His jaw moved and his tongue danced as the words rolled forward. The fog of smoke framed his mug like a dream. He stood looking at the blue outline of his face in the mirror: the healthy V of his jawline, nostrils, and his protruding eyebrows filled him with invincibility. He continued to stare, but something…something settled over him. Sadness? Regret? His eyes dropped from his reflection into oblivion…into history. For a moment, he just stood there.

The music had stopped, only the sound of the needle bouncing at the end of vinyl made any noise. The madman lifted his eyes again to his reflection. He drew in closer…

"But we need you for our legacy to endure…we need you for our legacy to endure…we need you for our legacy to endure…" With each repeated statement his voice grew louder, shriller.

Now, drawing even closer, he whispered, "And if you can be merry, then I'll say…a man may weep upon his wedding day!"

Returning to his chair, he sat down in the dark, clouded ambiance of the room. Only the lilting needle offered any frequency to the ear. "It sounds like soft kisses…kisses goodbye, does it not, Annie?"

Before drinking himself to sleep, he had decided a parting gift was proper.

◇

Morning light penetrated the room. Stale cigar stench stuck to it like the purple paint on the walls and the green carpet below. The madman awoke to a fresh day still seated on his throne, but in the hours between sleep and waking, the throne had returned to a simple chair. Rubbing his eyes and scruffy face, he rose and headed to the shower.

While washing the stink of last night's fantasy from his body, his phone began ringing. Pausing for a moment while washing, it continued to ring again and again. He needed to answer it.

"What is it? Who wants what now?" The madman complained to no one. He reached for the towel that was slung over the shower rod. Wiping his face, he fitted the towel around his waist and went for his phone. He saw the missed call alert.

"What does she want?" He hit recall. A female voice answered on the other end.

"Yeah, what is it?" the madman demanded. "Yes, I saw that, he posted it all over the place the other day." The woman on the other end went on and on. "Look, okay…maybe that's a good idea. Actually, I wish I would have thought of it…good way to get dirt on the guy. I'm sure there's plenty of it, too." The woman's tone now changed. "Oh God," was the madman's reaction. "We're not going to go into this again, are we?" The woman's retort was one of passionate confession. The madman's counter was one of cold rejection, "Look, we've been through this a thousand times. It's over, okay? We had some fun. I care about you, too, but it's over. We still have to work together, so let's leave it at that!"

After hanging up, he dressed and drove into the Cultural District. He had a notion he might find what he was looking for in one of the many antique shops that littered the old downtown. The day was tepid—typical for March. After parking, he walked the sidewalk and entered Guinevere's Attic, a large, but quaint shop of relics, across the street from Representative John David Dothan's office.

A young woman was behind the sales counter organizing items. The madman looked over a large arrangement of silver cutlery and exotic china displayed at the front of the store.

"That's some really nice stuff, by the way," she commented.

"Oh?" the madman asked, looking up, somewhat confused.

"Yeah, we brought most of that from an estate sale over in Tanglewild in Houston. Old money, you know?"

"No, I didn't." The madman started toward the counter.

"Yeah, rich kids just dumping their family legacy, I guess."

"Legacy…I know something about that."

"Oh, are you here to buy or sell? If you have some items you want to unload, you'll have to talk to the owners."

"What's your name, by the way?" He was now standing before the counter.

"I'm Elizabeth."

"Elizabeth…I had a daughter named Elizabeth. Very pretty name."

"Thank you. You said, you 'had?'"

"Yes, we lost her."

"I'm sorry, was this recent?"

"Recent? No. It was a long time ago."

"How can I help you today, sir?" Elizabeth was starting to feel uncomfortable.

"I'm looking for something…" The madman joined his hands as one taking communion.

"We've got a lot here. It's a very big place, and haunted." Elizabeth awkwardly tossed her arms open.

"I'm not looking for ghosts…necessarily."

"Okay, then, *what* necessarily?"

"What I'm looking for is a pendant, or a piece of jewelry that has eight points."

"What do you mean by eight points?"

"Like an eight-point star."

"Well, all our jewelry is down this hall, the second room to the left," she gestured toward the hallway. "Oh, and there's some brooches and stuff on display over here." She pointed to a glass-enclosed case to the right of the counter.

"Brooches…that may be what I'm looking for."

"Some of them are really old."

"That's what I'm looking for, something very old."

"Well," again her arms widened, "like I said, it's very big place. I need to tend to some things. Excuse me."

Eleven

Resumes began stacking up in Dothan's state-issued inbox. The entryway snail mail was stuffed as well. It seemed odd that so many people would be interested in a job that was little more than that of a glorified secretary. Though he saw the task of reviewing them as a burden, it was secretly an ego boost. Still, he loathed hiring staffers. It was something he usually deferred to Mason. Since Mason was in Austin, and because whoever he hired had to be the right fit, Dothan had to handle the matter himself.

A total of twenty-six applicants had applied. Dothan spent the day tearing open envelopes and printing out email attachments. The resumes were varied, some were college age and some were much older, as determined from their respective work timelines. Nearly all were women. The older applicants had far better writing skills, and a writing sample was a requirement. Morning bloomed into afternoon as he struggled with whether to hire an older or a younger woman. He knew it would be wise to hire the former, but...

He reached out to six of the twenty-six the next day, and interviews began in earnest over the subsequent two days. All were a disappointment. Dothan sat in his office at the conclusion of the second day and was going over the stack of resumes again when his phone pinged. It was a message from Kat, his new social media friend.

I would like to schedule a time when I could come by and discuss some of the issues facing Ft. Bryan City.

Dothan was intrigued. It was as if a beautiful witch had waved her wand. His heart rate increased, and with it, his breathing. In his impatience to absolve his self-perceived, long exile from the realm of belonging, he wanted to reply telling her that his schedule was open, but it wasn't. The back end of the week he was to be in Austin for a Culture and Recreation Committee interim hearing. He was going to spend the weekend visiting his daughter, Delilah.

How about Monday morning, say 11:00 a.m.?
Sounds good. See you then.

Tryphena waited for her ex-husband at her apartment in South Austin. She was apprehensive and nervous. Delilah began crying from her crib. She'd wet herself. Motherhood was not something that came naturally to Tryphena, which filled her with much guilt. As she changed Delilah's diaper, she wondered if having the baby had been the right thing. John David seemed to have little interest in his sole legacy, and this angered her. *But maybe I haven't given him a chance?* A tap on the front door broke her trance. After tossing the dirty diaper in the garbage, she welcomed Dothan into her guarded world.

"Come in. I just changed Delilah, let me wash my hands."

"No problem, is she in her room?"

"Yes, go in and see her. Speak softly," Tryphena said from the kitchen sink.

"She probably won't remember me. It's been so long."

Tryphena didn't like his tone, but she let it go. Dothan looked around at the well-decorated apartment. Pictures were hung, and there were vases filled with flowers. "Wow," he said.

"What is it?" Tryphena asked as she scrubbed away.

"Nothing, it's just that you have made your own little life here." He made his way back to Delilah's room.

Dothan awkwardly lifted his daughter from her crib and held her in his arms. He began speaking nonsensical baby talk. Delilah started to cry. Tryphena entered.

"I've told you before, she's afraid of men's voices. You have to speak softly and not so low." Tryphena nudged past John David, took the baby from his arms, and began to comfort her.

"Shit, I'm sorry," Dothan pleaded.

"I told you not to cuss in front of her."

"I'm sorry, Tryphena, I mean, fuck."

Tryphena shot back a contemptuous gaze.

"She's only five months old, for God's sake. I'm sorry."

"She's six months old."

"I'm sorry."

Delilah was left to rest as the two adults quietly exited the room. The two took seats at Tryphena's kitchen table. "Nice table," Dothan commented.

"Yes, it's mahogany. I'm almost afraid to eat off of it."

"How much did it cost?"

"It was a gift from a fellow lobbyist at the firm."

"Is that right?" Dothan said, tapping his fingers gently on the surface.

"I'm not sleeping with him," she protested.

"Hey, it's none of my business."

Tryphena looked at her ex-husband and felt a surge of

emotion, surprisingly it was positive. "So, how have you been?" she asked, moving her hands across the table toward his.

"Okay, I guess. I'm trying to find an assistant at the DO." They held hands.

"Oh, how do you like living upstairs from your office?"

"Not bad. It saves on gas."

"I'm sure." The supple look in her eyes registered with Dothan. "So, are you seeing anyone?" Tryphena asked.

"What? Me? No. I think I must have the mark of Cain at this point, or the black plague. I'm walking around in a cloud of miasma."

Tryphena laughed. "Hardly. Actually, you look really good. I see you dyed your hair and finally shaved that beard."

"I had to do something to make myself look younger."

"It worked. You look very handsome."

"Thank you. You look good yourself."

"Yuck, I look horrible. I'm sorry I've been so distant. I haven't meant to keep you from Delilah."

"It's okay. I'm been pretty self-absorbed lately, with this prick running against me and all."

"So, tell me about him. Zane Rayne? That sounds ridiculous."

"Hey, all you need is something catchy these days."

"John David Dothan is catchy…to me."

"Probably antiquated."

"I'm not so sure of that." Tryphena tightened her grip.

"Anyway, about Zane… He's the son of some big agricultural family in south Ft. Bryan. They own some grass farm or something."

"Yikes, that might help him in Wagoneer."

"Exactly."

"So how do you feel about it?"

"I'd feel better if I didn't feel so damned alone. These young Democrats are like fucking Maoists. They hate anyone over thirty."

"Is that the only reason you feel alone?" Tryphena asked. The light played off the glaze of her eyes. Dothan leaned toward her and stared, tracing every blood vessel.

"I think you know the answer to that."

Tryphena rose from the table and began undressing. She knew John David's fetish for bottomless women. She dropped her pants and panties. Only her top remained. She unfastening her bra and it dropped to the floor. Dothan watched as her round, brown bottom shook toward the bedroom.

When sex was finished, the two turned their backs from one another as they caught their breath.

"You were a little rough baby," Tryphena commented.

"Yeah, sorry. I got a little carried away."

"It's okay, I liked it."

"I'm thirsty," Dothan said, getting up.

"I don't have any beer, only Tito's."

"That'll have to do," he responded, heading toward the bedroom door.

"Pour me one as well, and please be quiet, baby, you'll wake Delilah."

"So what do you want to do this weekend?" Dothan asked after returning with their drinks. "We never really talked about that, just me visiting."

Tryphena pulled up a pillow and placed it against the headboard. She sat up and raised the drink from her nightstand. Her hair was in disarray and her breasts were exposed. Dothan followed her lead and pulled up a pillow as well. Situated, he stared over at her naked torso. Tryphena caught notice. She concealed herself with the available covers, up to her throat.

"Stop looking at them. They're hideous. Lactating has made them look awful. Pregnancy destroys a woman's body. You have no idea."

"I have an idea looking at you, and I think you look great. Your boobs are gorgeous."

"Gorgeous? What, swollen with milk?"

"Uh, yeah…"

"You are perverted, John David."

"Why, because I think my woman's breasts look good functioning for the purpose which nature intended? If a man can't find his post-pregnancy wife sexy, then there is something wrong with him. I just wish I'd seen you naked more often while you were pregnant."

"You really think that's sexy?"

"Yes, I do. There is nothing more beautiful."

"You're so sweet. I didn't mean to reproach you, baby."

"It's okay. You know what I'm thinking right now?" he asked.

"What, tell me." Tryphena took his hand as Dothan stared straight ahead.

"I wonder what kind of father I'll be."

"I think you'll be a good father, if you want to be."

"What does that mean? Of course I want to be."

"You'll be a good father, John David. I know it. I just wonder what kind of mother I'm going to be. I don't want to be one of these overly protective mothers, but sometimes I think that's what's coming out. My mom was so stern. She was loving, but stern. I think she did a good job."

"She did a great job," Dothan said. He turned his head and stared into her dampening eyes. "On another topic, how's the new lobby gig?"

"Not bad," she replied, wiping away modest tears. "Right now I'm just doing backline work, going through potential legislation for next session. Jimmy, my boss, is working on helping me get some actual contracts."

"Is he the dude that gave you the table?"

"Yes."

"Has Jimmy made a move on you?"

"Oh, my God, of course not! I can't believe you'd ask that."

"He's a guy…he's your boss…he gave you a fucking big-ass mahogany table…"

"Nothing like that. I'm not attracted to him, anyway."

"So what kind of lobbying do y'all do?"

"Water issues, mainly."

"Well, you do know something about that."

"Yes, I do, baby. Right now, we're looking into creating subsidence districts along the coast."

"Can't have that damned terra firma sinking under our feet now can we?"

"Some of these farmers in rural areas are just going to have to get used to the idea that they just can't pump water out of the ground like they have in the past."

"Wave of the future: Water Wars!"

"Change happens, and people adapt, John David."

"Oh, really? If for centuries, if not millenniums, people have fought over and slaughtered one another in droves over abstract ideas. You can damn well bet they'll do the same over a tangible, absolutely necessary resource like water—just saying."

"You've become very fatalistic, John David. I don't like it."

"It's not fatalistic. It's naturalistic."

"Whatever you say, Robinson Jeffers."

"Ha ha, that's funny you'd say that."

"Why?"

"I was reading a biography of the California poet recently, and it actually stated that Jeffers would be an environmentalist."

"Why wouldn't he be?"

"He was a naturalist! He would have seen environmentalism as not only the greatest human folly but the greatest expression of human vanity. How dare we puny humans think that anything we do will have any lasting effect on anything? It's ludicrous."

"Well, you know more about his writings than I do. I guess we'll see. I'm glad you came up this weekend. How was the Culture and Rec. hearing?"

"Boring."

The duration of the weekend was pleasant. Dothan, Tryphena, and Delilah acted out the nuclear family for the first time without pretense. Tryphena even had her ex-husband change his daughter's diaper once. Protest was minimal.

Back at his residence in the heart of his district, the poet legislator spent that Sunday night drinking and struggling with himself. He simply did not know how to read his ex-wife. She was all over the place. His whole weekend had been hot and cold. *Is she fucking with me?* he wondered. He had also noticed her dress was different. He had always lavished her with tasteful clothes. *Now she almost dresses like an old woman.*

The cause for his unease was very simple: Dothan had finally arrived to a point where he had accepted his reality which was apart from Tryphena's reality. He thought about writing, but wasn't up to it. He did have necessary writing work to do, though. UT Press was waiting for him to approve the second set of galleys. He had learned through email that volume two of his collected poems was set to be released in late fall or early winter. The thick envelope that sheathed his manuscript sat unopened in his closet. What struck him most about his recent sojourn at Tryphena's was that she had never inquired about his recently published book.

Not wishing to work on his own writing, he resigned himself to something at least associated with it. A DVD of Roman Polanski's, *Tess* had recently arrived in the mail. He'd just reread Hardy's tragic novel, and on a drunken whim, ordered the movie online. *Tess* was quite the rage when he was a young boy. He decided he might give it a chance. Though well-crafted, it grew laborious, at least in his present state. Another recent purchase was the 180mg vinyl of The Alarm's *Strength* album. With the keyboard intro of the first track rapidly chiming from the loft, he decided to sneak into his downstairs office. He checked his paper calendar on the desk.

"Oh, Lord, I forgot! She's coming in tomorrow!"

Annie Casey's life was habitual and ran like clockwork. The madman had been mapping out her movements and knew exactly what she did and when she did it, but he had no wish to harm her. He drove out to her residence repeatedly and surveilled from the woods. When watching her, a faint feeling of regret coated his sensibilities like a light mist. He always brought the brooch he had purchased in his pocket. The madman removed it from the small cotton sleeve he kept it in and would cup it in his palm, feeling its weight. It weighed on him.

One such evening, after departing his pedantic, voyeuristic fantasy, he decided, once in town, to drop by a local used bookstore. He was seeking something to offer explanation, and with explanation, perhaps guidance. With guidance perhaps would come redemption? He was like a sinner seeking out The Holy Bible.

He browsed the creased spines of old paperback classics and finally purchased a beat up volume of Robert Louis Stevenson's *The Strange Case of Dr. Jekyll and Mr. Hyde.*

Twelve

The morning sun was still making its way to her region of the hemisphere when Kat Morgan's alarm rang. Reaching over, she slammed it silent. Her mind and body lay in groggy twilight. Though dawn was distant and the notion of sleep the stuff of dreams, it was time to rise. Kat's morning routine, when she needed to impress, was an exercise in detail and perfection. She knew she was beautiful, but beauty was not enough. She needed to be stunning, and more importantly… prepared. The previous night she had purchased a leather-bound notebook specifically for this morning's occasion.

Kat started by shaving her legs in the shower. She wanted them as smooth as polished alabaster. After applying a clay mask, she straightened her hair, and then painted her finger and toenails. Makeup would come last. More than a week ago, she had chosen her attire for the coming meeting. Her palette matched the cover of John David Dothan's book of poems: dark blue and orange. Sunlight was just stripping the blinds as she put the finishing touches to her ruby lips.

Kat had spent the past two weeks reading *Collected Poems Vol. 1*. She was not well-versed in verse but had approached it as a project. She enjoyed the challenge. Much of it she did not quite grasp, as many of the poems were filled with allusions and metaphors that were obscure to the untrained eye. But there were a handful of poems that truly spoke to her. She knew her meeting this morning might prove one of the most unusual of her life; that, or a disappointment.

She did not know what to expect at all. After all, Representative John David Dothan had snubbed her at their first meeting. Sliding into her Prussian blue dress, she felt her stomach grow into tighter knots. She never ate before meetings or events. As Kat slipped on her orange pumps, she began to doubt herself. She decided to take a cigarette on the patio of her second-story apartment. She called a confidant.

"Hey…well, I'm all dressed up and ready to go."

"Good, how do you feel?" The voice on the other end asked.

"I'm so freaking nervous I don't know what to do with myself."

"Are you smoking?"

"Yes. I'm on the patio so it doesn't kill my perfume."

"It'll be fine."

"I've spent several hours getting my shit together for a meeting that will probably last ten minutes."

"You don't know that."

"Are you kidding me? This guy's an asshole."

"Not going to argue with that, Kat."

Kat Morgan crushed out her smoke and slid a fresh tube from her pack.

"Are you smoking another one?"

"Yes," she answered, as she exhaled. "I think I'm going to cancel. I don't think I can do this."

"You don't want to cancel. Just keep it together. If he's an asshole to you, then he's an asshole. It's just a meeting."

"I know…okay. When I'm done with this smoke I'm going to head over there. Will you follow me?"

"Of course."

Dothan woke up around 9:30. *Nothing Like the Sun* by Sting provided mood to the sunlit loft. He drank his coffee as he stood in boxer-briefs before the long mirror that hung from the outside of his bathroom door. The middle-aged man had been working out quite a bit lately. He flexed his recently reinvigorated biceps and admired the cut of his pectorals and lats. *I need to work on my legs more*, he thought.

With his morning routine finished, he pulled on his well-creased blue slacks. He chose a purple Polo, and then sat and drew his black cowboy boots over his socked heels. After gobbling a couple of slices of lightly toasted, buttered whole wheat bread, he was ready to rock and roll.

Still, he had a suspicion there was something more to all of this. In his gut, he knew without a doubt that there was something special about this morning's meeting…and that there was something special about Kat Morgan.

He sat in his office and tried maintaining the normalcy of routine. He felt restless. He dialed up YouTube and found his familiar playlist that varied if left to its own algorithm. As the designated time of her arrival grew closer, he rose and went into the foyer, unlocking the front door.

He waited.

The phone rang. The number on the caller ID told him he should not answer.

Van Halen's "Love Walks In" began to play from his computer.

The opening of the front door could be vaguely heard as he sat in his office. Nothing followed but silence. Rising, he strode into the foyer. Standing there was a most beautiful creature, like some celestial alien from a far-off planet. She was tall with long brown hair, long legs, big brown eyes, and his favorite…olive skin.

"Kat?" Dothan asked.

"Yes, hi," she answered, smiling.

"Representative JD Dothan. Please, come back to my office."

Kat's breathing was heavy as he offered her his hand. After she passed, he tarried in behind her. "Please, take a seat." he said authoritatively.

Both looked for a ring on the other. Dothan had none, Kat did. *Is that a wedding ring?* he wondered.

"Thank you." Kat sat down. Dothan followed. Before Dothan could engage, Kat pulled a book from her purse, stood up with an embarrassed, girlish smile, and placed it on his desk. "I'd like you to sign this for me…if you would."

"Oh, my book of poems…sure…"

Kat returned to her seat as Dothan searched for a pen. She folded thigh over thigh. Her long, olive calf dangled bare. Dothan hovered with his pen over the title page. He had signed many books. Usually with something he thought clever. There were a series of sayings…he must find something original. "I'll get this in a minute," he said, placing the ballpoint beside the shuttered volume. He leaned back in his chair. "Have you had a chance to read any of it?" The phone rang again. It was from the same number.

"Are you going to answer that?"

"No, not right now."

"I read it cover to cover," Kat answered, pursing her lips.

"Really? How did you like it? A bit esoteric, I know. No one really reads poetry anymore. It's kind of an arcane practice, really, like witchcraft or something,"

Kat switched folded legs. The harsh, overhead lights glittered like silk along their smooth naked pattern from the knee down.

I'm showing him my shoes…he's not noticing my outfit, Kat noted.

"Actually, I was impressed, Representative," she said, smiling again while tipping her head.

"Call me JD, please."

"That's short for John David?"

"It is."

"Can I call you that?"

"John David?"

"Yes."

"If you like."

The phone rang again. Dothan did not answer.

"Well, John David, like I said, I was impressed. I have to confess that some of it was over my head, but some of the poems I found really beautiful."

"At the risk of sounding narcissistic, may I ask which one that spoke to you in particular?"

"There were a few, but the one I remember the most was, 'The Girl That I Hailed.'"

"Ah, yes. That's one of my favorites, too."

"I enjoyed it so much, I memorized it."

"Really?"

Kat pursed her lips again, looked up at the ceiling, and then lowered her gaze to Dothan's startled eyes. She recited:

"I who understand the burning contempt cold,
Of labor without reward:
A tune caught as light ignites a snaking stream,
That I could never ford.
Or a conjured verse from the cauldron buoyant,
Yet scalded every word.

A legislative ends, plain, fair and just,
A governor deemed absurd…
But most contemptuous, by far, of all these fails…
The Love unrequited, from the girl that I hailed."

"Wow, I have to say I'm not only flattered but blown away! I don't think that I could have read it verbatim, and I wrote the damn thing!"

"Really?" Kat giggled, switching legs again.

"Definitely," Dothan confirmed, looking down with humility.

"Are you surprised I knew it that well? I did get it right… right?"

"Word for word," Again the phone rang.

"Who is that, if you don't mind me asking?"

"Just this pitiful old woman, her son is in prison. It's a mess."

Kat continued, "There are a few I've memorized by heart."

"I believe it. What about that poem worked for you?" Dothan asked, professorially.

"I don't really get all the metaphors and stuff, but it expresses a great disappointment…a deep regret. It's very sad and also very ancient sounding."

"Well, it spoke to you, and that pleases me," He replied, not knowing what else to say.

Kat was smitten by his obvious superciliousness, not toward her, but his work. She decided to venture another "'The Cave Painter.'"

"You memorized that one?"

"Yes…here it goes.

His tribe had cast him out.
His only crime that of…

He had wooed a woman.
Not with gut force or strength,
But with an artist's mind.

She rose not in defense,
But rather cold disgust,
Toward he that set her free.
And over his shoulder saw
Her take that savage arm.

The dawn was cold and frosted.
His brush could plant no seed.
He must come to accept it:
Like the sunset lurking…
With no promise of beckon.

But in her womb guarded…
A fugitive fresh grew."

"You're killing me here," Dothan joked, genuinely taken aback.

"Am I?" Kat jested, very pleased with herself. "That poem I found intriguing. Did I get it right again?"

"A trifle really—and, yes, you recited it word for word… again."

"What do you mean by 'a trifle?'"

"It was something I fired off really quickly. It's a version of a very loose trimeter."

"I'm not sure what that means. I did take a poetry class in college, but my memory escapes me."

"It's not important. I'm glad you liked it."

"What were you trying to say? It may be a trifle, but it suggests quite a bit."

"I think I was just trying to demonstrate the birth of the idea of an artist, apart from the art. It's how one could conceivably see how things might have occurred, at least in a benign fashion. The savage whose woman the painter had coveted would probably have bashed the guy's head in with a saber-toothed tiger's fang. The artist is an exile, ultimately, whether representative of a culture or in rebellion of it."

"That's heavy," Kat said. Dothan was beginning to think he was being too pedantic. Kat thought the opposite. "You don't mind if I make a comment about that last poem do you?"

"Of course not. Fire away." Dothan prepared himself.

"Well, you don't think that maybe…maybe it's kind of, well…sexist?"

"How?"

"She denounces him."

"Of course she does. It's a rare woman who chooses love over security. It's bio-anthropological, and in womankind's defense, it's usually a wise choice. The painter could have never offered her survival. In fact, it's insinuated in the third stanza that he will perish. His only vindication is that his seed will survive and produce another of his kind. No one knows for sure, but this is how intelligence most likely came into being. That's my theory, anyway."

"You are a very interesting man, John David."

"Not so much… We've talked enough about me, tell me about yourself."

"I'm not nearly as interesting."

"I'll be the judge of that."

"Well, I'm very driven, but I've made mistakes in my past."

"As we all have."

"Yes we have," Kat replied. "Mine was a very bad marriage to a guy who treated me very poorly. A byproduct of that treatment was that I got really down on myself. In fact, I let it damage my self-esteem." Kat batted her eyes in deference.

"I'm sorry to hear that. I have to say, in my opinion, the whole of feminine experience since we crawled from the proverbial slime has been one of complete irony."

"What do you mean?"

"Too often women seek that which works against their best interests while believing that what they seek is in their best interest. That's all."

"It's funny you say that, because we, my ex-husband and I, met in college. Both of us were political science majors. He acted like he was an ambitious future candidate for…something, but he was really a serial philanderer."

"Sounds like the Clintons." Kat nervously laughed at Dothan's comment. "Let me guess," he continued. "The dude's running for governor in an impoverished Southern state as we speak?"

"Uh, no. That would give him too much credit. Actually, I can't believe I'm telling you all this," Kat moved her long fingers toward her face in mock shock. "Last I heard, he was in jail."

"Jail?"

"Yes, he was arrested in Corpus Christi in a drug sting. From what I read, it had something to do with narcotics."

"Jesus! Did this transpire when y'all were still married?"

"No, thank God. It was a year or so after our divorce."

"So, if you don't mind me asking, what was the reason for the two of you splitting?"

"That's a pretty sick story. We were living in Austin. He had a job working as a valet at The Four Seasons downtown. I was working at the Capitol. Turns out, he was sleeping with everyone who worked at the hotel." Kat stuck her index finger near her throat and mimicked vomiting.

"That bad?" Dothan asked.

"Oh my God, it was terrible. It got him fired. I went and got tested for everything under the sun. Thank God it all checked out."

"That sucks. I'm really sorry to hear this, particularly in light of the fact that it hurt you so much."

"It did, but I got over it," Kat stated, perking up. "It slowed me down for a few years, but I graduated and moved on."

"And now you're in my office."

"I am."

The two were in the moment. Neither thought of anything but the impulse striking at that instant. Then something else happened that instant. "What's that?" Dothan asked alarmed.

"What?"

"I think someone came into the office," Dothan rose from his chair, grabbed his cane, and headed toward the foyer. Kat's big brown eyes followed every movement of his body. Dothan was stopped in the purgatory of the hallway by an unexpected visitor.

"Mr. Dothan, I'm so sorry I just showed up like this," the woman said. "I've been calling all morning. My Roderick is in some kind of trouble at the Rosharon Unit, and TDCJ won't tell me what's going on. I think he's ill. I know they don't care about no poor country black folk, but I got's to know what's wrong with my baby. He had pneumonia back a month or so. I can't get no information, sir."

"It's okay, Mrs. Henry," Dothan sighed. "I'll put in a call to the Department of Criminal Justice and find out for you. We'll call them now. They won't tell me no." Dothan looked at Kat with a combination of regret and duty. "I'm sorry, but I'm going to have to deal with this."

"I understand," she said. She grabbed her purse, took the book off of Dothan's desk, and stood. "You have work to do, and I've wasted enough of your time."

"You didn't waste any of my time, I assure you."

Kat left and the elderly Mrs. Henry replaced her in the chair. Dothan pulled out the State Directory and searched for his contact at TDCJ.

After the matter was cleared, and Mrs. Henry was gone, Dothan messaged Kat.

Sorry about that. Nuts. Crazy on a ship of fools. Can you shoot me some contact info?

My contact info? she replied.

Yeah, like an email.

Sure.

Thirteen

etective Garza sat at a traffic light near downtown Ft. Bryan City. His mind was lost in thought. Loneliness was his passenger. Frustration could be felt in his fingertips. He was an unhappy, troubled man. The light from the left turning lane on the opposite street ahead turned green. His thoughts were tuned to the here and now.

"What's this?" A green Ford pickup with a load of turf sections that weighed down the rear suspension turned left. His intention was to go straight. He hit his blinker and turned right. The sluggish acceleration of the vehicles ahead of him compounded his frustration.

Garza followed the slow moving truck as it made its way through the city toward the country. The green Ford's left blinker signaled. Garza drove past as the truck exited. He turned around and parked along the side of the highway. There was a sign some distance from the road. The green truck passed under it in a cloud of dust. Garza grabbed his binoculars from the glove box. He stepped out of his car so he could get a better angle. "Well, what do you know?" The sign read, "Rayne Turf Works." He headed back into town and called Lieutenant Young.

"Young, you got a minute?"

"Garza, you bet. What's up?"

"When you ran background info on green trucks, did you search everything?"

"Everything? How do you mean?"

"Did you check businesses—Corporations, S Corps, LLCs?"

"I had staff do the background checks, actually."

"Damnit, man, you didn't do it yourself?"

"No. Like I said, I delegated it to staff."

"Well, find out. I suspect 'staff' didn't check everything."

"I'll find out and get on it, sir."

On his way back to the station, Garza picked up a late lunch from Sonic then chewed his hamburger as he drove. By the time he pulled into the station, he felt indigestion coming on and was in a foul mood when he entered the building.

"Any word on the status?" he barked at Lieutenant Young.

"They never did run those other searches, sir."

"Are you on it now?"

"I have them looking into it."

"Get up off your ass and supervise this immediately! This may be the break we've been looking for, man! Goddamn, think dynamically!" Garza was clearly agitated so he turned right around and left for a walk to help his digestion. After several blocks, he came upon the Cultural District. He stood catty-corner to Representative Dothan's office.

Dothan was in his office alone when Garza came in. Until that moment, the only thing on the Representative's mind had been his meeting with Kat Morgan.

"Yes?" Dothan called out, having heard the front door open. Before he could lift himself from his chair, the dark figure of Detective Garza was standing just outside his office. "Detective?"

"Hello. Sorry to show up unannounced. May I come in?" Garza asked.

"Of course."

"You're not too busy are you?"

"Would it matter?"

"Actually, yes."

"Really, how? Haven't you come to inquire about my alibi?"

"May I sit down?" Garza asked. Dothan signaled an affirmative. "Representative Dothan, I know you have nothing to do with our case, that's not why I'm here."

"Why are you here?"

"I've been thinking about something Sheriff Neilson suggested."

"Neilson? He's a staunch Republican probably out for my scalp."

"Hardly. He's a Republican, yes, but he thought you might be able to help. You're a creative type, right?"

"A 'creative type?'" Dothan sniped, mockingly.

Garza felt that he had somehow offended the man, though he had no intention whatsoever of doing so.

"Yes, I would say that—although, not necessarily in that way."

"I didn't mean to offend you, sir."

"I don't allow people to offend me," Dothan relented. "It's just funny that's all. How can I help?"

"What we have on our hands is a psychopath, possibly with schizophrenia. He's leaving clues, but I don't think they are meant to be clues."

"How does that work?"

"Exactly. How *does* that work? To tell you the truth, I haven't a clue. What are his motives? That's the question. I don't think that he's finished, though. This is like some sick work of art. I've no idea what's coming, but I know in my heart of hearts that this isn't done. That scares me."

"If you're right, it scares me, too," Dothan said. "To tell you the truth, I haven't thought much about it for some time. By the way, I haven't brought this up with my ex-wife. Things are weird enough between us as it is. Do you understand?"

"I do, and like I said, I know you are clean. I was wondering, if I described some of the 'clues' this guy has left, your creative background could help with the investigation."

"I'll have to think about that one. I have an election to win."

"An election…of course. I've heard that before."

"Whether you've heard it before or not is immaterial to me. I'm a legislator, not a cop."

"I understand, sir. Will you think about it?"

"I will."

Garza returned to the station much in the way he had left, with his hands stuffed in the pockets of his black slacks as he walked. Once he arrived, he paced his office with his eyes focused on the floor.

Lieutenant Young tapped on the door jam. "Sir, we've got the information you requested."

"Already?"

"Yes. Only one company comes up: Rayne Turf Works. It's an S-Corp. It appears they have title to eleven green pickups—a couple of Chevys, but mostly Fords. The specific makes and years vary. Here's a printout of the license plates."

Dry weather had set in recently, so the madman left his truck at a secure location. After walking more than a mile, he now stood on the perimeter of Annie Casey's yard. He was dressed in a tuxedo. A rose in full flush was pinned to his lapel. The eight-point brooch was tucked away in his coat pocket, housed in a small, elegant box. Another gift swung from a canvas bag. Clenched in his sweating fist, a bottle of Chateau St. Georges waited for presentation as he made his way across the lawn that was in need of mowing.

There was a knock on Annie's back door. Don Gato leapt from the bed. Startled, she put on her slippers and shrugged into a robe. The sun had almost set, and she wondered who might be calling. She thought that it was perhaps a construction worker from the area, coming to inform her of some goings on. Recently, she had been informed by the crew on the adjacent property of a temporary road closing or waterline interruption. As she peered through the slats of the back door blinds, she was surprised to see a well-dressed man with a bottle of wine standing there.

"Can I help you?" Annie asked through the door in her thick Southern drawl.

"Annie, I'm the homeowner from next door. I've just come by to introduce myself. My name is Dothan. I know it's awkward, but the house is almost complete, and I thought I'd just stop by to make your acquaintance."

"So you're my new neighbor…or should I say my only neighbor?" Annie laughed.

"Yes. Forgive me for the theatrics."

"Did you walk? You look a little sweaty. I do have air-conditioning. Come on in, Mr. Dothan. Or is that your first name?" Annie unlatched the door.

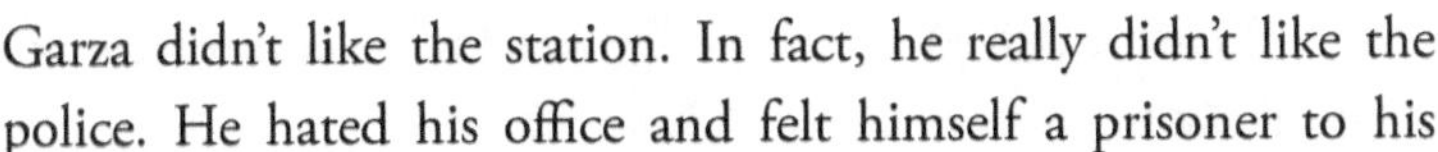

Garza didn't like the station. In fact, he really didn't like the police. He hated his office and felt himself a prisoner to his self-imposed limitations. His pride was swelling, and soon to rebel. He stuffed the information he had received that afternoon from Lieutenant Young into his expanding case file and shoved it impatiently into his briefcase. The light to the chief of police's office was visible down the hall. He was going to make another impromptu visit.

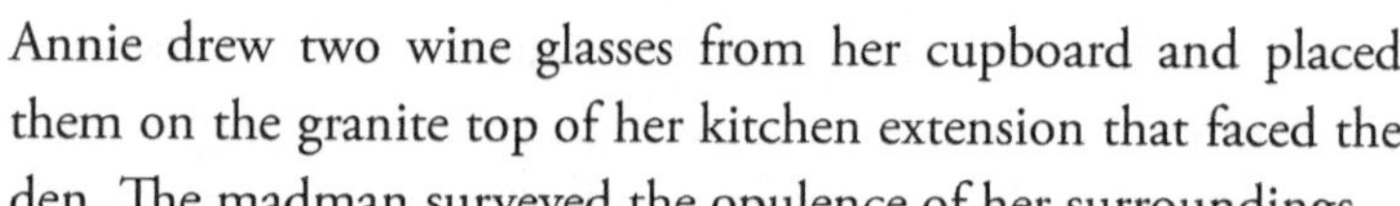

Annie drew two wine glasses from her cupboard and placed them on the granite top of her kitchen extension that faced the den. The madman surveyed the opulence of her surroundings.

"You've got a very fine place here, Annie."

"Thank you, Mr. Dothan. The house you're building is very fine, too." Annie pulled a corkscrew from a drawer and began peeling the foil from the bottle top. "I don't get many visitors. I know this makes me sound strange, but I don't have any friends, really."

"Let me do that, please," The madman interjected, taking the corkscrew. After he opened the wine, Annie and the madman took a seat across from one another in the den.

"So, Mr. Dothan, you never answered my question: Is Dothan your first or last name?"

"Oh, forgive me. John David is my Christian name, Dothan my surname."

"If we're going to be neighbors and all…do you mind if I call you John David?"

"Of course not, although my friend's call me JD."

"I prefer John David. So when will you be moving in?"

"There are still some things that need to be completed, but I would say by this summer."

"Wonderful. I have to tell you that it's so nice out here. It's like living in the country but with the conveniences of the suburbs." The two had already consumed their respective glasses.

"Would you like another?" The madman asked.

"Well, thank you, John David," Annie surrendered her glass. "As I said, I have so few friends…well…since my divorce."

"I'm sorry to hear that," the madman said as he handed her glass back to her.

"Most of my friends were 'our' friends, if you know what I mean. So when Tom and I divorced—Tom is my ex-husband—I really kind of—"

"Found yourself alone?"

"I did." Annie had already killed her second glass. "Don't you get up," she said, "I can serve myself." It was apparent the wine was working its magic. She returned to her seat, carrying a full glass. "So what is it that you do, John David?"

"I'm in politics."

"Politics? I don't do politics. Really, I don't even ever vote. I know I should. What do you do in politics?"

"I'm your State Representative."

"What's that?"

"It's like a congressman, only not in Washington but Austin."

"I see," Annie said, confused.

"I make state law, Annie."

"Oh, like seatbelt laws and stuff!"

"Exactly!" The madman lifted his glass in a toast. Annie smiled obligingly.

"We need to talk!" Garza insisted as he closed Chief Olivo's door behind him.

"I'm busy, Garza. It'll have to wait." Olivo sat at his desk reviewing a pile of paperwork.

"Did you know that those dipshits out there didn't even think to run a search on green trucks that belonged to companies? What kind of fucking amateurs are you hiring around here Olivo?"

"Whoa, you're out of line Garza. I suggest you take your righteous ass out of here right now!"

"I'll do no such thing."

"Then I'll have you removed," Olivo said derisively. "It's not their fault you've got nothing on that case. Besides, you could've got up off your lazy ass and done the backline work yourself. All you do is delegate. You know Sheriff Neilson called me a few weeks back. He thinks we need to bring in the Feds because you're so incompetent!"

"Why, you son of a bitch."

Olivo stood up. "Get the fuck out of here right now before I fire your ass!"

"You won't have to fire me. I quit!"

"Fine, get your shit and move on, you fucking prima donna."

"You are a clown, Olivo. A goddamned clown!"

"You say that any closer and I'm gonna knock a fuckin' hole in your skull! Get out of here!"

Garza thrust the door open and stampeded out through a throng of listeners just outside Olivo's office. Olivo followed. "And take your fuckin' grandmother's tequila with you. That nasty shit ain't worth running a lawnmower."

Garza stopped. He turned around. "You fucking prick, how dare you bring my family into this. You're Hispanic."

"I just did. And what the hell does that matter? I'm Venezuelan, not Mexican. You're lucky I haven't had your ass arrested for smuggling contraband across the border."

Garza grabbed his sports coat from the rack, stormed out into the night, fired up his engine, and sped out of the station parking lot.

--- ◇ ---

"Do you like music, Annie?" the madman asked.

"Of course. Who doesn't like music?"

"Great, I brought you a gift."

"Other than the wine?"

"Yes, you do like the wine, don't you?"

"It's wonderful, Mr. Dothan."

"John David, please." The madman got up and went to the counter where he retrieved his canvas satchel. "Here you go." He pulled out a vinyl album still wrapped in plastic.

"Oh, my, what's this?" Annie read the artist and title. "I've never heard of this person before. Is it new?"

"Far from it, it's from the 1970s."

"Oh, I love the '70s! I even have a turntable. It was my husband's, but I took it to spite him." Annie went toward the entertainment center. "Luckily, when I had all this installed, the technician connected everything. I really have no clue about electronics."

"Here, allow me." The madman took the album from her, and with his pinky fingernail sliced the seam at the spine. He slid the thick black disk from its sleeve and placed it gently on the turntable. The madman sat next to Annie on the sofa as the orchestral keyboard music filled the room.

"This is interesting." Annie said, gulping her wine.

"You're track two."

"What do you mean?"

"You are track two. It's about you."

"Oh? Why track two? Is there any singing?"

The madman handed her the album jacket, backside up. He tapped his finger on the picture under the designation of track two.

Annie giggled.

"I have something else for you, Annie." From inside his coat pocket, he removed a small, elegant jewelry box.

"Oh my, what's this?" Annie placed her glass on the coffee table along with the album jacket.

"A parting gift."

"Parting? But we only just met…John David." Annie fingered the soft ruby felt of the lid.

"Open it."

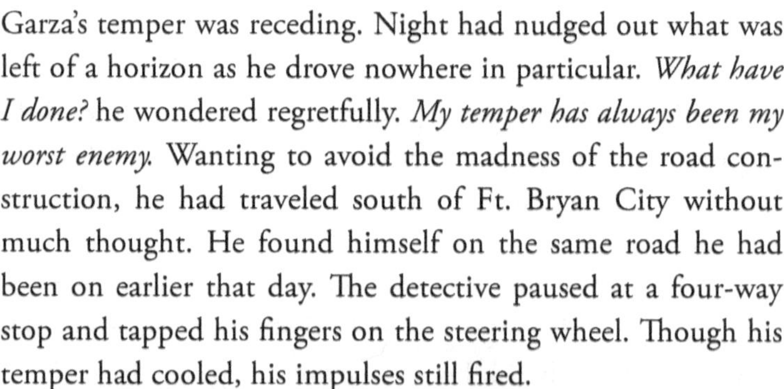

Garza's temper was receding. Night had nudged out what was left of a horizon as he drove nowhere in particular. *What have I done?* he wondered regretfully. *My temper has always been my worst enemy.* Wanting to avoid the madness of the road construction, he had traveled south of Ft. Bryan City without much thought. He found himself on the same road he had been on earlier that day. The detective paused at a four-way stop and tapped his fingers on the steering wheel. Though his temper had cooled, his impulses still fired.

The turn off for Rayne Turf Works appeared in his headlights. Garza decided to risk it. *Maybe they've all gone home for the day.* He needed to find something of substance to salvage the job he had just thrown away. *It's all I have,* he lamented.

He pulled carefully off the highway and drove slowly into the entrance of the establishment. He killed the engine and stepped out into the temperate night. With the exception of a tall, overhead spotlight, the grounds were enveloped in darkness. No lights illumined from the office widows, only a single outside bulb shone above the entrance. The small office buildings, sitting on blocks, were to his left. A sizable barn towered to his right some fifty yards away. Beyond, in the darkness, sprouted acres of grass; and beyond that, fresh suburban outcroppings.

— · · ◇ · · —

"Oh my, what is this?" Annie asked as she removed a brooch in the shape of an eight-point star from the small, red box.

"It's called an escarbuncle. At least, that's the design."

"A what?"

"It's for you, Annie, to commemorate our time together. I have set you up nicely here, I think."

"You what?" Annie turned toward the madman. "I'm confused, John David."

"Nothing to be confused about. I just wanted to stop by and leave you with this. I must get back to my duties." The madman stood up.

"How did you know my name was Annie? Did you look through my mail or something?"

"Silly woman…we were married."

"Is this some kind of joke?"

"You will live and flourish without me. I have given you that. That is my greatest gift."

"Okay, this is weird. I'd like you to go…please."

"I'm leaving."

"Please take this," Annie insisted, handing him the velvet box, "and your record. I'd like you to go now."

"What?" You spoiled, mundane, domestic bitch! I tried to culture you, but you are too homely to appreciate beauty!" he said, enraged.

"Oh, my God. Please leave," Annie implored more than demanded.

The madman fell to his knees in a plea. "Annie, please, please take the gifts. Please, it is a part of my design."

Annie stood up and ran toward the landline, which hung from the wall near the back door. She lifted the receiver, but only managed to punch the number nine. The madman approached from behind, grabbed her by the shoulders, and threw her across the floor. Annie flew in violent disfiguration. Her head smashed into the corner of a kitchen cabinet. She collapsed limply. Her tangled body shook involuntarily. Dark-red blood dripped out of her brown hair. The spot grew and grew on the floor until it puddled.

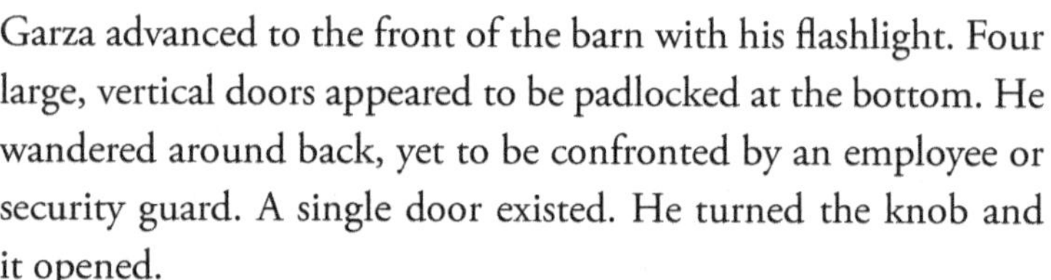

Garza advanced to the front of the barn with his flashlight. Four large, vertical doors appeared to be padlocked at the bottom. He wandered around back, yet to be confronted by an employee or security guard. A single door existed. He turned the knob and it opened.

The flashlight revealed what one would expect—flatbed trailers, forklifts, farm equipment, and green pickup trucks.

Had the madman's providence been only luck? He viewed the kitchen and den with great dismay. *What am I to do?* he anguished. *I have nothing to erase my presence here tonight.* Panic shot through his soul, but only for an instant. He settled down and began to ponder. *I could turn the gas on and blow the place up…but fire won't erase anything, really. It will take some time to determine that a crime was committed, but they will figure it out. It won't be easy though…I should sleep on it. Annie told me she has no friends. She has no job. Family?*

He decided to sleep on it.

Garza tried to open every truck door. Some were locked, some unlocked. He approached his inquiry methodically, moving from left to right. Some five pickups had been inspected. The last in line was oddly placed. It was parked crookedly just inside the barn. He tried the driver's side door. It opened.

The madman made his way through the small copse and open dell of turf crop. He had no flashlight. He stumbled numerous times. The distant spotlight of Rayne Turf Works doubled as his premature morning star.

Garza's first rule of order was to check glove boxes. This particular one yielded a wallet. He shined the yellow beam down as it unfolded. *What's this?* The crunch of footsteps sounded. The echo made it hard to determine from which direction. Replacing the wallet, he removed his torso and head from the cab. He turned and was struck with an epiphany: "YOU? It's you."

Fourteen

You want to get lunch this Thursday, John David? We never did discuss business.

Sure. Where?

Awesome. Pick a lunch place. I took the day off. I have a facial appt. that a.m. LOL.

Kat, looking tall and stunning in her pumps, stood outside a Mexican food establishment called Gringos. She wore blue pants and a blue jean jacket over a crème top. Through her oblong sunglasses, she caught Dothan looking her up and down as he approached. She was less obvious with her observations, but was impressed by his classic black suit and tie.

They stepped to the bar area and immediately ordered drinks. Dothan killed his beer in a matter of minutes. When the waitress returned, he brusquely ordered a second.

"Well, that was rude," Kat remarked. Her lips were pursed and her brows clenched, knotting the otherwise smooth flesh above her nose.

"What…?"

"Your tone with the waitress was rude."

Dothan made sure to correct himself when the waitress came by again, and again…and again.

What was to be a brief appointment, at least for Dothan, stretched well past the allotted hour. It was the middle of the afternoon, and they had talked very little about business. Instead, their conversation was about travel, college, Dothan's writing, and his failed marriage.

"So how long have you been divorced?" Kat asked.

"Lord, I don't know…about a year now."

"What happened? If you don't mind me asking."

"I don't know. I guess I was selfish. Tryphena has always known what she wants, but then somehow she doesn't."

"Sounds female."

"We just drifted apart, I guess. I made some bad decisions. I think I was too busy doing what needed to be done with my job and not enough with my marriage. We have a child."

"Yes, I know. How do you like being a father?"

"I love it, though it scares me. To tell you the truth, I don't see my daughter that much."

"Because of Tryphena?"

"I suppose." Dothan changed the subject. "So your mom is a city councilor. I get the impression she doesn't like me."

Kat laughed and finished off her margarita. She ordered a second. "What makes you think that? You've never met her, have you?"

"I sat with her at the museum shindig."

"Oh, I forgot about that. Mayor Andy's table, right? Yeah, she told me, come to think of it." The margarita quickly arrived and her full lips drew on the straw.

"Well, did she have anything to say about it?"

"She said you were rude."

"Seems to run in the family."

"Ha, ha. I wouldn't take it personally."

"Honestly, I think she was kind of rude."

"Look, she doesn't like me either. "

"Well, I like you."

"You do?"

"Yes. I'm glad you contacted me. We had a good meeting the other day, I think."

"We didn't even discuss Ft. Bryan at all—then or today. Let me get the check."

Outside, their eyes adjusted to the sunlight as Dothan followed Kat to her car.

"Thanks for meeting me for lunch," she said. "I didn't mean to drag you away from work." "I don't think I'll get much done this afternoon. I'm a little high."

Kat hugged him and kissed his cheek before they parted.

Dothan returned to his office, and the afternoon buzz started to dull. He sat down to check his work emails. He had a reminder from the Ft. Bryan County Legislative Liaison, Raymond Ricardo, regarding an upcoming concert at the city's new event center. A month or so back, Ricardo had contacted him about a legislative night out to a concert of Dothan's choosing. Ricardo pitched Judas Priest. Dothan laughed hysterically. He commented that it might be offensive to some of the area elected officials. They'd settled on Jason Isbell. Dothan had forgotten all about it. It was scheduled for Wednesday of the coming week.

Dothan pondered at his computer screen while rubbing the five o'clock shadow on his jaw. "To hell with it!"

Kat sat on her couch drinking a glass of wine and mindlessly channel surfing. She rarely watched television, but she was in an odd state. Her phone pinged with a message from Dothan.

Ft. Bryan County's holding a legislative concert event in their suite at The Imperial next Wed. A lot of state and county officials going. Interested? Great way to politically network.

She immediately texted him back and accepted the invitation.

After Dothan received her text, he set out for more beer.

———◇———

Though Dothan was hungover the next morning, it looked like it was going to be a fine day. The April sun pierced through his bedroom like a renaissance. He felt more renewed than he had in months. The curveball that Tryphena had thrown him was but a figment from the past.

Dothan had recently purchased a set of weights. He splashed water on his face and dressed in shorts and a tank top. He choked down a protein shake mixed with a freshly cracked egg white.

Iron Maiden's *Piece of Mind* was going at top volume when Mayor Andy discovered Dothan doing lunges up and down the long hallway.

"Hey, dude!" the mayor yelled.

Dothan's back was to him, and he didn't realize he had company until he reached the end of the hall and turned around. "Oh, hey." Dothan dropped the weights. "Hang on." The sweating representative paused the music and descended the loft stairs to welcome his guest. "Sorry about that, man, just trying to do something about these skinny ass legs of mine."

"You're looking fit to me, JD."

"Yeah, I've been working on it. Ever since my stroke I've had problems with my right leg, particularly the outside of the foot."

"Can ya feel it?"

"Yeah, I can feel it. It comes and goes. Trust me, I'm being careful as hell doing these lunges."

"Well, don't hurt yourself."

"I'll risk anything for vanity, you know. Let's go into my office." The mayor followed. "What's up, Andy?"

"Ah, nothing, man. I was just stopping in to see how things were going. Last time I came by you were just gettin' settled in."

"Take a seat. Yeah, it's coming along, I suppose. I need to hire an assistant, but I haven't had any luck so far."

"Well, I'm sure it doesn't pay much, and in this job market it's probably hard to find good people."

"Pretty much. So, how can I help you today?"

"Like I said, just stopping in to see what's up."

"Anything going on I need to know about?"

"What, with Ft. Bryan City? Just the usual city council drama. I guess there's the road construction issue. Did you ever talk to the highway department about that?"

"I call them with every complaint. They don't do anything, of course. Nice folks, though. It's just going to have to run its course."

"Yeah, I guess."

"By the way, are you going to that concert next Wednesday night?" Dothan asked.

"You mean at the Imperial?"

"Yeah, I got an invite from the county."

"Yeah, I did too. I'll have to see. I'd have to find a date…a little late for that, I think."

"You're not married?"

"Not anymore—been married too many times. Oh, I've got a lady friend, and then there's another gal I've got my sights set on."

"I'm going with Kat Morgan."

"Oh, the councilwoman's daughter?" Andy's tone and expression was both surprised and cautious.

"Yeah, do you know her?"

"A bit."

"What does that mean?"

"Nothing, really. She's an ambitious one, that Kat Morgan."

"Yes, she is…and beautiful."

"Watch out for her, JD."

"Why do you say?"

"She's friends with Zane."

"Like how?"

"I just know they're close."

Blooming flowers spilled from the large pots placed about the Cultural District's capacious sidewalks. Dothan stepped out into the early evening sun dressed in an apricot dress shirt that hugged his increasingly muscular torso. Just moments ago he was in his loft laboring in indecision as to what shirt to wear. Apricot seemed very spring-like. From the waist down, it was his usual jeans and boots. His brown boots were special, though, as they brandished a fine stitching of the Texas State Seal in bright yellow. Everyone who had ever seen them was impressed. Often times, admirers would actually take a picture of them to post to social media. While dressing, he repeated a YouTube video of Jason Isbell's, "Traveling Alone." The song, though melancholy, was stuck in his head. Breathing in the fragrant smell of honeysuckle, he started his truck while feeling like a stud.

The plan was simple: Dothan would meet Kat in front of the Home Depot at the local Town Center. This center consisted largely of big-box stores found nearly anywhere, but it was a safe, central location. From there, the two would Uber to The Imperial. Before his wardrobe dilemma, he had downloaded the Uber app. Dothan was a poet and skilled in the arcane arts. He was not adept at burgeoning technology.

Kat's blue car was already sitting in the parking lot as he arrived. *A few minutes early,* he thought. She was on the phone as he pulled beside her. He saw her laughing and giggling through the driver's-side window. Dothan remained in his car until she stuffed the device in her purse.

"Hi," she greeted giddily, shutting her car door behind her. Kat was dressed all in black—tight black shorts, and a taut black top. Her already considerable height was accentuated by black pumps. Her dark brown hair cascaded over her shoulders. Her lips were blood red.

"Hey, are you ready?" Dothan asked.

"Yeah, we're going to Uber, right?"

"You look great by the way," Dothan added.

"Thank you. I had a wardrobe malfunction, actually. I'll tell you about it later."

Now, Dothan's lack of techie acumen was about to prove troublesome. As Kat opened the passenger door of his truck, he was tinkering with his phone.

"Okay, I've got the addresses in my pocket, both for the Home Depot and The Imperial." His butt squirmed as he procured the handwritten information from his back pocket. When he tried entering the information, it registered as if he was to serve as the Uber driver. "Shit." He tried a few more times with the same result. Kat stood holding the door. Her lips pursed, and her brows tightened as she became impatient. Even worse, she seemed irritated.

"I can call a friend to take us to The Imperial…really," she offered.

In his mind he knew that he was about to blow it. *Have her friend chaperone us on a date?* The thought was anathema to him. "I'll drive."

"I thought you didn't want to deal with parking? What if you start drinking?"

"It's cool. Hop in."

Kat noticed the floorboard of his passenger's seat was a mess of cans and wrappers.

"Here, let me clean that up for you," Dothan pleaded.

"It's fine, really."

Their conversation was tense as they drove the five miles to the venue. Mostly, Dothan talked about his truck, of which he was very proud. Kat had yet to comment.

"I notice your clock hasn't been changed. Daylight saving time started a few weeks ago," she quipped.

"Yeah, you know this old girl got hit by a hurricane some-time back," Dothan prattled. "I had to have it gutted. I probably would have had to sell her for scrap if not for a constituent who owned a full body repair shop. He fixed me up via an in-kind contribution. I use this as a campaign car. When he redid the electrical system, he put this high-tech, digital clock in here, along with satellite radio, which I love. I hate to say this, but I don't know how to change the clock."

With the long fingers of her left hand Kat hit a few buttons and forwarded the hour. "There."

Dothan was starting to feel he was making a fool of himself and was grateful when they finally made it to The Imperial. He pulled into the complicated parking lot and was directed through the maze toward a parking space by men in orange hazard vests. Dothan was relieved to park the truck. Kat seemed over it. The sun was still high in the spring sky as they trekked toward the entrance. Kat strutted. Dothan struggled hard to maintain a stiff pace. He had left his faithful cane at home.

"I can't believe you're wearing that shirt," Kat quipped.

"What's wrong with it?"

"Nothing," she answered with a mocking snicker.

"Hey, check this out, though!" The two paused. Dothan bent down and pulled his jean leg up to reveal the state seal on his brown boots.

Kat laughed. "Oh, the state of Texas."

He released his pant leg, disappointed. They continued forward. Kat paused to take a picture of the brightly lit fountains that sprouted in arches. At the front gates, an army of staff awaited them.

Their tickets were at Will Call, but after Dothan directed Kat through the security gate, they found themselves at the front doors without tickets.

"Tickets, please?" the usher asked.

"Uh, I'm Representative JD Dothan. I do have tickets. They're supposed to be at Will Call?"

"You'll have to go back through these ropes and reenter through the first gate. It's marked 'VIP and Will Call.'" Dothan turned to find Kat with her arms folded and her left leg cocked in derision. *Was this all a mistake?* he worried.

When they finally made it inside the beautiful venue, there was a specific route up to the suites. Dothan had been a guest here before and thought he remembered the appropriate path. He didn't. He had to solicit directions. Kat laughed while they rode the elevator to the second floor that housed the suites. The door opened and before them unfolded a long, curved hallway of dim exclusivity. Dothan struggled to remember exactly what suite they were seeking.

"Do you know where we're going now?" she asked.

"Yeah, it's in the center of the curve. We do have center stage, by the way," He remembered the letter 'G' and abruptly angled toward the large, dark door labeled as such.

As they entered the suite, ambiance hovered with an air of sophistication. It was not spacious and no bigger than a small bedroom. The far wall served as a glass partition through which the neon outline of the stage could be viewed. A dozen or so political bodies stood between the door and the glass.

"JD, you made it!" Ricardo called out. "How it's going, buddy?" He was nursing a beer and leaning against a table that was full of finger foods.

"Great, Raymond," Dothan greeted. "This is Kat Morgan, she's on the FBC city council."

"Fort Bryan City? Really?" Ricardo replied sarcastically to Dothan's gaffe.

"I mean, her mother is a city councilor."

"I believe we've met before," Ricardo said. "It's nice to see you again."

"Hi," Kat shook Ricardo's hand.

Dothan was feeling awkward and needed a beer. He pointed to the small fridge that sat just to the right of the entry. "Is that thing stocked?"

"You know it, buddy. Knock yourself out." Dothan returned with two beers. Kat was talking with Mayor Andy. He had just entered from the other side of the glass partition which disguised several rows of VIP seating along a balcony.

"Andy, I see you made it, after all," Dothan remarked.

"Hey, how could I not?"

"Take a picture of us," Kat insisted, handing Dothan her phone.

"Sure. How does this thing work?"

"Simple, hit the camera icon—"

"I know that much, it's just different from mine." Kat's energy had been pretty contemptuous, but he assured her, "I can handle it."

Dothan angled the camera as Kat and Mayor Andy stood arm in arm. "Wait, let me get it focused," Dothan said. Kat cocked her head. Dothan took several pics and returned the camera.

"Next time, we'll get someone else to take the pictures," she teased.

It was getting close to show time. The room was full. Dothan had yet to isolate Kat, as she was making the rounds from official to official. As the lights went down beyond the glass, the VIPs made their way toward their exclusive seating. Kat grabbed Dothan and led him into the shadows. She took a seat on one of the stools near the wet bar in the back corner.

"So, I've been rereading your poems," she said.

"Really?"

"You're so interesting," she stated.

This statement was a surprise to the poet-legislator. These three words had the potential, in his mind, to save the evening. His apricot-clad shoulders relaxed. He was getting his footing again; just in time for the room to completely empty. "This counter is uncomfortable. Do you want to get a spot near the glass?" he asked.

After moving to two stools near the glass, Kat sipped as Dothan downed his beer. The band was getting started.

"I'm really glad you accepted the meeting the other day," she continued without moving. "I was so nervous, you have no idea."

"Really? Why were you nervous?"

"Are you kidding me? You are intimidating, Representative Dothan."

"I don't bite." *But you do,* he thought.

"You don't remember the first time we met, do you?"

"Yes, when you first came into my office."

"That's not the first time we met."

"No?"

"No. You want to go take a seat and watch the show?"

"Yeah, I do. Jason Isbell is awesome! When did we first meet?"

"We'll talk about it later." Kat took his hand and they entered the venue.

The music jangled and kicked. Kat was feeling it. "You really are so interesting," Kat said loudly to combat the decibels. Through the concert darkness, Dothan turned toward her. Kat reached over and grabbed his head then madly kissed him. Dothan was self-conscious, as they were seated among his colleagues. Isbell was barely into the second song, and he felt her tongue lick his ear. Her hot breath tickled his eardrum. Dothan felt he should ask her about something he'd seen on her social media profile.

"I thought you were in a relationship," he said.

"It's on-again-off-again."

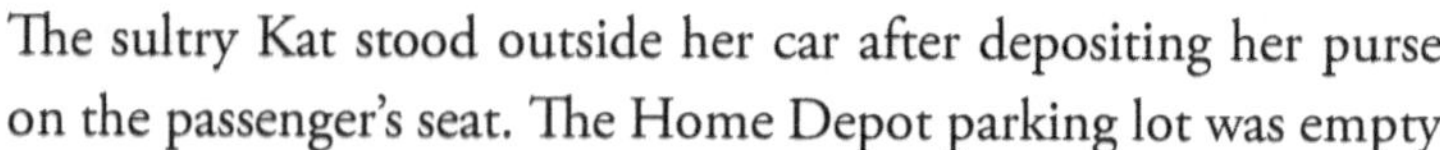

The sultry Kat stood outside her car after depositing her purse on the passenger's seat. The Home Depot parking lot was empty except for their automobiles. Both were significantly buzzed. Dothan looked around for the authorities. They were alone. He moved forward, bracing Kat between her car and his body. His stare added to her intoxication. They kissed tenderly, and then kissed some more.

"I really had a great time tonight," she whispered.

"I know, I did too. May I ask you a question?"

"Sure…anything."

"How much are you making lobbying for the city?"

"Why?"

"I need an assistant at the district office. I think you'd be great. It could be just a part-time gig. If you want it, it's yours."

"Do you think we'd get any work done?"

"I don't care." Dothan cupped her jaw and brought her lips to his. Mad kissing ensued. With his left hand he caressed her long, naked thigh.

"I accept. When do I start?"

Fifteen

"All I can say is, son, please stop doing what you're doing."

"Dad, you worry too much. The man is a sitting duck. I've got this thing in the bag."

"Listen to me, son. If the voters discover your extra-curricular activities, it won't be."

"With what I've got working now, there will be so much dirt on Dothan, it'll take an acid bath to clean him off. Trust me."

Zane Rayne sat with his father in the office of Rayne Turf Works. Outside, the rumble of returning trucks could be heard making their way back to headquarters after a long day.

"I'm leveraging the bulk of your candidacy, and I'm paying that damned overpriced consultant. As far as I'm concerned, I have the first and last word. You have a wife and a child, for fuck's sake."

"Lesley doesn't know anything, Dad. Believe me, she just loves being a new mom."

"Are you that cynical, son? Jesus, if your mother were here she'd be puking. I can't believe you're risking it all for…for *this*." Mike Rayne rose from his seat ready to strangle his insolent son.

"Whatever."

"Whatever? You little bastard, I can pull the plug on this thing anytime I choose, and I will if you don't listen to what I'm saying." He pushed the contents on top of the table that separated father from son onto the linoleum floor. Zane was unmoved.

"Chill, Dad. I'm going to end it soon. Trust me."

"You keep saying that, Zane." The father now sounded defeated and slouched down in his chair. His son got up to leave.

"You know, Zane, things aren't what they used to be. I was outbid on that new football stadium contract. I've had to take on a silent partner. Aren't you grateful for anything?"

"You know, Dad, that was an expensive bottle of single barrel Jack Daniels you just shattered on the floor."

"Get out of here! Go home to your wife and child!"

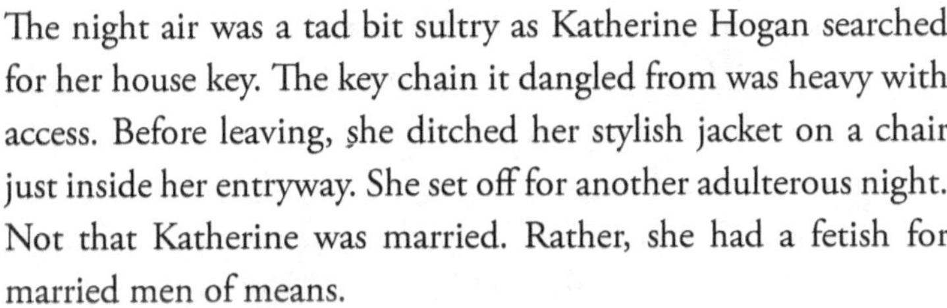

The night air was a tad bit sultry as Katherine Hogan searched for her house key. The key chain it dangled from was heavy with access. Before leaving, she ditched her stylish jacket on a chair just inside her entryway. She set off for another adulterous night. Not that Katherine was married. Rather, she had a fetish for married men of means.

Her rendezvous point was a motel on the outskirts of Houston's extra-territorial jurisdiction. The man she would meet was already checked in when Katherine arrived in her Toyota Camry. The adulterer peeked through the cheap blinds again and again. This time, he spotted Katherine's beige car parking in the sparsely inhabited lot. He loosened his blue tie and undid the top button of his white shirt. Jostling the bottle of white wine that chilled in a steel pitcher, he stared nervously at the bouquet of roses that adorned the cheap dresser.

There was a tap at the door…

"Hello," he said, opening it while trying to restrain his passion.

"Hey, baby. Sorry it took so long. Friday night traffic from Ft. Bryan, I guess."

"I would have thought you were going in the opposite direction, but I guess with all the road construction..." He backed up to allow his mistress to enter.

"Aren't you glad to see me?" Katherine placed her purse down on the small, abused table in the corner.

"You know I am."

Free of feminine accoutrements, Katherine opened her bare arms for an embrace. The adulterer complied. After a brief, singularly passionate kiss, Katherine broke off. She drew her fingers to the relaxed knot of his tie.

"You know how much I like you all spiffy. Why did you loosen your tie?"

"It's just a little warm in here, that's all."

"Yes, it is," Katherine pecked his lips. "What's this?" she asked excitedly, pointing at the flowers.

"Oh, those are for you."

"Roses." She walked around the bed toward the dresser, poked out her skirted bottom, and drew in a whiff of the bouquet. "Roses are my favorite, baby."

"I know." The adulterer had moved in behind her. His aroused groin pressed into her backside.

"What is that?" Katherine asked with a dash of mischief. She turned around and they stood face to face.

"I can't take this anymore...I feel like I'm living a cheap cliché."

"Cheap? How do you mean? Do you think I'm cheap?"

"No, of course that's not what I mean. It's just that I can't go on like this. I want you with me all the time. It's all I think about. I'm going insane."

"What about your wife and kid? I thought you told me you were trapped."

"I was…or I still am. I just want to run off with you, that's all."

"Me, too."

"You do?"

"Of course, you know how cute I think you are, baby." She put her middle finger to his mouth and drew a circle around his lips. "Oh, by the way…my rent's past due."

"Oh, yes. I brought the cash. It's in my coat." He turned and withdrew a thick bank sleeve from the pocket.

"I hate asking you for this, but since the company made changes…"

"It's okay, I don't mind. I want to help you."

"I need to get back into school, but it's so much to take on."

"I've told you I can help you with that, too."

"What can I help you with?"

A couple of hours had passed when Katherine and her benefactor dressed and readied to part. Katherine left first. He watched her pull out of the motel and feelings of remorse and malevolence overtook him. *What am I doing this for? It's like she wasn't even here.* He sat for a moment with his head in his hands. He finally stood up, applied his cufflinks, and pulled on his coat. He gazed back at the room before switching off the light. The flowers remained.

Kat arrived promptly at nine that morning, dressed to kill. Dothan had only just risen and wore a ball cap to disguise his wild mane.

Clothed in dirty blue jeans, a tank top, and sans shoes, he'd had yet to unlock the front door. He reproached himself for not giving her a key, although that broke with basic office policy.

"Cute. I don't think I've ever seen you in anything but a suit and boots. That hat is adorable," she commented upon entry.

"Yeah, it's unprofessional of me, I know. I'm just getting a late start. How are you this morning? By the way, you look incredible." Dothan was stunned by her long, blue slacks and sleeveless blue top tied at the neck with a bow. Her olive arms were tempting him.

"Thank you. I feel great. I'm just looking forward to getting started."

"I filed all the paperwork with House payroll a few days ago. That's why I asked for your social security number. I went ahead and put in a request for a state email account. I'm waiting for it to be approved. So, let me jump in the shower and when I get down we'll get you going."

"Sounds great." Kat wore a smile as bright as the May day that shot through the glass doors.

"Oh, if you'd like some coffee, there's some right down this hallway," Dothan said. "That's where the kitchen is. You'll have to make it, of course, sorry. Or, I could make it for you before I go upstairs."

"Not a problem. I can manage."

Dothan turned toward the hallway, but stopped in his tracks. "Uh, I don't have any cream or sugar, come to think of it, so I hope you like it black."

"I'm fine, really. I don't need any coffee. I got up really early this morning, and I've had plenty."

"What time did you get up, if you don't mind me asking?"

"Five."

"Five?"

"Yes."

"Jesus. Now I really feel like a loser."

Kat laughed. "You're fine, really. Go get ready. I'll be fine." Kat sat in Dothan's office—behind his large oak desk—and waited. When she heard the 1970s music spilling down the stairs and through the hallway, she got up and dawdled patiently.

Dothan appeared shortly. He walked past his own office and into the foyer.

"I'm in here!" Kat called out, innocently.

"Oh, there you are, in *my* office."

Kat was struck at how handsome he really was. His hair was blow dried and perfectly disheveled. The loose garb had been replaced by slacks and a short-sleeve collared shirt. The boots were back. "My, what a transformation," she remarked.

"Oh, thank you."

For the next few hours, Dothan had her fill out tax documents and insurance information. Then, he showed her where supplies were and how the file system worked. He checked his emails on and off. The approval notification for Kat's state email finally arrived.

Dothan stood above her as they went through the process of setting up her House email. He leaned his head down near hers and the smell of her perfume coaxed his senses. She could smell him, too. His deep voice and the breath it took to expiate it made her aware of his close proximity. She was getting hot. He was getting hotter. Dothan bent down further. Their profiles were now parallel. He placed his hands on the back of the swivel chair. She could feel his knuckles gently poke into her back. With the index finger of his free hand he pointed to the computer screen. Kat turned her head to face him. The coil of his ear and the jawline of dark stubble consumed her vision. Dothan felt her soft breath tickle his eardrum again.

They faced one another—Dothan above and Kat below. Their lips met and their tongues entwined.

"I want you," Kat insisted as Dothan grabbed her from his chair and pushed her against the large bookshelf that stood just left of his sprawling desk. Kat turned around. Dothan pressed up behind her. Crouching down, he reached around and undid her belt. Kat felt her pants and underwear fall with a single tug. "Fuck me," she coaxed. "I want you to fuck me now."

Dothan scrambled with his own belt.

"Hello?" A voice called from the foyer, above the music that had not ceased playing.

"Oh, my God," Kat muttered fearfully.

Dothan buckled his belt and ran his hands through his hair. "Give me a minute, please!" he called out.

"Sure thing. Take your time."

"What do I do?" Kat whispered as she pulled up her pants.

"Just chill in here. When I go up front, I'll close the door. Take off upstairs."

Dothan entered the foyer and closed the door behind him. It was Neilson.

"Sheriff, how are you?"

"Sorry to drop in unannounced, Representative, but I would like a moment of your time."

"No problem. What's up?"

"Do we talk here?"

"Uh, no…back in my office…please." Dothan cracked the door to the foyer and peeked down the hallway. Seeing that it was empty, he welcomed the sheriff back. The music abruptly stopped as they entered Dothan's office.

"So, what's on your mind, Sheriff?"

"Are you at all familiar with the, how should I say this, bizarre murder case the city has been handling?"

"Somewhat. I was visited by Detective Garza a few weeks ago and he actually asked for my assistance."

"What did you say?"

"I said I'd think about it."

"Have you?"

"Not much. To tell you the truth, I've got a lot going on right now. I just hired an assistant and am in the process of getting her oriented."

"Is that who I heard when I came in?"

"Uh, maybe? She stepped out to grab some things. She should be back soon."

"I see…"

"How is Garza, by the way? I haven't heard from him since that day he showed up out of the blue."

"Garza's missing."

"Missing? What do you mean?" Dothan wiped residual sweat from his forehead. Neilson noticed.

"He went missing. A few weeks back, he got into a tiff with the police chief and walked out; said he quit. He hasn't been seen since. His house hasn't been packed up, or anything. Chief Olivo tried getting in touch with his family back in Mexico, but hasn't had any luck. His car is gone, so maybe he just split. Who knows? I told Olivo that if his electricity gets shut off then someone should file a missing persons report."

"That's strange. What day was this—when he quit?"

"I'd have to ask Olivo. He told me, but I can't remember the exact date. It was a couple of weeks ago, like I said. Would you be willing to help me with some of these details Garza wanted to run by you?"

"I can."

Neilson spelled out all the details, including the macabre symbolism—the pomegranate and rose; the feather; the strange ash bird upon the breast. He briefed Dothan on the dagger and the sliver of grass and his frustration over how long the crime lab in Houston was taking.

"What I've told you is strictly confidential, obviously. Please tell no one. I just need help with this stuff. I'm *this* close," Neilson flashed his index finger and thumb in close proximity, "to calling in the real pros. I don't want to do that because, frankly, the city doesn't want to look like the rank amateurs they are. I know I'm out of my league. This is Sherlock Holmes shit."

"I'm no Sherlock Holmes, that's for sure."

"But you're a writer—a poet, so I've been told. Garza sought your advice because I told him to. Garza's vanished. Who knows where? Hell, he might turn up in Cozumel on a beach, I don't know. What I do know is, he was right about one thing. This isn't done."

"His disappearance might be the signpost to confirm that."

"Exactly."

"So what do you want me to do, Sheriff?"

Neilson stood up and headed toward the door. "Find out what those freakin' symbols mean. That's the key, Representative. Again, keep all of this close to the vest, please, sir." He walked out.

Dothan sat stunned at what had just unfolded. He had forgotten that prior to this fateful visit from Sheriff Neilson, he had been about to "take" his fresh assistant in his office.

A text alert pinged on his phone. It was from Kat. Dothan smiled.

Kat sat on Dothan's bed, naked but for a short, green gown that plumed at mid-thigh. "Dream Weaver" wove its magical notes through the loft's thick ether via satellite radio.

Kat rose up on her knees, undid the gown's tassel, and exposed her breasts. "I want you…now."

"Do you?" Dothan asked as he got undressed. "Where did you get that beautiful outfit?"

"I brought it with me to work this morning. It was in my car."

"I see. Green is my favorite color."

"I had a notion."

Outside, Earth erased the sun. The night was consummated simultaneously. Darkness overtook the loft. The sweating lovers lay wrapped tight as a rope. Kat could still feel the convulsing remnants of an orgasm between her thighs. Her lover's seed cooled on her abdomen. Dothan, freed an arm and reached over to switch on the nightstand lamp. The two stared into each other's eyes in the glow of soft light. Pecking turned to full kissing.

They were dozing off, and their eyelids grew heavy. Dothan went to kill the lamp again.

In the darkness Kat inquired, "What did Sheriff Neilson want?"

"I don't want to talk about it."

"Uh, okay…"

"I'm tired. Let's sleep."

Sixteen

Kat left early in the morning for a change of clothes. Dothan was sluggish as he prepared for another workday. It felt good, sharing the night with his new assistant. While cracking eggs into a skillet, he thought of what he was doing and could not bring himself to think there was anything wrong with it. *I'm a divorced man. I need love,* his mind insisted. The sizzling eggs smelled like home. For the first time in a long time, he felt at home. Dothan knew it would be some time before Kat arrived. He took his hot plate of breakfast down to the office to eat and begin his day.

With his stomach full, the euphoria from the night before settled into calm intellect. The conversation with Neilson overtook his thoughts. He picked up the state phone and dialed the Capitol. Mason answered.

"Where's staff?" Dothan asked.

"Down at the Capitol Grill. What's up, JD?"

"You're not going to fucking believe it."

"Oh yeah? Try me."

Dothan told Mason everything Sheriff Neilson had told him the day before.

"You got me," Mason said. "That's freaky, dude. He wants you to help?"

"That's what he said."

"So he has an ancient idea of what a poet does?"

"He's not a redneck, Mason. He's from somewhere up around the Great Lakes."

"So he's a Viking. I guess he believes in the concept of the warrior-poet?"

"Maybe so. What do you think?"

"How does this shit always find us?"

"I don't know, but I agreed to help him, but I don't know if I can."

"So what do we need to do, figure out these symbols?"

"Bingo!"

"I'll ponder it, JD."

As Dothan hung up the state phone, his cell phone rang. It was Tryphena. He didn't answer.

The madman paced back and forth through his den. "Once" by Pearl Jam snarled from the stereo speakers. Though the lights of the room were switched off, the dazzling morning sun outside exploited cracks in the window coverings here and there. To his quaking mind, it felt as if something was scratching into his domain of peace and power. Mind and music fused, and he began destroying his den. Pictures went flying, furniture overturned. After, the floor was carpeted with glass and wood debris.

This nervous pacing, done without direction, only destruction, was finally directed toward his attachment garage. Bracing against the door jamb, he summoned his composure, but not his reason. With the exception of a fine blade of light at the base of the garage door, it was pitch black as he entered. A superstition had whispered its edict that no house light should hold dominion, but again, he was betrayed by the elements. Turning back toward the laundry room that hugged the attachment, he scurried through cabinets searching for a flashlight.

Gripping the shiny cylindrical handle, the madman stepped into the garage. What appeared before him was a dudgeon and the smell…

⸻◇⸻

The representative and his new assistant sat in Dothan's office just staring at each other; he behind his desk, she sitting with her elbows on the glass surface on the opposite side.

"You are so beautiful," he said.

Kat brought her hand to her mouth and giggled. "There's nothing special about me," she retorted, shaking her head. The smile had vanished, replaced with a plaintive stare.

"No, you really are. You may be the most beautiful woman I've ever been with."

"What about Rachael?"

"More so."

"And Tryphena?"

"Tryphena is beautiful in a different way."

"What do you mean?"

"Tryphena is earthy. You are not of this earth."

"That's silly."

"No, you're like the ether…the air… You drift in like…a breeze."

"If I'm the air, what are you?" Kat teased.

"I'm like an alien planet rebelling against my revolution."

"You are definitely different, John David Dothan."

"I'm like no other man you have or will ever know."

"Maybe so. You don't like to talk about either of your past loves do you?"

"I don't know what you want me to say."

"I just want you to tell me how you feel."

"Sometimes I feel nothing…"

With this statement Kat raised an eyebrow—not in judgment but sorrow.

Dothan continued. "And sometimes I feel everything."

"Feeling everything…is that good?"

"My synopsis of life is that it is basically regret."

"All of it?"

"No. Rachael is gone, and being divorced…well, that's kind of like being excommunicated from your own life."

"I know how you feel. Do you regret right now?"

"No."

The next series of moments the two just stared at each other. No words were passed between them. Then Dothan jolted from his chair with authority and approached her. Standing above, he looked down at her thighs which revealed themselves as she wore a rather short blue skirt. Kneeling down to where she sat, he ran his left hand along her right thigh, slightly nudging her skirt upward. In the prior half-shadowed night, she'd been like a mirage. He had discovered little detail of her topography. Now, under the harsh light of his office, something revealed itself.

"That's so beautiful," he said looking up at her.

"It's horrible…I hate it." She retorted. She then tugged at her skirt in an effort to conceal the birthmark.

"No…no it's not horrible. It's beautiful." Kat withdrew her protest. Dothan kissed the quarter-sized, oblong imperfection. They retired to the loft.

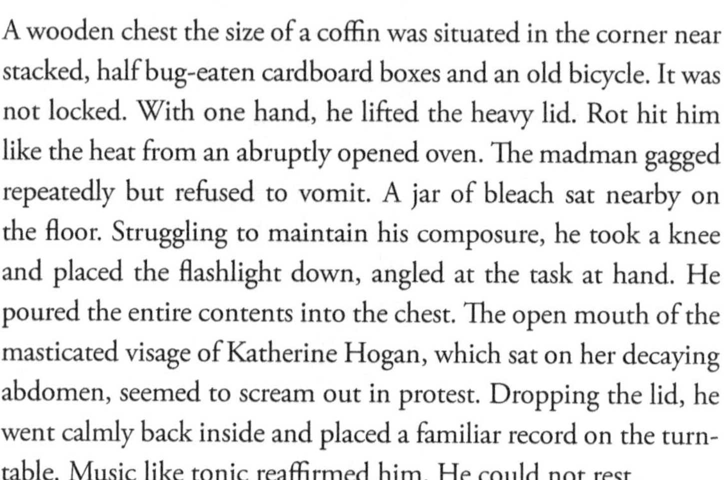

A wooden chest the size of a coffin was situated in the corner near stacked, half bug-eaten cardboard boxes and an old bicycle. It was not locked. With one hand, he lifted the heavy lid. Rot hit him like the heat from an abruptly opened oven. The madman gagged repeatedly but refused to vomit. A jar of bleach sat nearby on the floor. Struggling to maintain his composure, he took a knee and placed the flashlight down, angled at the task at hand. He poured the entire contents into the chest. The open mouth of the masticated visage of Katherine Hogan, which sat on her decaying abdomen, seemed to scream out in protest. Dropping the lid, he went calmly back inside and placed a familiar record on the turntable. Music like tonic reaffirmed him. He could not rest.

Absolutely no more room was left in Annie Casey's mailbox. This didn't sit well with Leroy Sebastian, who had handled this route for over twelve years and was on the eve of his retirement. When he'd started this route, which was rural at the time, he was already a veteran of the postal service. Even though the route was longer, there was less mail then. Country folk just seemed to get less junk. Now, with suburban growth, all kinds of nonsense found its way into his small red truck. Leroy was also a veteran of the USMC during the Reagan administration. He had participated in the invasion of Grenada.

He put the truck in park and walked up the white sidewalk toward Annie's front door. His bad knee and back were acting up. The morning sun was already too warm. The bundle of mail under his arm didn't wish to cooperate. Repeatedly, he had to bend down to fetch a fallen article. The breeze didn't help.

He made it to the shadow of the awning and knocked.

He waited, then knocked again. Then he rang the doorbell. No answer.

"Hello!" he called out. Leroy decided to take a look around. After all, when the house first got assigned to his route, he delivered the mail, and on the following day the box was empty. He peered through every first story window along his way but saw no signs of life. There was a protocol for such instances. *Maybe I should follow it?* he considered, but he kept on around the house. He arrived at the back door—rectangular glass framed by an elegant, varnished wood casing. Below, on the other side sat a skinny cat. He placed the pile of mail on the tiled porch and bent down. He tapped on the glass softly. The cat wearily stood up and began pawing at the transparent partition. Its pawing turned to desperate clawing. Leroy, who had never taken to cats, felt a cramp of compassion.

A glare coated the top portion of the back door. It was hard to see beyond just a few feet. Leroy cupped his hands near his eyes and put his nose to the surface. He squinted. On the floor, some fifteen feet away, he saw a dried puddle of…something… Something was not right.

Leroy Sebastian removed his USMC ball cap and scratched his thinning afro. In all his years as a postal worker, he had never come across what he perceived as an emergency situation, but his military training kicked in. He checked his pants for his cell phone. "Damn!" he shouted, "It's in the truck!"

A figure appeared at the door. "Can I help you?" the man asked. He wore latex gloves and a damp rag dangled from his hand. The cat had vanished.

"You live here?"

"Why yes I do."

"Why ain't you got the mail in weeks?"

"I'm sorry. You know today I do most everything online, sir."

"What's your name? All this mail is for a lady named Annie Casey."

"I'm Mr. Casey…her husband."

"Everything's in her name, ain't nothin' come for you? Is that cat in her name?"

The madman opened the door. "I work out of town a lot, sir. Cat?"

"Yeah, man. That cat looked like it ain't had nothin' to eat in forever."

"Picky."

"I see…well, here's your mail. I'd appreciate you folks emptying your mailbox. It makes my job harder, you know, when you don't."

"My hands are filthy, as I'm doing some cleaning. Would you mind just setting it on the counter here in the kitchen?" The madman turned slightly and signaled inside.

"I can do that." Leroy stepped in. "Say, ain't I seen you someplace before?"

"Oh, I don't know…"

Leroy walked past the madman and stood at the counter. His back was now to the madman.

"I think I grabbed too much here. Looks like I got your neighbor," Leroy said, shuffling through the envelopes.

"Neighbor?" The madman asked from the opposite side of

the large kitchen as he slowly pulled open a drawer.

"Yeah, you got somebody moving in soon…looks like." Leroy finished sorting the mail. "Speaking of cleaning, what's with that blood stain on the floor?" He stacked the mail on the counter and turned.

"Blood stain? I'm not sure what you mean," the madman replied as he stepped in front of Leroy.

"That's dried blood, man. I was in the milita—" His last syllable was cut short abruptly. Leroy fell to the floor. Fresh blood gushed from his throat. His hands grasped his neck where a large steak knife, lodged in the C-5 vertebrae of the spine, protruded from his esophagus.

Kat and Dothan fell into a deep sleep after lovemaking. Dothan had passed out with his head on her stomach. The purple sheets were in disarray. It was getting dark out when his eyes unsealed. Though twilight was at hand, there was still enough light to peer at the birthmark on her right thigh near her groin. Softly he lowered his head so he could just stare at it, but his movement disquieted Kat from her dreams. Sensing the locale of her lover's head, she began playing with his hair, massaging his scalp with her long nails.

"Why did you have to be so beautiful?" Dothan asked in his gentlest baritone.

"Because you needed me to be."

"I've only felt this feeling once before in my life," he continued as he began rubbing her leg.

"With Rachael?"

"Why do you keep asking about her?"

"You have a history. We all do."
"Rachael's dead. Can't she just rest?"
"Can you let her rest?"
"I can, if I have you by my side."
"I want to believe that. I really do."
"You can."
"I'm falling for you, John David Dothan."
"It's okay, I'll catch you."

Seventeen

Despite all the extra-curricular activities, Dothan's office was starting to shape up. Kat had a talent for organization and offered a much-needed woman's touch. The new District Assistant had spent most nights with her employer since starting work. Whether she made her bed in the upstairs loft or at her apartment, she was quickly learning that the representative was not an early riser. Kat was sitting behind the representative's computer working on a constituent issue when Dothan finally drifted down.

"Whatcha ya working on?" He sat across from her and set his coffee down on the desk.

"Just a Department of Criminal Justice issue." Kat was typing; her fingers flitted over the keyboard like a scurrying mouse in a tight maze.

"Oh, what about?"

She stopped and swiveled around to face him. "It's a prison transfer issue. A family wants to have their son moved to a unit closer to their home."

"What are you writing?"

"A nice 'no.'"

"Wrong."

"You mean you want to move him? But he's a criminal!"

"What are the circumstances? Is one of the family members, mother or father, ill or disabled?"

"Uh yes, I believe it says that the father has recently been diagnosed with cancer."

"Then have him moved."

"But according to the letter, it appears they're already within the allotted distance and don't qualify for transfer."

"Override the Department of Criminal Justice, then."

"But he's a criminal," she repeated.

"The father's dying of cancer, and the family didn't commit any crime. Do it."

"You can do that? Just say move him, and it happens?"

"I can, I do, and I will."

"Okay." Kat swiveled back toward the screen. Dothan stood above her awkwardly.

"Say, you don't mind if I use my computer for a bit do you?" he asked.

"Oh, no. I'm sorry. I didn't mean to be presumptuous," Kat began to nervously gather her materials.

"It's cool. I just have something I need to do really quick."

"Of course, you're fine. I'm sorry." Kat stood up to vacate.

Dothan stood some feet away. "Hey, come here," he ordered gently.

"What?" Kat asked, inching forward with her arms stuffed with papers and her purse slung from her shoulder.

"It's okay. I don't mind you using my desk and computer. Like I said, I just have something I need to hammer out. It won't take long."

"I understand…I'll go up front." Kat's tone and expression were very submissive—and out of character.

Dothan leaned in for a kiss. "Thanks," he whispered. "Oh,

and by the way, you look gorgeous with your hair up like that."

"Thank you. I had to pin it up in a hurry to get down here."

In the foyer, Kat continued her work on the prison transfer. Dothan carefully closed the door behind him. Something was fluttering around in his mind like a bird that had just flown in through an open window. He must capture it and pluck a feather before it found its way back out into the void. He sat down at his computer and called up a fresh document. In the time it took to exit the loft, descend the stairs, and traverse the hall, it had all come to him. He began typing.

A BEGINNING

From the threshold of the exhausting heat
That wrinkles the world,
Out into the traffic yet away from it,
A planet he spun.

Turning from worn to young, primal as sin,
Yet hallowed as love,
By a breeze as blue as a spring eternal
Blowing through his door…

If he be the aged earth, then she the air…
The ever-changing air…
She the mystery, he the steady spinning;
Turning now from her touch?

And like wind tickling the sun-dry grass…
His naked chest…Her nails long caressed…

It was done. He hit save and then printed it.

Kat was furiously punching her keyboard when he entered the foyer. Papers were spread out all over the desk.

"I think something just printed." She sat with her back to his as Dothan made his way to the printer behind her in the left corner of the room.

"Yes, I know. I printed it."

"What is it?" she was still engrossed in the task at hand. Dothan withdrew the single sheet and placed it on her keyboard. "What's this?" she inquired.

"Read."

It took her only moments to scour the lines. "Is this about us?"

"It's about you and how you make me feel."

"Oh, it's beautiful, John David," Kat said, turning to look up at his hovering face.

"You're beautiful."

"I didn't think guys like you even existed."

"They don't. There is only me."

"I know." Kat batted her eyes. Her long dark eyelashes fluttered like the bird of inspiration that had just found its way to the page before her. Reaching down, Dothan hoisted her from the chair. They could be seen kissing through the front doors by any passersby. The roughness of his darkened jaw aroused her. Dothan grabbed her by the hand with the intention of leading her upstairs.

"I can't."

"What...why?"

"I started this morning. It's shark week."

"Shark week?" he asked as she giggled.

"That's what I call it."

The phone rang and Kat reached over and answered. "It's for you. Do you want to take it?" she asked him after placing the caller on hold.

"Who is it?"

"I don't know. The caller ID isn't working."

"Fucking state phone. Okay, give it to me. Hello?" It was Tryphena. All morning, she had been texting and calling his cell. He had ignored her as he had a bird to catch.

"So you no longer have any interest in your daughter, I guess," Tryphena reproached him.

"What are you talking about, Tryphena?"

Kat got the picture and slipped back into Dothan's office.

"What am I talking about? I've been trying to reach you for the last week."

"I've been busy."

"Too busy to care that your daughter has a nasty earache?"

"Now, wait a minute. You didn't say that in any of your messages."

"Poor thing, she's just been as miserable as she can be."

"I'm sorry. Is she feeling any better?"

"Who answered the phone?"

"What? Some chick that just started working here. Why?"

"Right, no wonder you haven't been answering my calls."

"You know I've needed help up here since I opened the damned thing. Mason is in Austin, and I need a right-hand man...or woman, rather."

"Yes, I'm sure you do."

"What the hell is that supposed to mean?"

"Nothing. So do you care about your daughter anymore, or should I just stop calling you about her?"

"Of course I care about my daughter. What the fuck? The

fucking checks clear, don't they?"

"Why are you getting defensive, John David? By the way, that's your obligation."

"Defensive? You're the one accusing me of shit."

"I'm not accusing you of anything."

"Do I need to come up there?"

"It would be fatherly of you, yes. You can even bring your new girlfriend."

"Girlfriend? She's not my goddamned girlfriend."

"Can you or not?"

"When?"

"As soon as possible."

"It's that bad? I thought you said it was just an earache."

"Oh, my God, you are such an asshole! *Just* an earache?"

"Okay, I'm fucking coming. Let me see what I can negotiate."

"Good. You can stay here if you like."

"We'll see."

"Don't you want to?"

"After this conversation?"

"You worry me when I don't hear from you, baby."

"Like I said, Tryphena, I've been busy as hell."

"Okay. I still think about you all the time. I love you."

"I…I love you, too…and Delilah."

"Are you sure?"

"Of course I'm sure. I need to go. I have someone waiting up front." Dothan got off the phone with his ex-wife and stormed back into his office. Kat sat in his chair with her legs crossed and her hands folded neatly at her waist.

"Everything okay?" she asked with the lift of a dark eyebrow.

"No…she's a giant head-fuck, from top to bottom.

Apparently, my daughter has an earache, and I suck."

"Well, it's none of my business, but the way you got shafted in the divorce…" Kat swiveled around to face the screen.

"Yes?" Dothan implored to her back.

"Nothing. Like I said, it's none of my business."

"Just say it, goddamnit."

Kat swiveled around. "She's a bitch, okay? I said it. She doesn't know what she wants, and she's confused. So she's fucking with you. What pisses me off is she's using your daughter to manipulate you."

Dothan plopped down in one of the chairs in front of his desk. "She wants me to come to Austin, like now, basically. My daughter has an earache."

"Not a big deal. Infants get them all the time."

"I know, but I have to go. By the way she's acting, you'd think it was polio. Do you want to have a little getaway to ATX?"

"What am I supposed to do while you're with your wife and daughter?"

"We'll figure it out, Kat. We'll figure it out. Just go with me, please. I don't want to go alone, and I—" Dothan hung his head in exhaustion.

"What, sweetheart?"

"I don't want to be away from you, even if it's just for a day or two."

"I've been reading and rereading your poem. I grabbed it when I came back. I don't know if you noticed…"

"I didn't. I'm sorry."

"It really is beautiful. I treasure it. No one's ever written me a poem before."

"I'm sure there's a lot more where that came from."

"I'll go with you to Austin."

"Great. Then it's settled. Say, what time is it?"

"Getting close to noon."

"Perfect. You want to go get some lunch?"

"I'd love to, but I made plans."

"Oh, no problem," Dothan said with an air of surprise and disappointment. "What are you doing, if you don't mind me asking?"

"Nothing really, just meeting a friend, but I can cancel."

"No…don't. Just do what you planned." He turned to leave his office.

"No, wait."

Dothan turned from where he stood in the doorway. "Really, I can cancel, but only if you take me where I want to go," Kat pursed her lips.

"You name it."

"I've never been to the Railroad Café."

"Down the sidewalk?"

"Yes, I've never been."

"Would you like to go?"

"I would. Let me text my friend."

"Your friend doesn't want to join us? It's fine if so."

"No. I'm canceling."

The Old Rail Road Café was a stone's throw away, located at the end of the block. The May sun was heavy with moisture as the two strode the canopied sidewalk. Antiques filled the shop windows along the way. At the sidewalk's end, Dothan held open the one hundred-year-old wooden door, and a bashful Kat passed through.

"Take a seat anywhere you like, it's open seating," he said.

Kat surveyed the room and chose a table against the far wall. Dothan presented her chair and she sat down.

"I've never been here before," Kat reaffirmed. "I've heard a lot about it."

"It's not bad and not a big menu. I always get the same thing."

"And what's that?" she asked, looking around the restaurant. The walls were high with exposed brick from chipped and decayed stucco. The floor was long, worn, wooden planks. Black-and-white photos depicting the early days of train traffic hung in varying sizes from the aged walls as did paintings from local artists. On the opposite wall was a series of windowed doors that had once announced an early twentieth century parlor. There was a fully stocked bar toward the back of the room. Steam and smoke rose from beyond the bar. The whole place reeked of atmosphere.

"I always get the Santa Fe chicken sandwich," Dothan replied as she surveyed their surroundings.

"Is it good?" she asked.

Just then, a hearty, Bohemian, bearded waiter arrived. He placed two menus down and recited the day's special. He took their drink orders and vanished.

"The sandwich is good, to answer your question," Dothan said.

"There are a lot of people here. We're lucky we got a table." Kat looked behind her at the trellis that scaled nearly two stories of the tattered wall. "I want us to always sit right here. I love this location. You can watch the whole place. It's perfect." Kat lifted the menu and began to read. Dothan watched her eyes.

Going forward this would be their regular table...without exception.

— ◇ —

Night was all. The streetlamps below warbled their bubbled light in oblong orbs along the loft's leaded glass windows. Dothan sat in bed reading a biography on D.H. Lawrence. Kat stood in the bathroom getting ready to go to sleep. When done, she slipped under the covers only wearing black, ragged panties.

"I'm sorry I can't do anything tonight. I really want to," she said.

Her lover placed his book down on the nightstand to the left of the bed, which was his side in their new arrangement. Kat lay in the fetal position with her back turned. Dothan nestled up next to her, kissing her neck and ear. Kat twitched. Below, their feet met and played deep in the cavern of covers.

"It's all right. It's enough just having you here next to me. There's nowhere in the world I'd rather be than right here." Dothan wrapped his left arm around her tummy.

"You're so sweet," she said.

"I want the whole world to know you're my lady."

"They can't, John David. We have to keep this a secret."

"Why? I don't care what people think."

"We can talk about it tomorrow, baby."

Eyes closed, and soon they were enveloped in unconsciousness.

Eighteen

A pearly hue lacquered the loft windows as Kat yawned and stretched. All that was left of her lover was a trail of creases and mangled covers. Without dressing, she padded down the loft's stairs. The sound of lovely piano music could be heard from the end of the hall. *He must be writing*, she surmised. She trotted back up to prepare for the day.

As she waited for the water to heat, she heard her cell ring from the bedroom and went to grab it. "Hey, what's up?" she answered.

"Where were you last night?" the caller asked. "I came by your apartment around eleven."

"Oh, you did? I was over at my mom's pretty late."

"Where are you now? I need to see you."

"I'm at my apartment…"

"Great, I'm coming over. I'll be there in about twenty minutes."

"Wait—"

"What's the problem?"

"Nothing, I'm about to get in the shower. Give me thirty." Kat hurriedly gathered a few essential items and threw them in one of her bags. "What do I tell John David?" she muttered, heading down the stairs.

"Sweetheart?" she called, poking her heard into Dothan's office where he sat typing away.

"Oh, hey," he answered, swiveling around.

"You're up early."

"Yeah, I had some poem ideas. I couldn't go back to sleep, so I got up."

"Look, baby, I left my tampons at my apartment. I need to run home and get them. I'm going to shower over there and I'll be back."

"Okay, see you soon."

Kat tore out of the Cultural District and headed back to her apartment only a few miles away. Road construction was everywhere and traffic wasn't moving.

"Fuck! Hurry up!" she yelled, pounding the steering wheel. She checked the car's clock every other second as if she were watching tumbling grains of sand. Her thirty minutes had dropped to the bottom of the proverbial glass as she screeched into her apartment complex. She looked around for the truck. *Thank God he's not here yet!* She had barely placed her purse and bag down when a knock at the door startled her frazzled nerves.

"I thought you told me you were about to get into the shower," her visitor said when she opened the door.

"What? Oh, yeah. I got stuck on the phone with my mom. FBC drama—what else is new?"

"I really need to talk to her later. Can I come in?"

"Yes, of course. What's going on? What's so urgent?"

"You're not going to fucking believe who paid me a visit last night."

⋯ ▬▬▬▬▬◆▬▬▬▬▬ ⋯

Salvation or damnation hangs on a single syllable for the wordsmith. And like an engineer designing a construct, one miscalculation and it all comes tumbling down. Dothan sat as stuck as stuck gets. In his present state, there was no getting unstuck. He needed a walk. He grabbed the key for the PO Box from Kat's desk drawer and went out through the front. He deduced it was going to be a sultry day as he paced toward the post office. For the first time since he and Kat had started their affair, his leg was acting up. He wished he'd brought his cane.

Not much was in the mail, mostly junk and newspapers. He limped back in irritation and loathing due to his condition. Though there was considerable glare on the glass, he could see that someone was standing in the foyer as he approached. The shape through the glass was too masculine to be Kat. Dothan entered.

"Oh, hey, Young. That's your name, right?"

"Yes, Lieutenant Young of Ft. Bryan City PD."

"I see you made your way in. I must have forgotten to lock the front door."

"Yes, I announced myself, but nobody answered. I was going to leave, but I'm meeting Sheriff Neilson here."

"Really? I imagine this has something to do with your string of murders?"

"God, yes. Don't you read the local papers, man?"

"Well, as you see," Dothan lifted his shoulder to demonstrate the periodical under his arm, "apparently not yet." The door opened and Neilson appeared. "Don't you guys ever make appointments?" Dothan quipped.

"Sorry about this, Representative. Can we have a word with you in private?" Neilson asked.

"What's up?" Dothan inquired as he flipped through the numerous newspapers before him on his desk.

"Representative, our worst nightmare has come true. I'll let Lieutenant Young explain."

"Thank you, Sheriff. In the past seventy-two hours we've had two missing persons reports."

"Not two more girls?" Dothan asked.

"A young woman named Katherine Hogan. She went missing over a week ago but was reported missing three days ago."

"We have a suspect," Neilson chimed in.

"Yes, we have a suspect," Young restated. "The other is a postman. A man named Leroy Sebastian."

"A postman? Do you think the two instances are related?"

Neilson chimed in again, "We don't know, but we're not ruling anything out."

"Any leads on that one?" Dothan asked.

"Nothing," Young answered.

"Okay. What about the lead on…what's her name?"

"Katherine Hogan. That one was rather easy," Neilson commented.

Young continued, "Ms. Hogan texted a girlfriend that she was meeting a certain man—we can't tell you his name due to the investigation—at a certain motel on the last evening she was seen or heard from. She mentions the suspect's name in the text. We checked with the motel to see if the suspect had registered that evening. He had, and that was it."

"What's interesting is what was left behind," Neilson added.

"According to the management," Young said, "a large bouquet of red and white roses was left in the room. When the maids entered to clean the room, they discovered it. Thinking nothing of it, one of the ladies took the bouquet home for herself."

"And you think this is a clue?" Dothan asked.

"We don't know," Neilson answered.

"It fits in with everything else—well, kind of—wouldn't you say?" Dothan added.

"Exactly, sir," Young responded.

"Our backs are against the wall on this, Representative," Neilson pleaded.

"Call me JD, please."

"JD, do you have anything at all to shed light on this… anything?"

"Not yet, but I will." As Dothan commented, Lieutenant Young smirked doubtfully.

"Any news on Detective Garza?" Dothan asked, noticing Young's derisive expression.

"Nothing, we think he may be a component in all of this insanity as well," Neilson answered as Young squirmed.

"It's unfortunate that he's no longer on the case. Hopefully, he's kicking' it on a beach somewhere," Dothan said.

"I doubt it," Neilson concluded.

Lieutenant Young and Sheriff Neilson left Dothan with the unfinished obsession of his poem. For some moments, he pondered the document before him on his computer. He was still stuck. He needed a beer, but it was way too early. He turned back toward his desk and grabbed a pen and some paper—the old-school way of writing verse. Without much thought he wrote:

Pacing Avenue G
How I long for a time,
Years hence,
When I can trace
These sidewalks away from
The present tumult…
And recall with fond conclusion
This place that led you to me.

It was noon before Kat arrived back at the office. She came in through the back door and found Dothan sitting alone staring into nothing. "Sorry it took so long," she said as she made her entry.

"What?" The poet was broken from his trance.

"Are you okay?" she asked, placing her purse on his desk and sitting down.

"Yeah. What's up? You've been gone forever."

"I know. I was on the phone with my mom. FBC drama."

"Ah, city politics… Let me guess—someone's pissed because they don't like where the fireworks display will be this Fourth of July? Or, the hedges on Such and Such Road need to be trimmed tighter?"

"Are you done? You don't have to be so sarcastic."

"I know…I'm sorry. It's just that city politics seem so petty to me. They spend time on stupid shit; meanwhile, there's a fucking psychopath on the loose." Kat turned pale. "Are you okay?" he asked her.

"Sure."

"No, you're not. What's wrong?"

"Nothing. Like you said," Kat lifted her purse and set in on her lap. She began rummaging through it. "There's a psychopath on the loose. It's kind of scary."

"May I tell you something?" Dothan asked.

She looked up at him. "Of course. What is it?"

Dothan rolled out the situation with the police from beginning to end. Kat sat perplexed. "So, they think because you write poetry you can solve all these murders?" she asked with a bit of sarcasm in her voice.

"Sheriff Neilson does. He thinks I might be able to decode all the bizarre clues this nut job has left behind."

"All the items you just described—fruit, flowers, ashes, and more flowers?"

"Sounds kind of poetic when it's recited that way."

"You don't think you're out of your league, maybe?" Kat said with a shrug of her shoulders.

"Why are you being so goddamned negative? I didn't think so, but maybe you're right."

"Baby, I'm not trying to be negative…not at all," Kat tried to backpedal. "I mean, where do you even start?"

"That's what I have my Chief of Staff, Mason Dixon, for."

"I see."

"So, are we still going to Austin?"

"You say when."

"How about tomorrow?"

"Sure. How many days?"

"Oh, just a couple, I think. I'm not planning on spending too much time with the family, it always gets weird after not too long. I do want to hit some bookstores while I'm there, and I need to go by the capitol. Anyway, you've never met Mason, and this will be a great opportunity to introduce you."

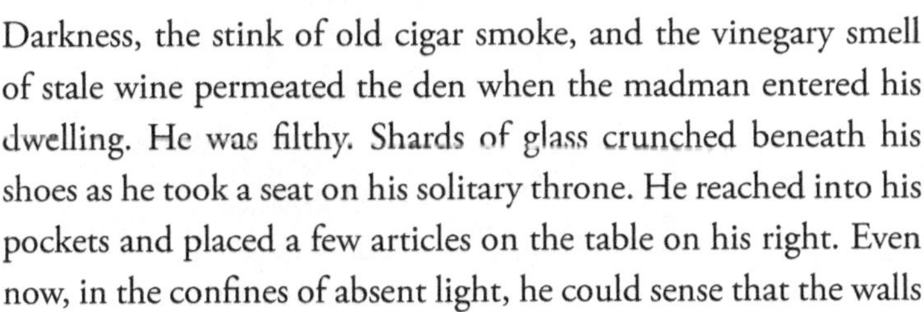

Darkness, the stink of old cigar smoke, and the vinegary smell of stale wine permeated the den when the madman entered his dwelling. He was filthy. Shards of glass crunched beneath his shoes as he took a seat on his solitary throne. He reached into his pockets and placed a few articles on the table on his right. Even now, in the confines of absent light, he could sense that the walls had inched in closer. No music spun from the turntable; he was alone in silence. His phone began to vibrate on the table.

"Yes?" he answered, pained.

"What are you doing? Where have you been? Why haven't you returned any of my calls, texts, or emails? What's wrong, honey?"

"I haven't been feeling well, Janet, darling."

"Please don't call me that. And do you have to use that accent?"

"It used to turn you on," he said.

"*Used* to… I know you don't want me anymore, but you've missed two meetings, and I keep making excuses for you. Doesn't that mean anything to you?"

"Thank you."

"What's going on with you? Please tell me," she begged.

"You wouldn't understand."

"Oh, don't tell me… Wait, you don't know anything about what's happening, right?"

"What's happening?" he asked.

"Those girls?" she bemoaned.

"I'm sure I don't know what you're talking about, Janet."

"Please say you don't know something about all of this."

"Okay, I don't know anything."

"I spoke with Kat earlier."

"How is Kat?"

"Working for our illustrious representative, like we discussed."

"Yes, it must have slipped my mind."

"Tell me, have you been approached by the police?" Janet asked abruptly, as if she couldn't hold her inquiry back any longer.

The madman began laughing sardonically.

"Why are you laughing like that?"

"I have to go."

———————◇———————

Kat did not spend the night, but rather went home to pack her things.

Dothan got up early and was getting his articles together for their trip when a text arrived from Kat.

I can't go with you to Austin. Something's come up. I'm sorry.

Dothan was infuriated and immediately called her. "What the fuck?" he demanded.

"I'm sorry. There's just too much going on with the city right now, and my mother needs me to stay here this weekend."

"Well, goddamn. I was looking forward to this, Kat!"

"I know, baby, I'm sorry. It would be awkward, anyway, with you having to deal with Tryphena and your daughter."

"But I booked us a room at the Driskill."

"We really need to be careful, anyway. I mean, I'm your assistant. Can't you see how all this can hurt you?"

"So this is what it's all about, huh? What are you telling me?"

"I'm telling you I can't go to Austin with you. There really are some things I need to deal with, John David. Please understand."

"Are you quitting?"

"God, no! I just can't go this weekend. When you get back, I'll be here. I promise."

"You told me you were falling in love with me."

"I have."

Nineteen

"Here you go, babe," Tryphena smiled as she placed a slice on Dothan's plate.

"Man, that looks like a million dollars," her husband commented with exceeding joy.

"Brenna, do you want a slice?" she asked.

"I think I'll stick with the salad, Tryphena, but thanks."

"And you, Mason?"

"Tryphena, I think I'll stick with the pizza."

Mason's wife, Brenna, smiled at him as she chewed, and a sliver of greens protruded from her mouth.

"Babe, are you going to have a slice?" Dothan asked Tryphena.

"I don't know, it's tempting, but maybe I should take Brenna's lead."

"When you're a woman you have to suffer for beauty," Brenna proclaimed with a sprinkle of sarcasm.

"Just eat a slice, already. You two are the best looking women within a five-mile radius," Dothan said.

"Only five miles?" Tryphena slyly asked as she cut a slice into two slivers.

"There are a lot of people in a five-mile radius."

The old clan sat enjoying a pie in the stone masonry of Brick Oven, a pizza parlor on Red River not far from the capitol building. Patrons shuffled about as the foursome enjoyed their lunch. Austin traffic piled up outside the large window that flanked the booth where they ate. It was the first time they had communed together in over a year, but their group had increased in number by two: Delilah, and Brenna's son, Will. Delilah was in her stroller in the aisle just to the left of Tryphena. Will, who didn't like pizza, had eaten earlier and now roamed the parlor, impatient to depart.

Dothan wiped his mouth with a large napkin and laid out the itinerary for the afternoon. "So, as everyone knows, I am a great lover of books. Austin has the best bookstores in the state. I suggest we hit Half Price Books on both South and North Lamar. What do y'all say?"

"I think Brenna and I might be in the mood for some shopping, John David," Tryphena said.

"I agree, besides, Will has more books than he can read at the moment," Brenna said.

"You want to hit The Domain up north?" Tryphena asked Brenna.

"Right on, girl," Brenna responded.

"Well, JD, both us will be broke by the end of the day," Mason opined.

"Are you going with them? Because I'm going to the bookstore," Dothan declared. "I'm on board with you, JD," Mason replied.

"So we'll split up. Mason and I will take my truck, and y'all can take the van," Dothan said.

"Yes, sir," Tryphena replied with a playful, mocking smirk.

"We'll meet back up at the capitol later. Sound good?" Dothan asked.

"You're the boss, JD," Mason replied.

Dothan rubbed his full belly. "I'm glad I didn't order any beer; this pizza is sitting like an anchor in my gut."

"That's what I'm saving my allotted calorie intake for," Brenna joked.

The ladies headed north with the kids, and the men went south. For the first half hour of the men's journey Dothan went on and on about Kat.

"I'd like to meet her, JD, now that she's part of our team," Mason said.

"You will. Things just didn't work out this weekend."

"At least you're spending time with Tryphena and Delilah."

"This traffic is incorrigible!" Dothan insisted, pounding the steering wheel.

"Welcome back to ATX, JD—the land of poseurs and traffic."

"You're right about that one."

"So, anything about our case?"

"I've been thinking about it, Mason, and I've had a break-through. Regarding the pregnant woman… Do you remember her name?"

"Jane Sellers."

"She was the one who had the ashes in the shape of a bird on her body. That has to be a phoenix."

"Makes sense, JD."

There were no available spaces in the Half Price Books parking lot. "Goddamned, you can't ever park in this city," Dothan complained.

"Just keep circling around for a bit. Someone will pull out," Mason said.

"You think?"

"Dude, I live here. Trust me."

"I'm glad I don't."

Parking was negotiated. Once inside the bookstore, Dothan calmed down.

"So what are you looking for exactly, JD?" Mason asked.

"Christ, I don't know. I'm going to cruise the poetry and fiction sections first. After that, I'll hit the rare books aisle.

"That's my favorite, too."

An hour passed before the two adventurous minds met up in the rare books aisle. "You've already got quite a stack there, JD," Mason commented.

"Yeah, and I need to set them down somewhere. I can't tell you how much of a pain in the ass this cane is."

"I thought you were getting better? Why don't you ask them to set your books behind the counter?"

"Good idea."

"I really thought things had improved, JD."

"I did, too, but my leg is like a portentous barometer. I suspect it senses the ominous on the horizon."

"You sure it's not a pretention barometer?"

"Ha ha... Funny, asshole. What are you looking to read?"

"History. I think I'll lurch around in search of old forbidden chronicles of past occurrences. You?"

"Next up, poetry and literary criticism."

"That may be forbidden knowledge, too, JD."

"Some things never change."

As they stood in the checkout line, Dothan and Mason quietly debated their respective selections.

"So, what do you have there, professor?" Dothan asked.

"Well, this is a pre-World War II volume about the Civil War, but it's called *The War Between the States*. I think that's more accurate than 'Civil War,' actually."

"And it's got an image of the Confederate Flag on the cover."

"The Stars and Bars, which was the actual flag, not the battle flag, and it's crossed with a Union flag as well."

"I'm not that stupid. I know what it is, but it's a Confederate flag, nonetheless."

"So, what are you getting at, JD?"

"You'd better hide that shit—that's all. And the other one?"

"A book on sixteenth-century England."

"What for?"

"It's an interesting subject. I *was* a history teacher in another life."

"And you got out of that in a hurry."

"It was a shitty profession—no respect."

"So you've found respect working for the state legislature?"

"Not respect, so much, but sometimes fear."

"You shot your old boss. Shit, I'm afraid of *you*."

"What's that tome you got there?"

"*The Platonism of Shelley.*"

"Heavy."

"Yes, it's heavy reading. It's what I like."

"No, I mean the book. It looks heavy."

"Whatever, smart-ass. What's that big black tome you've got there?"

"Oh, a Holy Bible."

Out in the parking lot, Dothan chastised Mason. "You're not going to go 'born again' on me, are you?"

"And what if I did? We live in a world without redemption, JD. Once you screw up, or lose, there is no second chance. Doesn't that bother you?"

"Of course it bothers me. But that doesn't mean I'm going to go running to a book of fables."

"So what if they are fables? The Bible can be a code for living. So, no, I'm not going 'born again' on you. I'm just reading."

They arrived at Dothan's truck and leaned on opposite sides of the rear wheel well with the empty bed between them. Dothan's keys swung from his right index finger.

"By the way, JD, you don't have to sound so damn superior," Mason continued, "What do you actually believe in?"

"First of all, I'm not acting superior. The way of the world bothers me profoundly. You want to know what I believe in?"

"Yes."

"I believe in love."

"Oh, that's vague. Are you John Lennon now?"

"No, smart-ass. I believe in love—not in some lofty, abstract sense, but between two people. I don't know if it's meant to last, but it's what I believe in. It's about all I believe in, okay? Now, get in so we can go meet the ladies."

The madman stood in an immense, open field. Below him, a slight sagging was detectable within the rectangular tracing of raw earth. A corresponding yellowing was apparent in an otherwise healthy expanse of green sod. This troubled his already troubled mind. The sun was setting, and the light was less than erudite. If it could be seen with this degree of definition now, he reasoned in his anti-linear mind, what about at the height of day? *And I still have three more bodies to deal with.* This notion weighed on him considerably. If the walls of his den were inching closer in, then the walls of his mind were nearing collapse.

He trekked through the grass farm and entered the wild copse that skirted Annie Casey's silent home. Paranoia was well advised, given the situation. For a mind already afflicted, fantasy and reality were by now in tenuous agreement, and fantasy was moving in for the kill.

The madman pressed a clicker for the garage door, and it rattled open. He squeezed between Annie's Mercedes and Leroy Sebastian's postal truck. The rank scent of death greeted him inside the home. He switched on the outside lights, as well as a house lamp here and there, which he had done regularly for some time now.

Fortunately, Annie paid her utility bills by traditional mail. Her checkbook was always handy. He would wait until the witching hour to retrieve what mail there might be from the box. Though he had kept Annie's cell phone charged to monitor calls that might come in, and a few did, he never answered. He had no idea how to pay her cell phone bill. Adding to this anxiety was the fact that he had no way to actually access it, as he was ignorant of her password. "Don Gato" had not worked. Don Gato, himself, had finally died, and was now buried in the backyard. The burial scar was far less obnoxious than that of Katherine Hogan's.

———◇———

Dothan arrived home early Sunday evening. It had been a good weekend with Tryphena; much better than he expected. What dismayed him was that Delilah cried whenever he held her. Though he confided in no one, this made him angry at Tryphena.

He sent Kat a text to announce his return, unpacked, and waited. He was working on his troublesome poem up in the loft when she entered. The lights were low, and a satellite seventies station crooned lowly. She wore no makeup.

"You know," he mentioned from where he sat on the bed with the laptop, "you are truly naturally beautiful."

Kat drew her hands to her face in an act of humility. "I wasn't sure you'd be back tonight, and I didn't want to spend too much time getting ready."

"You don't need to spend one second. Just come as nature made you."

"You're blind." She went into the bathroom without closing the door. "What are you working on?" she called out to him.

"A poem."

"For me?" she was looking at herself in the bathroom mirror as she disrobed.

"Yep."

Kat came out of the bathroom, wearing only a pair of panties. "I look awful, John David. I can't believe you like to see my face in the raw."

"I like all of you in the raw."

"Well, not 'all.' I'm still on my period. I should be okay after a shower in the morning."

"I can wait until then."

"You're so sweet." Kat got in bed beside Dothan. "But I do have a question…"

"No, I didn't sleep with her, if that's your question."

"It was. Did she want to?"

"Yes, but she's on shark week as well."

Kat laughed and then yawned. "You tired?" Dothan asked.

"Yes. It's getting late, and we have to work tomorrow."

The poet-legislator hit save and placed the laptop aside. He inched forward and embraced her. They kissed intensely. After breaking for air, Kat looked him in the eyes. "Would you have if she weren't?"

"No."

"What would've been your excuse?"

"Shark week?"

Kat broke into hysterical laughter. When the muscles of her face finally relaxed, she just stared at him.

"What is it?" Dothan asked.

"Let's snuggle, baby." She turned around and squeezed her bottom into his groin. His hot breath on her neck aroused her. She could feel him growing, but knowing she couldn't play, she turned to cerebral topics. "Do you really want to win reelection, John David?"

"Of course I do. Where did that come from?"

"I was just curious. You seem so disengaged. It's like none of it matters to you anymore."

"I've just been wrapped up in you, to tell you the truth. Little else has mattered."

"You know I have ambitions, too."

"I do. My ambition is to carry you off to an island and write you love poems."

"Silly. I'm being serious."

"I am, too."

"What do you think will happen to us if you lose your election?"

"Do you only want me if I'm an elected official?"

"Truthfully, it might have been at first. Now I think I just might follow you anywhere."

"What about that island?" Dothan tightened his grip on her and smothered his face in her hair.

"I wish it existed. I'd go there with you. I would."

"I just want to exist with you as an island, away from all the ever-encroaching madness of the world," Dothan fantasized.

"I wish it were that simple."

"It is."

"I have to think about the future, John David."

He loosened his grip. "You women are so damned practical. Romance is certainly a creation of the masculine sex."

"Don't let go," She drew her arm back and grabbed his thigh. "I like you close."

Dothan returned. "What are you telling me?"

"You've got to get back into the fight, baby."

"I will. I don't like to lose. Losing is great for art, but it feels better to win in actual life, and I've yet to lose an election."

"When you lose you don't get anything."

Sleep overtook them. Dothan had failed to set his alarm.

The lovers awoke to Kat's phone pinging.

"Who is that? Dothan asked, half-awake. "What time is it?"

"It's my mom, and it's late…after nine. We need to get up. I'm going to get in the shower." Kat grabbed her phone and rushed into the bathroom, closing the door abruptly. Dothan lifted up in confusion. He had failed to prepare coffee. Though the apparatus was just a few feet away, it could have been across the sea.

Dothan sat in bed drinking his coffee as Kat finished in the bathroom. Dothan had something on his mind when she emerged totally naked. Her flitting form was turning him on as she scurried about getting ready.

"Hey."

"What?" She stopped where she stood, with a pair of panties and a bra in hand.

"Remember what we talked about last night?" he asked in a sultry voice. His thick, black eyebrows bowed in the way she found irresistible.

"Baby, I can't. Not right now."

"Still on shark week?"

"No, but I've got to run. I have to go meet my mom. Something's come up. When I get back, I promise we will."

"What's the goddamned emergency about? Would you like to fill me in? Your phone's been blowing up all morning."

"Drama, John David. Just more drama."

"I like drama, as long as it's not mine. Bend my ear."

"I will later. Really, I've got to get going." Kat slid on her underwear and fastened her bra. She headed to the bathroom to apply her makeup and left her phone sitting on top of the dresser. The sink was gushing water when her phone pinged. Dothan stayed seated and waited to see if Kat heard it. She had not. Dothan was not a snooper. Long ago, he had learned that a woman will do what she will do, and if there is anything to encourage her actions, it was suspicion. So there the phone sat. When Kat's hairdryer suddenly roared, curiosity won out, and Dothan made his move. Though he did not know her password, he had seen how her phone worked. A fresh text would always partially appear. More importantly, it would reveal the sender. He took the gadget in his hand and punched the bottom button. The phone screen lit up. What he saw shattered him. He staggered. His breathing was now labored, and a sickness gripped his gut. He swallowed with difficulty. The hairdryer stopped. Dothan reached for a pair of jeans draped over a rocking chair.

"You okay, baby?" Kat asked from the bathroom.

"Yeah," he answered, sitting on the end of the bed.

A few moments passed. Kat popped her head out from the bathroom. "You sure are silent." The look on Dothan's face was blank. "Oh, baby, don't sulk. We'll have some fun when I get back.

He pulled on a pair of socks, and rose to fetch his boots. His balance was compromised.

"Are you okay? Is your condition acting up?"

"Funny, you've never inquired about that before," he said.

"You're condition? I'm asking now."

Dothan took a seat in the rocking chair and pulled up his cowboy boots. "Oh, your phone beeped a second ago. Better see what it is this time."

Kat applied the last few, quick finishes to her makeup with a brush. She came out of the bathroom, entered the closet, pulled out her clothes and put them on. Dothan sat silently in the rocking chair. Kat knew something wasn't right. She quickly finished dressing and darted around the bed to retrieve her phone from the dresser.

"Lord, it's my mom again. I've got to go. I'll be back in a couple of hours. You okay, baby?"

"So, are you fucking Zane Rayne or just spying on me on his behalf?" Dothan asked, looking not at her, but off to the side into the essence of all misery: betrayal.

"What?" Kat was shocked.

Dothan slowly locked eyes with her. There he sat shirtless, in jeans and boots, his mane wild from a night's sleep.

"What are you talking about, John David?" Her expression said it all. Guilt had totally taken over her face. She did not need to say anything. Henceforth, every syllable from her exquisite mouth would be the conjuring of lies, the steeping bubbles from a witch's cauldron.

Dothan came clean. "I looked at your phone. You can't lie to me, though I know you'll try, Kat Morgan."

Kat's chest heaved. "So we're friends. What of it? It doesn't change the way I feel about you."

"Doesn't it?" A man expresses himself with anger. It is encrypted in his nature. It is the single mechanism that has ensured survival from the time of creation. Rage against those who wrong you—before reason evolved and civilization was established. Dothan could suppress it no longer. He lifted with some difficulty from the unsteady rocking chair. Limping, he set out for his cane, which leaned against a corner across the room.

"Are you okay, baby?" Kat's tone was desperate.

"You fucking Gudrun!" he accused, swiping the cane from the corner.

"What?" Kat trembled.

"You suck the life from a man's soul and leave him to die on a frozen mountainside."

"What are talking about? I've fallen in love with you, John David."

"Keep it, you poisonous bitch!"

"Don't say these things, please. I can explain everything."

Dothan paused. The inertia of love is stronger than the pull of hate. "What?"

"I'll confess."

"Then fucking confess!" Hate tugged.

Kat was shaking. "Yes, Zane sent me here to spy on you. You're right."

"I knew it!" Dothan swung his cane and smashed the lamp at his bedside. The shards scattered chaotically. Kat's own innate hunger for security was challenged by the beast. In the time it takes to strike a match, her fear turned to attraction. She wanted him above all else.

"You're scaring me, baby," she began. "Look, yes, I came here under false pretenses, but then I fell in love with you. I'm in love with you. I love you, John David Dothan. Please believe me," she pleaded.

"But you run to him at his beck and call." Dothan's voice had gone from devilish rasping to calculated consternation. "So go to him."

"I won't go. I'll cut it off right now."

"Get out of here, NOW!" Dothan swung the cane at the ceiling fan that spun above the bed. A blade cut in half and jettisoned across the loft. Security won. Kat rushed to the bathroom, grabbed her purse, and ran down the loft stairs. Dothan pursued, but he was moving too quickly, lost his balance, and fell. Kat stood at the end of the hallway at the entrance of the foyer.

"I can't believe you're capable of this!" Dothan yelled. "I'm not going to let that fucking grass boy beat me!" He pulled himself up and steadied his footing with the cane.

"You don't need anyone to beat you," she hissed. "You'll always just beat yourself."

Dothan hurled the cane across the hallway. It circled as it flew.

Kat, fleeing from his rejection, had ducked into the foyer. The cane hit the doorway. Kat witnessed the coiled shaft slide across the foyer tile in fragments and flashes. Passion clouded, but looking down, she saw the cane had broken in half. She slammed the foyer door and made her escape.

Dothan collapsed on the first step and leaned against the adjacent wall. His whole body ached—in particular his right deltoid. He grabbed his shoulder and thought he might be having a heart attack, but he settled. Rising slowly, he limped exaggeratedly toward the closed door at the other end of the hallway.

He opened it.

The Kraken had vanished.

CODA Act II

Summer hit hard. Heartache and loneliness in the summertime is a fiery furnace. The endless daylight and the instincts of warmth and thriving burn as antithesis to the flesh, nerves, and brain it bombards. Worse, it afflicts the mind. In Dothan's mind it was simple. The spring never lasts. The summer beats us down. The fall is fleeting. The winter comes to stay, and no season of fanfare can negate an emotional nuclear winter. This melodrama is what he woke to every morning and what he went to bed with every night. Dreamless sleep was a blessing. This alchemy designated his soul as sick. The sickness that of Kat Morgan

June fell to July and July oozed into August. Dothan spent the bulk of his time drinking and listening to old film soundtracks like The Name of the Rose, *Basil Poledouris' score to* The Blue Lagoon, *just about everything John Barry ever wrote, and, from time to time, Michael Nyman's* The End of the Affair. *But campaign season was upon him. He had to somehow pull himself from self-pity and emerge as what he was, a public figure. He detested the thought. Why leverage what was left of his soul for a thankless, six-hundred-dollar-a-month—before taxes—job?*

The poet-legislator had seen enough of the world to know that a man in pain has no market, and, ultimately, no friends. He is consummately alone. There was no feel-good support group, only the

silence of getting on. And, somehow, he had to get on.

In his state, he found it hard to raise campaign funds. The few fundraisers he staged were half-hearted and he was unconvincing to his shrinking following. Zane Rayne was a burgeoning star, and his coffers were growing.

What hit the hardest was discovering that Kat was now Zane's campaign manager. Hatred overtook the man, and that hate collapsed him. Yet, even in the throes of this demonic emotion, he continued to write. If life was about winning, art was about losing. And he had lost. Writing served as exorcist.

Three poems consumed him. The first, the one he had labored over, and the second, the one he thought had the least merit, her call to his action.

THE COUNCILWOMAN'S DAUGHTER

THE FIRST MEETING

I.

Nervous as the wind through a cracked door,
Shaking like a shutter in his foyer,
She stood in the vacancy awaiting…
Awaiting a hand she thought a wall.

But it wasn't.

And as she struggled between cold and hot,
Which rattled undecided through her ribcage,
Her dress blue yet shoes the color of sun,
He led her to a seat in his office.

II.

The thought of his hand on hers still present,
She crossed her legs in contradiction.
An azure and orange book, she drew and set
Upon the glassy glare of his oaken desk.

Unknowing she sat, as he pondered with pen,
That by inviting his scribbled name,
Out of orbit, his axis rebelled.
Still pausing with pen…her knowing knew.

III.

No, his hand hovering, no artifice,
No construct, nor conjured impediment.
More her ambitions and latent dreams
Awaiting the drawbridge of her mind?

And in the warm air she exhaled softly,
As he set aside the unwritten page,
The conversation so unrelated,
Alluring would prove, and a portent…

THE QUIET GARDEN

The State Seal both fed and exiled him:
Feeding his need for the body politic,
Yet standing sentry to the quiet garden
Green on the periphery of his imagination.

He could see her, smell her, and hear…
Her soft breathing ensconced within

The cursive gate that teased like a torso.
But he could not touch her, nor taste her.

Often he thought, as he stared through
The coiled bars,
That he would trade the former senses
For the latter.

But were not the lips and skin he so desired,
Not within but without?
Was not the soft breath he heard merely an echo
Tempting him back into the fight?

The third he scribbled with pen and paper. He would wait to type it because he knew if he did, he would feel compelled to send it her.

Twenty

Oftentimes, the obvious eludes. While lying on his bed listening to Chopin's nocturnes—as life can afford those in tune with the elemental and the inductive—the obvious finally appeared. Dothan sat up with an epiphany. *The blade of grass!* "Holy shit!" he declared. "That's it!" He grabbed his cell phone and dialed Mason. It was 3:00 a.m., so there was no answer. He kept calling.

"Yeah, JD. What's the emergency?" Mason answered drowsily.

"Dude, I'm sorry to bother you this late, but something's come to me. I know what to do."

"Have you been drinking?"

"Of course. Look, I won't keep you, and I'm sorry I woke you up, but can you come down this weekend?"

"I don't know. I'll have to check with Brenna. What's up? And what's so dramatic that you had to call this late?"

"The blade of grass."

"What blade of grass?"

"What Detective Garza had discovered at the scene of Anne Spencer's murder."

"Oh, Jesus, not all this again. I thought you'd forgotten about it, to tell you the truth."

"I had. I was too busy feeling sorry for myself to think of anything else. I can't believe I didn't see it. Of course that's the answer!"

"Dude, this is way too much excitement for…what time is it?"

"About three in the morning."

"Can I call you in the daylight, please?"

"Fine. Just call me back when you get up. Check with Brenna. I have a plan."

Dothan was wired. He knew his present state would screw up his sleeping pattern, but it was already screwed up. He frantically zipped around the loft rummaging around for a pack of cigarettes he knew he'd stashed somewhere. No luck. He decided to go down to the office to see if he'd hidden them there.

Enclosed in the silence of his office, exhaling a buxom plume of carbon monoxide, the inevitable doubt that always follows a great notion gripped him. The Marlboro was making him light-headed. He reached for a bottle of Four Roses Bourbon in the immediate right-hand drawer of his desk. A whiskey glass waited in the left. He leaned back in his chair, taking healthy swigs. *Maybe my hatred for Zane Rayne is clouding my judgment?* he struggled with the thought. *I do hate the motherfucker. I wonder if the crime lab in Houston has analyzed that blade of grass yet. Neilson would have probably contacted me if so…or maybe not. But it all makes perfect sense. He's a grass brat. The company has green trucks. I know because I've seen them on the road. Is it worth risking? If I'm right, then he's toast, but if I'm wrong, and I get caught, I'm toast. He used Kat, though, and Kat used me at his behest. Now she's running his campaign and probably fucking him as well.* Then a second epiphany struck him. *Oh, my God, maybe he's already a suspect. Maybe he's the person of interest Neilson and Young couldn't reveal.*

He polished off his bourbon and the euphoria waned; he was getting sleepy at last. Fatigue or not, he had arrived at resolve.

Dothan was crashed out when his phone started to ring. He saw that it was Mason.

"Yeah?"

"You up, JD?"

"Yeah. What time is it?"

"Almost noon. Did I wake you?"

"Yeah."

"Funny how the universe works: What goes around comes around, huh?"

"Okay, I get your point. What's up?"

"I talked to Brenna about coming down. You do remember asking me, don't you?"

"I said I get your point. Yes, I remember."

"I can come down. When you get up, why don't you call me and tell me what the hell your plan is. I have an idea, so I'm in, but call me back."

"Okay." Dothan dropped the phone and passed back out.

After all this time, it was finally done. The madman locked up Annie Casey's house after placing the day's mail in a drawer in the kitchen. The smell of bleach stung the indoor air. He removed the latex gloves and stuffed them in his pants' pocket. Crickets and frogs thundered in the summer night. Stripping off his attire down to his underwear and socks, he grabbed a duffel bag left in the backyard grill. He pulled out a change of clothes and replaced them carefully with the filthy articles. As he inserted one leg after another and then one arm after another, he began sweating. He slipped on his shoes and reached down to tie the laces.

A trumpet sounded. He stood up in wonder. Hooves on stone grew in volume with a regal cadence. Turning around, a white carriage girded in gold appeared. The cloven march slowed and then stopped. The madman approached the coach. The door opened. A purple footstool dropped. Raising his left foot to enter, he toppled to the ground. His skull slammed to the cobbled edge on the back promenade.

Coming to, he looked upward in disorientation. Pre-dawn was ripening. Fantasy was broken by reality. He lifted his slimy form up with his palms. The dry grass crackled under his backside. He looked back at the spot of injury. The beige cobblestone was discolored. He wiped his forehead and looked at his hand. Tepid blood appeared, dotted with clotted fragments. He wiped the remnants on his pants. He retrieved the duffel bag and moved to the back spigot. He haphazardly scrubbed the soiled stones with a damp shirt. It was time to get the hell out of there. He tried to determine the extent of his wounds by peering into the glare of a back window. What he could make out looked bad.

He emerged from the skirting wood and heard the sound of diesel trucks roaring out of sight. Rayne Turf Works was starting the day. *Shit! How do I get out of here? I'm trapped!* The madman had no choice but to return to Annie Casey's residence and wait until nightfall, though he had already scrubbed the house clean and lacked the constitution to repeat the task. Once inside, he began to feel faint. Nausea sunk in his middle. He inspected his wounds in the bathroom mirror. There were several scratches above his right eyebrow, but near his scalp line, the skin perforated. *What if I need stitches?* he worried, pushing lightly around the damaged flesh with his fingers. He got a damp paper towel and cleaned around the wounds as best he could. He did not wish to go searching for medicinal alcohol as that would leave too many traces. In the den, he placed a stray garbage bag which he had left on the kitchen counter by mistake across the large leather sofa. Sleep came quickly.

When he awoke, the natural light had changed from one side of the house to the other. The sun was going down. He rubbed his eyes and stood up. He went into the bathroom, retrieved the discarded paper towel, and disposed of it in the garbage bag. He had been careful not to touch anything with his bare hands. He wrapped the flaccid bag around his grip and exited.

There was still a slight water stain on the cobblestone where he had bashed his head. He bent down and examined it, trying to determine if the blood had left a mark. It was impossible to tell in the fading light. *How did I fall?*

<hr>

Mason texted Dothan that he was nearly in district and would arrive shortly. The day prior, Dothan had gone to the hardware store and brought two sharp shooter shovels. Mason had instructed this, as he had a hunch of his own. Every instinct in Dothan's body concurred.

The chief of staff arrived at the district office. Dothan texted him to come up to the loft. He was looking for his keys as Mason ascended the stairs.

"You ready?" Mason asked.

"Not yet, I can't find my fucking keys!" Dothan was throwing clothes about, searching through pockets, irritated.

"No telling where they are in all this mess. Are all these beer bottles empty?"

"Probably. The housekeeper was a spy for my nemesis, so I had to let her go."

"That's kind of a sexist statement, JD. It implies that your girlfriend doubled as your help."

"Well, she kind of did." The keys were discovered. "You ready?"

"Sure. You know, this is the first time I've ever been up here, JD."

"Sorry I never invited you, but you've got the wrong equipment between your legs."

"Understood."

"We'd better take your car. I've got state official plates."

Dothan pulled the dual shovels from the back of his cab seat and set them in Mason's white van and they were off.

"I can't believe you're still driving this whale," he commented from the passenger's seat.

"I love it," Mason said. "It's old school, like your truck."

Dothan leered over at him in disbelief and then asked, "Did you tell Brenna about any of what we're about to attempt?"

"Fuck no. Where are we going, actually?"

"Just keep on this road. I cased this whole thing out earlier in the week. We're going to be turning into this new, largely undeveloped planned community in a few miles. As for Brenna, why not? She ain't no stranger to this kind of thing, as I recall."

"If you're referring to the Carlson break-in, that's moot at this point."

"How do you figure that?"

"After we got married, we both became really domestic. Besides, there's Will."

"There was Will before y'all got married, dude."

"I just didn't tell her, JD."

"Well, let's hope we don't get nailed for trespassing. I don't want her opinion of me to get any lower."

"She doesn't have a bad opinion of you."

"Then she's the only woman alive who doesn't at this point."

"Speaking of women who have a bad opinion of you, Tryphena called about a month ago."

"God…let me guess."

"Don't you at least want to see your baby?"

"Yes, of course, but I've been in a bad place this summer. By the way, Tryphena's a hypocrite. She left. Her fucking bitch lawyer worked with that fucking district judge and made sure I was excommunicated. Just saying… She doesn't want me. She just wants me to trouble over her. It's a game. I'm sorry she bothered you, dude. If I could figure women out, I'd be the richest mofo in the world."

"So, it's about to be September, Representative," Mason changed the subject. "Campaign season's about to be in high gear. Have you thought about hiring a consultant?"

"Nope."

"So, what's your campaign strategy?"

"This *is* my campaign strategy."

Dothan instructed Mason where to turn, and they entered the new development. The whale passed right by Annie Casey's home.

"Okay, take a right here." Mason pulled off onto an ungraded road. "Park in this wood," Dothan instructed.

"What about that house over there?"

"I don't think anyone's moved in yet."

"What about that one over there?" Mason asked, pointing toward Annie's house.

"Seems pretty tame."

"I hope you're right, JD. I hope you're right."

Mason drove as far into the copse as possible, then snuggled the van into the trees. They got out and they slogged forward into the musky twilight armed with shovels and flashlights. "So, JD, any idea where to start looking?" Mason asked.

"Well, here it is."

The two stood on the peripheral of an expansive grass farm that stretched in all directions. Its only demarcation was the silhouette of trees in the distance from every angle with the exception of southward. In that direction, against the watery horizon, were the visible structures of Rayne Turf Works. In the middle, a carpet of sod was sprawled out and fitted with long, rolling, suspended sprinklers.

"Wow, this is a lot of grass. They should water it more often."

"It's been hot and dry all summer, Mason."

"That could work in our favor."

"I know. "

"Are you getting a feeling of *déjà vu*, JD?"

"How do you mean? "

"Last time we came out of the woods, we came upon a retention pond. This time, it's a grass farm."

"Yeah, and the wrong kind of grass. I think we should check the tree line. That's the area least likely to get watered." Dothan pointed down at the yellowing runners that snaked toward them into the wild.

"Well, you go that way and I'll go this way."

"You know what we're looking for, right?"

"Sure, rectangular areas outlined with dead or unhealthy sod."

"Good luck, Mason, and don't get caught trespassing. Text me if you find anything."

"Likewise, JD," Mason checked his phone signal. "Wait. It looks a little spotty out here."

"Then use your flashlight to signal me."

"What if we can't see each other?"

"Jesus, then walk into the middle of the field."

"What if the sprinklers come on? "

"You sound like a freakin' child. Then I guess your ass gets wet."

Dothan and Mason set out in their respective directions.

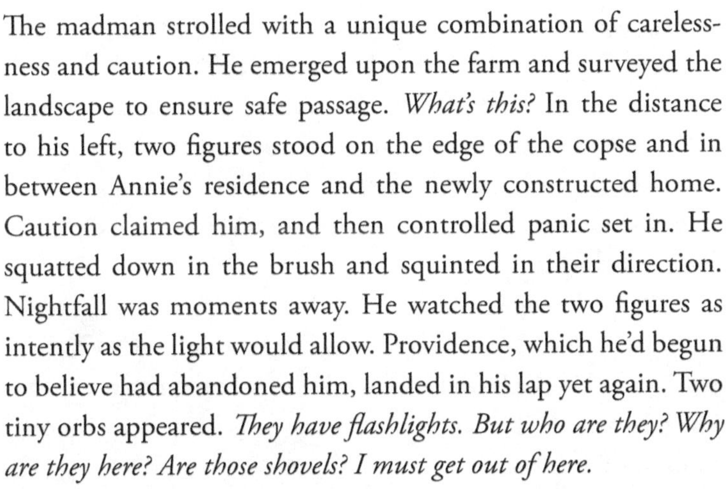

The madman strolled with a unique combination of carelessness and caution. He emerged upon the farm and surveyed the landscape to ensure safe passage. *What's this?* In the distance to his left, two figures stood on the edge of the copse and in between Annie's residence and the newly constructed home. Caution claimed him, and then controlled panic set in. He squatted down in the brush and squinted in their direction. Nightfall was moments away. He watched the two figures as intently as the light would allow. Providence, which he'd begun to believe had abandoned him, landed in his lap yet again. Two tiny orbs appeared. *They have flashlights. But who are they? Why are they here? Are those shovels? I must get out of here.*

A light was coming toward him. Its luminescence hugged the tree line. The beam scoured the ground. *How do they know? Are they police?* The madman was sweating hard. He hunched down, crept back into the copse, and waited for the northbound figure to pass.

Sticks and brush popped under every step. Dothan followed the opposite path of his chief of staff, the shovel doubling as a cane. The single spotlight from Rayne Turf Works glowed closer and closer. His boot snagged on a ridge of earth.

"What's this?" Below, Dothan discovered he was standing in what appeared to be a patch of non-uniform sod. Tracing the ground with the flashlight, dead or dying edges exposed an oblong rectangle.

The madman struggled through the brush and trees, his body soaked with perspiration. Every step announced itself, no matter how light his treading. He cringed with every crackling.

Dothan placed the flashlight between his thighs and removed his cell from his back pocket. "No service. Shit!" He signaled Mason, but Mason had by now vanished into the moonless night. "Fuck it," Dothan set down the flashlight, angling it as best he could. The earth cracked with the weight of his boot. The blade of the shovel sunk reluctantly. "Damn leg," Dothan complained. He hopped atop the shovel and pogoed up and down. He lost his balance very quickly, tumbled over, and the half-embedded shovel tore out a chunk of clay. He rose with some difficulty and reached for the flashlight.

From the edge of the tree line, the madman spotted a second light. He hesitated in indecision, as there was no way back to his truck stored in the Rayne Turf Works barn. He squatted and then inched forward. The figure on the green took definition. The limp unmistakable. *Dothan!*

The chunk of clay was the size of a football. The hard clump's roots resisted as Dothan tugged at it. With the shovel tip, he chopped at the tangle of runners. Dothan dropped to his knees and ripped at the small cavity with his fingers. He felt… something…not earth, rock, or grass. It was cold and clammy, hard, yet spongy. The texture induced gagging.

He stood up to recover the shovel and heard rapid footsteps pounding from behind. He turned. From the darkness came a bolting presence. He was tackled at the waist. Dothan hit the ground and grunted, expiating the last of his breath. The weight of the madman collapsed down on him with a powerful certainty. Rapid footsteps raced back into the darkness.

Dothan writhed on the ground in pain, not knowing what had just happened. Mason appeared.

"What the fuck, dude? Are you okay?"

Dothan lifted up slightly, a sharp pang accompanied each movement of his chest. "Go after him. Go!"

Mason took off toward the southerly compound. He darted into the yard of Rayne Turf Works. Out of breath and pumped, Mason searched frantically for a sign. From the barn some fifty yards away came a violent rumbling. He sprinted around to the opposite side of the barn as a car sped away in a swirl of dust.

Twenty-One

orning hatched through the tree-studded horizon like a five-pointed star. Heat and dew defined the infant day. The two grave diggers sat exhausted on the sod covered in dirt. They shared a single bottle of warm beer. Dothan belched loudly.

"So, JD, how do you want to handle this? Should we call 911?"

"Hell no!" he blurted and took the bottle from Mason. "If we call 911, we'll get some dummy who doesn't know jack shit and will probably arrest us for trespassing."

"So what *is* the plan, then, Mr. Representative?"

"Funny. I think we should get in touch with Neilson. He'll know how to handle this, and he's not a gung-ho cowboy. He's a pretty even-tempered guy, actually."

"Are you going to pass that?" Mason asked, motioning to the precious beer.

"Here," Dothan burped. "I wish you had another one of those in your van. My whole body hurts from that hit I took. It's Sunday, though, and we can't get anything to drink until noon."

"We got lucky I had a stray. That's a stupid law, by the way."

"You're such a libertarian, Mason. You know we can't have heathens indulging on the Sabbath."

"Are you mocking my interest in Christianity?"

"Yes."

"I'm too tired to tell you to go fuck yourself, JD."

Dothan looked around at the freshly lit landscape. "Jesus, what are we going to do about this? I didn't think about the fact that it's Sunday. The Sheriff's Department has probably got nothing but grunts working today."

"Well…it's killed…the beer, I mean. You want to get out of here and go God knows where?"

"Yes. So you think these graves are covered back up enough?"

"I think so. I don't know the carrion habits of buzzards, to tell you the truth, but I think we got it covered if they eat actual rotting flesh."

"Sick."

The two exhausted men sauntered back to Mason's van. Dothan struggled.

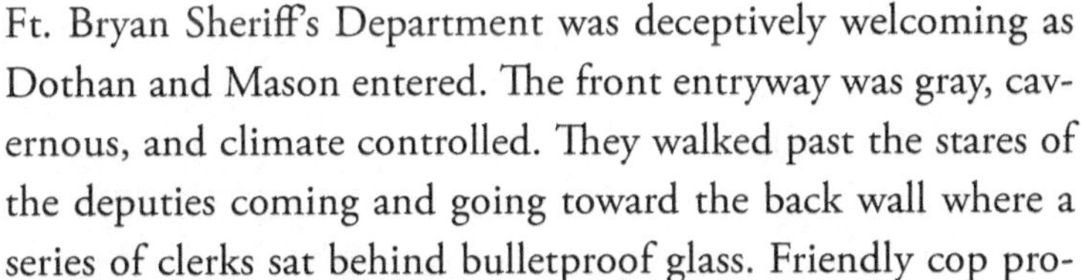

Ft. Bryan Sheriff's Department was deceptively welcoming as Dothan and Mason entered. The front entryway was gray, cavernous, and climate controlled. They walked past the stares of the deputies coming and going toward the back wall where a series of clerks sat behind bulletproof glass. Friendly cop propaganda covered the walls along with "wanted" posters.

"I think we underdressed for the occasion, JD."

"I think you're right." Dothan greeted a passing deputy. "Howdy." The returned look was ominous.

"See what I mean? We look like two early twentieth century farmers, dude…and we probably smell," Mason said.

They went up to one of the protected clerks.

"Can I help you?" A rude, husky, voice came through the speaker.

"Uh, yes. Is Sheriff Neilson available?"

"Sheriff Neilson? And who may I say is calling?" Her tone went from rude to suspiciously condescending.

"Oh, sorry. My name is Dothan—State Representative John David Dothan."

"Please wait." The large, uniformed woman got up and walked off.

"I think she's calling the cops on us, JD."

"Shut up. Look, goddamnit, I'm an elected official. I don't give a shit if I come in here dressed in a burlap sack with an empty bucket of chicken on my head. I want to see the sheriff."

The woman returned with a short male deputy donning a cowboy hat. "Can I help you?" he asked abruptly.

"I hope," Dothan was getting agitated. "I'm the state rep. for this area. My name is John David Dothan." Dothan pulled out his badge and pressed it to the glass. "I need to talk to Sheriff Neilson…please." The fat deputy and the short deputy looked at each other and then at Dothan with strange confusion.

"Sheriff Neilson is out of town, sir," the short one said.

"Out of town, where?"

The fat woman answered, "He's at a convention out of state. Can anyone else help you?"

"No, I'll talk to him later." Dothan turned to Mason. "Let's blow this hut."

"You're the boss, JD."

The atmosphere at the Ft. Bryan City Police Department was strikingly similar. The only difference was that the front area was smaller with only a single bulletproof window.

"Is Lieutenant Young available?" Dothan asked through the glass. "I'm Representative JD Dothan, and I really need to speak with him."

"The Lieutenant is off today, sir," the dispatcher informed him.

"Well, he needs to come in, so dispatch him here, please."

"If this is an emergency then you can tell me."

"It is an emergency, but I need to see Young!"

"Sir, I'm going to ask you to please remain calm."

"I am calm, ma'am, but get Young down here now. This is an inter-governmental issue that needs his immediate attention."

"Excuse me for a moment." The large woman went through a gray door. Dothan turned to Mason who stood behind him indifferently.

"Jesus. This is ridiculous."

"This is hopeless, JD."

The woman reappeared. "Sir, the lieutenant will see you. He will be here in about thirty minutes."

"Great, thank you so much." Dothan turned to his partner. "Man, I could sure use a beer about now."

"I'd go for just a glass of water, and I'm also starving. I'd love a shower, too."

"I know. You want to grab something to eat instead of loitering around here for thirty minutes?"

"Sounds good to me. Where?"

"Do you know if there's a Burger King around here?"

"Burger King? I don't really dig Burger King, JD."

"You don't like a Whopper? That's un-American."

"No one's selling burgers this early. Are they?"

"I don't know. They sell them in the middle of the night to drunks."

"To tell you the truth, I'm thinking about breakfast."

"Whataburger?" Dothan turned to the dispatcher behind the glass, who had overheard their entire discussion. "Ma'am, do you know if there's a Whataburger around here?"

"I don't know, sir," she responded.

"Don't you live around here, JD?" Mason asked.

"I rarely eat fast food."

After a hearty breakfast of egg, bacon, and cheese tacos at Whataburger to appease their appetites, they returned to the station with revived spirits. A door to the side of the dispatch fortress buzzed. Lieutenant Young emerged wearing civilian clothes with his arms folded. "What's this about, Representative? Today is my day off, unless there's an emergency, of course. I do have a family, you know."

"Hey, sorry about that, but this is an emergency…a real emergency."

Young's arms unfolded, but he still had a look of disdain. "Then come back to my office."

Dothan and Mason followed behind Young through the open, desk-cluttered station. Officers on duty looked at Dothan and Mason like they were derelicts. Young's office was toward the rear. He unlocked his door and welcomed them in tepidly. They all took a seat. "So, what's so important, gentlemen, and what's the story behind the outfits? Why are you both so dirty? By the way, you reek of BO."

"Sorry about that, Lieutenant," Dothan said.

"Yes, sir…very sorry," Mason affirmed.

"By the way, Representative, I'm not sure I know this person you've brought along with you."

"Oh, this is my Chief of Staff, Mason Dixon."

"Are you the Mason Dixon who shot his predecessor?" Young asked Mason, pointing at Dothan.

Mason looked at Dothan for instruction.

"Just tell him," Dothan directed.

"Yes, sir, I am. You're aware of that?"

"Of course, I was on the force here. Good job, by the way. I never liked that guy. He was a real elitist asshole."

"Yes, sir." Mason smirked and lowered his head deferentially. Dothan felt a bit of relief at Young's comment.

"You've got to watch this guy…let me tell ya." Mason said, cocking his head toward Dothan.

"I believe it. So you're keeping him in line, are you Mason?" Young asked.

"Yes, sir."

"Well, guys, what's this visit about?"

"I apologize for our appearance, Lieutenant, but that's kind of why we're here," Dothan said.

"Okay, I'm listening." Young folded his hands behind his head and relaxed in his chair.

Dothan drew a deep breath and looked at Mason. "How should we begin?" he asked his chief of staff.

"I don't know, dude? This is your ballgame."

Young sat up and placed his fists on his desk in impatient suspense.

"Well," Dothan began, "how many 'missing' are you up to now with our case?"

"*Our* case?" Young asked, slightly insulted.

"Three, right? Katherine Hogan, Detective Garza, and the postman?" Dothan counted them off on his fingers.

"That's correct. We don't know if their disappearances are related, by the way. We suspect."

"We'll, Lieutenant, I think we found three of them."

"What the hell are you talking about?" Young's posture

straightened and his arms gesticulated.

"Let me back up. Last night…" Dothan laid out the whole scenario from the night before and earlier that morning. Young listened, and during the course of Dothan's tale, his mood changed from shocked to fascinated to indignant.

"How could you do something so irresponsible, Representative? I mean, I know you have a reputation—you as well." Young flung his hand at Mason. "You both have a reputation for taking the law into your own hands, but this is insane."

"I know," Dothan replied, "but we went out to Rayne Turf Works on a hunch, and we found three graves. Like I told you a moment ago, though it's hard to determine facial features, two were clearly dressed in women's clothes and one in men's."

"You know I could have you both arrested for trespassing, Representative."

"That's so amateurish, Lieutenant," Dothan calmly quipped.

Young rocketed up in anger. "Look, you arrogant fuck, just because you're a 'big legislator' doesn't give you the right to go digging on private property. The fact that it's your opponent's place of business… That wouldn't have anything to with it, would it?" Young sat back down and gathered his composure the best he could.

Now Dothan was pissed. He stood up, too. "Someone had to do the job you fuckers couldn't! I mean, how long has it been since this shit started…a fucking year?"

"Fuck you, Dothan. We have rules and protocol." Young rose and leaned over the table toward his antagonist.

"You're too prideful and provincial to bring in the pros, Young, and you're incompetent to boot."

"You know what?" Young yelled.

"What, dickhead?" Dothan yelled back.

"Okay, that's it…I'm arresting you both!"

Mason, who remained sitting, tried to intervene. "Guys, Jesus. Just chill, JD. Sit down, Lieutenant." Both men begrudgingly did as they were told. Mason continued, "Look, Lieutenant, you don't want to have us arrested."

"Why the fuck not?"

"Because you know we just advanced your case. You could be the hero in this. I mean, no one even has to know that JD and I were ever involved."

Young did not look at either of them. Instead, he grabbed a letter opener from the top of his desk and began passing it from taut fist to taut fist. "You're right, Mason," he said. "You guys just beat me to the punch."

"What do you mean?" Dothan demanded.

"Relax. What I mean is the forensics arrived from the Houston lab for both the blade of grass and the dagger. The dagger is a stage prop that you can buy at any costume shop in town, but the grass is a type of Bermuda that Rayne Turf Works specializes in. I've asked the county court judge for a search warrant. I'm just waiting until it goes through, tomorrow. Seems we're about to arrest your opponent for murder, JD. That should make you happy."

"After what I saw on that property, none of this makes me happy. By the way, if it is Rayne, he missed his calling, he should have been a linebacker."

It was only noon when the two dilettante detectives straggled into the district office. On the way there, they'd grabbed a case of beer, but were too exhausted to partake. After they both showered, the fact that it had been thirty-six hours since either had slept hit them hard. Dothan passed out on his bed and Mason crashed on the couch.

Mason was jostled awake hours later.

"Wake up, Mason," Dothan said, shaking him.

"What time is it, JD?"

"Almost eight. I've got some coffee brewing."

After they were sufficiently wired on caffeine, hunger returned. "Are you hungry, Mason? 'Cause I'm starving."

"Yeah, dude, you want to order a pizza or something?"

"Sounds like a plan. Say, I'm going to crack open one of those brews. You game?"

"Hell, yeah! I'd better text Brenna and let her know I'm not coming back to Austin 'til in the morning. I told her I'd be back tonight. I didn't know this was going to turn into Raymond Carver meets Stephen King."

"Texting—the way to avoid unwanted conversation." Dothan popped a beer and handed it to him. While Mason texted his wife, Dothan ordered a pie and put on some music.

The loft was dimly lit as they sat together drinking and waiting for their food to arrive. Mason killed his beer and headed to the fridge for a second.

"So, hey, JD, I have a question."

"Fire away."

"Two questions, actually. What are we listening to?"

"It's *About Face*, by David Gilmour. I've never been a Pink Floyd fan, really, but his solo stuff is incredible. This album is actually the first cassette I ever bought, before I discovered post-punk."

"I dig it. My second question is, after everything that's happened, do you still believe in love?"

"Ha ha. That's a very good question."

"To clarify, I mean between two people."

"I don't know. To tell you the truth, I don't think I believe in anything at this point. It's almost as if I have suspicious contempt for everything. It's like everything is just a fraud. Even art put into action requires the most ruthless of means. People are just fucked up to no end, and their stink is on everything… tainting even the noblest of enterprises." Dothan leaned forward and placed his beer on the small table between him and Mason. "Tell me, you see what we do in the legislature. You've worked in education and in other areas of government. Is there any hope? As for love, I honestly don't know if it's possible to give love to a woman. Their idea of love and ours is totally different. I think, for a woman, love is just an extension of security, so they get bored with it. My whole life, I've snagged women because they thought I was some sort of bad boy. When they discover that I'm really not, they grow contemptuous. No, the only thing you can do is keep them guessing. You can't give yourself entirely, even though that's the only thing you want to do. Men labor to make and build things for women, but that's not what they want. They want mystery and intrigue, and that can only last for so long. Ultimately, it just all settles into security: What they both crave and loath."

"Did you ever think that maybe you just haven't found the right woman?"

"Have you?"

"Brenna? Oh, I don't know. I think so, but I have to confess, raising another man's son is no fun. I think he'll probably turn out as a spoiled brat. I hate to say that, but she won't let anyone discipline him. All she does is indulge him."

"The real question, Mason, is has she found the right man? I ask because as long as they're attractive, their options are endless. Are you just filling a slot for the time being?"

"Damn, dude, you are cynical. You don't think you're being too academic about this?"

"I'm just processing my reality and trying to make sense of it."

"That's the catch, though, JD. You really can't make sense of it."

"Maybe you're right, but wouldn't it be the ultimate irony if it was love that destroyed the world?"

"On a lighter subject, but one more pertinent to the present, it looks like you're in like Flynn with regards to the election, JD."

"Maybe."

"Maybe? Dude, your opponent is about to be arrested and charged with murder."

"Yeah, I guess it's Zane who tackled me. I never got a look at his face. He was a powerful bastard, I'll tell you that much. He probably won't be indicted until after the election. You know how slow the criminal justice system is, Mason. Besides, it won't matter. His name will still be on the ballot."

"That's just a technicality, dude." Mason went to grab two more beers. "So, tell me, how do think Kat Morgan will take this?"

"I've no idea. She'll probably hate me for it."

"She may never find out that you and I played a role in his arrest."

"It won't matter."

"I hope you're wrong."

There was a knock on the door below.

"Awesome, our pizza's here," Mason chimed.

"Just in time; these beers are giving me a buzz on an empty stomach," Dothan went to answer the door.

He returned with the food and dropped the box on the

table. The two began stuffing their faces. "This hits the spot, JD," Mason said with a full mouth. "Thanks for dinner."

"You earned it. It's the least I could do." Mason's phone rang. "I'll bet that's your wife."

"Yeah, shit. I'll call her in a bit. I want to get something in my stomach first."

"What are you going to tell her?"

"I don't know. I'll make something up. I'm not going to tell her what we did last night."

"So you're going to lie?"

"She wouldn't understand, JD."

"They never do."

Twenty-Two

The next day, Mason traveled back up to Austin. Through the subsequent week, Dothan kept a low profile in district, except when he limped through the heat to the post office to grab the local paper stuffed in his PO box each afternoon. It took several days, but, eventually, the front page bore the headline: *Local State Representative Candidate Zane Rayne Arrested on Five Counts of Murder.*

"Five counts?" Dothan read out loud in the lobby of the post office. Patrons getting and sending their mail were startled by his volume. Realizing this, he walked outside. *Who was the fifth?* He read the article as he labored back to the DO. A quote by Kat Morgan struck him:

"Zane is innocent of all charges. He is a good man who loves his family and his country. He will be found not guilty of all charges. I will continue to campaign for him while he is in custody. He's going to win this election and he will be the District 100 state representative."

Dothan was both floored and angered as he entered his office. His anger was soon submerged in a sort of sadness that cloaked his every movement. This sadness was inescapable. *I'll have to see her at every candidate function between now and November.*

He had good reason to be apprehensive. September had commenced, and that meant candidate forums. He already had several engagements coming up. He would have no choice but to attend and play his part. It may not be hard to run against an alleged serial murderer, but, in essence, he would be running against the woman who had taken a piece of his soul. It was all Golgotha to him. No matter how foolish he was and felt, he had yet to shake his love for her.

Something happens to one once they take office. They gain knowledge a candidate running without experience can't possibly grasp. It is a combination of the need to see things through and expanded knowledge of one's elected position. Hubris or not, it is as incorrigible to the elected as the perceived self-importance of the incumbent is incorrigible to the electorate. *Change can only occur by the hand of those who understand how to enact change. That takes time.* Even though he was a born performer, he had tired of performance and only wanted to retire into the deliberation of his duty. The idea of campaigning irked him, but it was also a duty. He knew he had it in the bag. *But her…not her.*

Dothan sifted through the invitations piled on his desk, looking for a forum invite he had opened recently. Envelopes went flying in all directions as he rummaged. He had forgotten about the invitation until now. He'd received it while in the grip of his malaise. Once he located it, he tugged out the card. *Shit! This is next week and I haven't RSVP'd.* To make matters worse, it was scheduled on his daughter's first birthday. *But I have to go.*

Did he, though? Was something else driving him to attend the forum in lieu of his daughter's birthday? Tryphena was already mad at him and would most likely never forgive him. He hadn't even contacted his ex-wife in three months; repeatedly skirting her calls to the point she'd stopped trying. Reason usurped paternal instinct. He emailed his RSVP.

Dothan was expecting a call from Tryphena when the day arrived. He had decided he would talk to her and tell her the truth. The call came as he knew it would.

"Is this John David Dothan?" Her tone was light.

"Yes, Tryphena, it is," Dothan answered, conciliatorily.

"I thought you had fallen off the face of the earth, John David. It's nice to hear your voice again. Are you all right?"

"I apologize for not contacting you. I've been in a bad place all summer."

"Well, summer's over. I imagine you know what today is?"

"Delilah's first birthday."

"Yeah, you remembered."

"Of course I remember."

"So, what are your plans for today?"

"I have a candidate forum I have to attend this evening."

"Oh, is that right? So does that mean you won't be coming up to see us?"

"I can tomorrow. I promise." A grave pause ensued. "Are you still there?" Dothan asked.

"Yes. If you can't come until tomorrow then that's fine. It is what it is." Though she was short, Dothan was astonished that she had not blown up at him. He began to feel increasingly guilty as he held the phone to his ear.

"So you don't hate my guts?"

"What would it matter? I mean, John David, you just can't help being yourself. None of us can, actually."

"I'm not trying to hurt you."

"I know. Where is the forum, who's hosting it?"

"It's some local chapter of some 501.c3, Catholic Women Voters of Texas."

"Oh, God! A religious group?"

"Yeah, I know. But there are a lot of Catholic Democrats, I think."

"There are. By the way, I read about your opponent. Sounds like he's done for this world. Not sure what you're worried about. If you lose to an alleged serial murder, then you're in the wrong business."

"I'm not worried. I just have a duty to the voters, Tryphena."

"It wouldn't be because your ex-girlfriend is still stumping for him, would it?"

"I don't know what you're talking about."

"Hmmm. Well, just call me and let me know when you would like to come celebrate your daughter's birthday. I know she's only one, but she'll remember. She loves you, John David."

"I love her, too. Thank you for being so understanding."

"Would it have changed anything if I weren't?"

"I'll call you tomorrow."

Dothan's nerves were up the whole way to the event. He had no idea what to expect. Though he had done plenty of these types of events in the past, this one would most likely be entirely differ-ent. The large church where it was being held appeared through an arbor of trees at the end of a suburban road. Though it was new, it was a beautiful pentagon-shaped structure. Stained glass mosaicked upward in slim gothic fashion above the handsome front door. The parking lot was nearly to capacity. Since his cane had vanished, Dothan had refused to buy another. Mainly because he knew that whatever aid he might find, it would be a visual deficit. He limped from his truck under the nestling sun to the entry .

Inside the church, the devout and the engaged bustled about. Two young Hispanic women greeted him from behind a long, white, draped table. Neither woman recognized him, but once checked in, he was escorted by a nun to the backstage area. She laid out the evening's proceedings in a methodical, pleasant voice. Dothan was left standing alone amid a shroud of red curtains.

Nervous, he ran his fingers around the inside of his white collar, wiping the sweat from his neck. It was warm, and he paced nervously in his fashionable black silk suit, back and forth almost in a circular pattern in short intervals. From the other side of the curtain, someone made announcements from the PA system. *Am I to do this alone?* he wondered, relieved. Just then, Kat appeared in the corner of his right eye. He turned toward her as she approached him. Led by the same nun who had previously escorted him, they spoke together inaudibly. As she came closer, Kat had yet to acknowledge him, her conversation with the nun continued. He noticed her hair was now blonde.

"Representative Dothan, have you met Ms. Kat Morgan?" the nun asked.

Dothan cracked a faux smile.

The nun continued, "She will be speaking on behalf of Candidate Zane Rayne. She is his campaign manager." Kat had yet to meet his eyes, her eyes were fixed solely on the soft-spoken nun. The sister went on to explain the rules of the forum. "Because Ms. Morgan is not the actual candidate, she cannot answer policy questions when we come to Q and A, but she will be allowed to give an introduction and provide closing statements." The nun departed and left the campaigners to fraternize. Dothan stood hesitant and Kat insouciant. Her arms were crossed, and her long leg cocked. They did not look at each other. The voice over the PA continued to ramble. Still not a look or word was exchanged between them. Then…

"You look nice," Kat complimented, looking forward into the heavy, dangling folds of the rich curtains.

Dothan felt her words down the length of his spine. "Thank you. When did you decide to go blonde?"

"About a month ago. Do you like it?"

"Why did you change it? Your dark brown hair was beautiful."

"Every woman secretly wants to be a blonde. Mayor Andy suggested it. Maybe he just has better taste than you?"

Dothan felt that he had offended her and then wondered why he cared. He felt his spleen rising. "How could you still stump for Zane, I don't understand."

Now it was Kat's turn. "It's none of your business what I do. Besides, he's innocent and I know what you did."

"And what is that?" They locked eyes. "What did I *do*, Kat?"

"You know." Kat turned away and pouted and refolded her arms. Dothan did not reply. Kat fired her eyes straight into his. "I have friends in the police department. Enough said."

"I don't know what you're talking about."

"Like hell you don't, motherfucker," Kat accused, thrusting her whole body in his direction. The nun, who was coming to inform them that it was almost showtime, heard Kat's vitriolic tone and paused. Neither Kat nor Dothan was aware of her presence.

"Whatever," Dothan said.

"*Whatever,*" Kat mocked.

"Look, you betrayed me. Why should I care if your designs are spoiled?"

"I would have given them up for you, but you threw me out if I remember correctly."

"Look, goddamnit…"

The nun interrupted. "Excuse me," she said meekly.

"Great, nice language. You're so disrespectful, John David." Kat scorned, shaking her head.

"I'm just coming to inform you two that we're about to start the forum. Is everything okay?" the worried nun asked.

"Fine," Kat insisted.

"Look," Dothan continued as the nun grew increasingly anxious. "I loved you."

"I hate you," Kat retorted as the curtain swished open. The nun looked at them in horror.

"I hate you back."

"You do?" Kat asked in a pained voice, as if the conversation heretofore had never happened.

Kat took the initiative and proudly stepped out to face the clapping crowd of women. Dothan tagged behind, working to disguise the pusillanimous limp. Two chairs and microphones at the front of the stage awaited them. Kat was already seated with microphone in hand as Dothan leaned down for his. His balance was compromised, and he paused before lifting it. He tapped the meshed dome to see if it was live—it wasn't. He sat down next to her. A middle-aged woman was finishing up the introduction when Kat leaned over to her opponent.

"Having trouble?" she asked meanly.

"Yes, since you stole my cane."

"You're ridiculous."

Kat introduced herself and then talked glowingly of Zane. She repeatedly insisted that he was innocent, never actually saying what it was he was innocent of. Dothan sat calmly with a boot propped up on a knee. He looked out among the littered pews at all the women. It was a struggle to keep his face from showing disgust. Repeatedly, he forced his sight on the arches, beams, and medieval glasswork and icons that lined the walls—anything he could think of to be in a good place mentally.

The forum quickly devolved into a debate and then an all-out fight. Kat was refusing to follow the guidelines, and the Catholic ladies were letting it go. After razzing him for failing to do anything about the highway construction conundrum, she laid into his liberal voting record, accusing him of being anti-business. Dothan really tried to keep his cool, but Kat was pushing it too far.

"The real question is: Do you want an atheist to represent you in Austin?" Kat asked the audience, though it was more of a declaration. She turned toward her opponent and pursed her lips with admonishment. The ladies sat aghast.

When it came time for him to reply, Dothan straightened his back and brought the microphone to his mouth. "Thank you for that, Ms. Morgan. Your commentary was both illuminating and ludicrous." Kat's body language stiffened considerably. Dothan continued, "First off, my faith, or lack thereof, has never influenced my belief in freedom of religion and respect, in particular, of Christianity. In fact, I find the Catholic faith something truly beautiful. Look at this church. It's gorgeous. What a history you have! I can assure you that I would never vote to impugn the church in any way. I have nothing but respect for your faith."

"But you're totally on board with abortion," Kat retorted, pointing her finger at him viciously. She leaned back in her chair with an air of satisfaction.

Dothan had had enough. "Ladies, the question you should ask yourselves is do you want an alleged serial murder as your representative in Austin?"

"Oh, my God—that's all you have?" Kat sat up, completely on fire.

"In any sane world, that would be all I need, but, no, I have experience, wisdom, and a genuine desire to serve the constituents. What you have is arrogance, self-righteousness, and a terribly misguided interest in taking money from a sick human being. If he can actually be called 'human.'"

Kat was incensed. "So you don't believe in due process? Zane is innocent until proven guilty!"

"Actually, I know more about that then you could ever comprehend. Ever heard of civil asset forfeiture? No? I didn't think so. Why don't you tell them why you're actually up here shilling for him, Kat?"

"What…what are you referring to?"

"Folks, Zane Rayne is, among other things, an adulterer."

"Oh, my God! What is that supposed to mean?"

"I'll let the good women of the Catholic faith draw their own conclusions."

The nuns cut the forum-turned-battlefield abruptly short.

In Wagoneer County, Dothan's former homestead, it was worse. Kat, knowing of his past war with the water district and contentious relationship with the county's elected class, lambasted him for being against agriculture.

"I mean, how does he think we get our food?" she shouted. Again, she was allowed to carry on without respect for the rules of debate. Dothan refused to swing at a third pitch. No more forums.

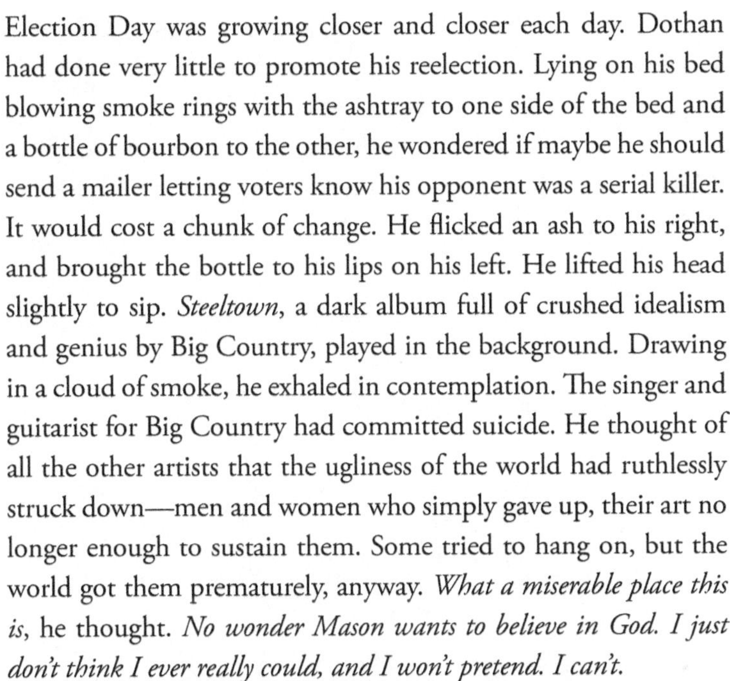

Election Day was growing closer and closer each day. Dothan had done very little to promote his reelection. Lying on his bed blowing smoke rings with the ashtray to one side of the bed and a bottle of bourbon to the other, he wondered if maybe he should send a mailer letting voters know his opponent was a serial killer. It would cost a chunk of change. He flicked an ash to his right, and brought the bottle to his lips on his left. He lifted his head slightly to sip. *Steeltown*, a dark album full of crushed idealism and genius by Big Country, played in the background. Drawing in a cloud of smoke, he exhaled in contemplation. The singer and guitarist for Big Country had committed suicide. He thought of all the other artists that the ugliness of the world had ruthlessly struck down—men and women who simply gave up, their art no longer enough to sustain them. Some tried to hang on, but the world got them prematurely, anyway. *What a miserable place this is,* he thought. *No wonder Mason wants to believe in God. I just don't think I ever really could, and I won't pretend. I can't.*

While engrossed in tragedy, his mind continually circled back to the female thread through his life. He pondered all the mistakes he had made repeatedly over and over and over again. *Have I never learned? When Tryphena said I act according to my nature, is she right? I wish Rachael were still here. If she were just still alive...*

When he thought of Kat Morgan, a flood of love and hate submerged him. *How could I be such a fool? If love is the king of emotion, then hate must have his kingdom, too.* From a young age, he had a liking for the Greek God of the Underworld, Hades, and, in Romantic fashion, he had always admired Milton's Satan. *I must learn to make peace with hate. I can't defeat it. It does motivate…better than coffee and nicotine.*

If all this wasn't enough to weaken the walls of his heart, an opened letter lay beside him on the bed. It was from UT Press. His second volume of poems, previously scheduled for release in a few months, had been put on hold.

He continued smoking, drinking, and listening to music where he lay. He might as well be floating on the other side of the universe.

Twenty-Three

"So, JD, do you have an October surprise ready to pull from your arsenal?" Mason asked from across the table. Dothan was in Austin visiting his family. Mason and Brenna met them at Serranos in Sunset Valley. It was a repeat of their earlier communal, only with Mexican food this time. Tryphena tickled Delilah in her stroller as Brenna was busy trying to get Will to eat.

"No. Why?" Dothan asked. "My opponent is a sicko in jail in Ft. Bryan County."

"I understand, but does the average general election voter know this? That's something you can't count on, JD," Mason said.

"Dude, get real. Besides, the Democratic Party of Texas doesn't seem to think I have anything to worry about, so they're focusing on other races. Makes sense to me. I've been trying to get block-walkers rounded up, but those precinct chairs are lazy as hell. I may just have to walk door to door myself."

Tryphena chimed in, "His ex-girlfriend is out wreaking havoc everywhere she goes, Mason. Next we'll hear that John David is in league with Satan. Zane Rayne is out on half-million-dollar bail. How corrupt is that? Supposedly, he's on house arrest and wears an ankle bracelet, but the Raynes have so many properties in the county, who knows where he is? I also read that his wife split with their kid."

"I guess if you've got the money… About JD and Satan, that's not far from the truth, is it, JD?" Brenna joked.

"They found another body since his arrest, a mailman who's been missing. He was in a victim's garage," Tryphena added.

"Look, I'm tired of listening to this bullshit," Dothan said. "Don't worry, Mason, your job is secure. People aren't that dumb…yet."

"Yeah, but there's no more straight party voting. You can't count on democrats to go down ballot," Mason insisted.

"You're spoiling my lunch." Dothan changed the subject, "So we're all game for Zilker Park after this, right?"

"Isn't that where you used to go walking with Rachael Logan?" Tryphena commented factitiously.

"Okay, one more remark about any of that shit, and I'm going home."

"Oh, JD, for a politician, you sure have thin skin," Brenna observed. "Are you and Mason sure you don't want to hit some bookstores? Tryphena and I could go shopping." Brenna lightly kicked Tryphena in the shin under the table.

"Baby, you know I'm really into my new book. I don't like having too much on my reading plate at one time," Mason protested.

"Oh, what are you reading?" Dothan asked.

"That book on sixteenth-century England I bought when you and I went to Half Price Books."

"Are you're enjoying it?"

"It's interesting, JD."

The weather was temperate, and Zilker Park was pleasant, but for the swarms of people and their unruly dogs. Dothan spent the night with Tryphena and left home for district the next day.

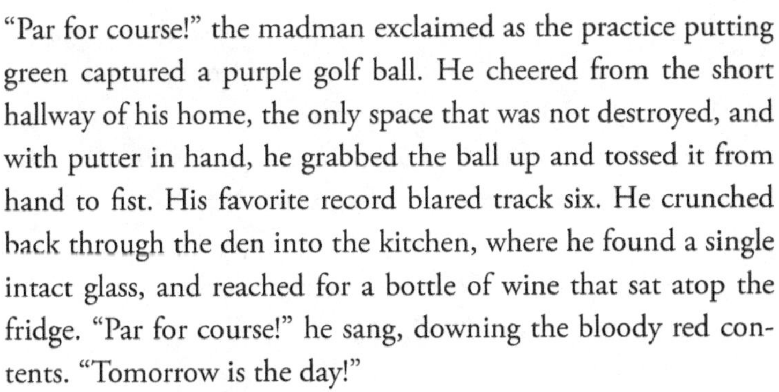

A day of block walking, going door to door, in precinct after precinct proved difficult. Dothan resigned himself to a new cane. On the second outing, he felt incredibly unhip as he hobbled street after street with his generic, geriatric walking aid. He had one volunteer, a young woman who wasn't even involved in the local party. After numerous conversations with her, he decided she was a potential revolutionary communist and did not ask her back for fear she might terrify the voters. Out of guilt, he gave her two hundred dollars in cash.

Kat had been out and about working her black magic. Nearly every door he knocked on was answered by a voter who had been visited by Kat previously. Dothan repeatedly got the impression the voting public believed they were voting for her. Some of the prospective voters didn't believe him when he disclosed the truth about Zane. As with the forums, he halted all block walking.

Election day drew nearer…and nearer…

"Par for course!" the madman exclaimed as the practice putting green captured a purple golf ball. He cheered from the short hallway of his home, the only space that was not destroyed, and with putter in hand, he grabbed the ball up and tossed it from hand to fist. His favorite record blared track six. He crunched back through the den into the kitchen, where he found a single intact glass, and reached for a bottle of wine that sat atop the fridge. "Par for course!" he sang, downing the bloody red contents. "Tomorrow is the day!"

But the mind was twitching again, and a tremor afflicted his hand. The glass dropped and smashed on the floor. He staggered back and shielded his eyes. Unveiling them, a tennis court replaced the kitchen and the floor was now taut green turf. He smiled powerfully, knowing that he would always win. *Providence has birthed me this way.* He began prancing to the music, though the only sound was the sound of the needle popping.

Anxiety, indifference, and traffic jams were the internal and existential conditions Dothan found himself in the latter days of October. He despised social media, but had to tend to it for the purposes of campaigning. To his surprise, Kat had not banished him. No doubt to rub in his face her ongoing promotion of his opponent. He was past caring at this point, or so he told himself. Their time together was a brief flash or a short-lived flame, at most. Sitting in traffic on the highway, he scrolled down his feed, after much nonsense and narcissism from people he once knew, or barely knew at all, he arrived at the latest post from Kat Morgan. He noticed his phone was about to die. He did not have the charger available. *So, she's meeting with Mayor Andy, is she? I knew I couldn't trust that guy either. He hasn't been around in a long time. No wonder.* Dothan bounced from pedal to brake and brake to pedal. *And at her apartment…wow. How close are they?* Nothing surprised him at this point in his life. By now, trust was just an abstraction, no less celestial than the notion of global peace.

A call came in from Mason, interrupting his scrolling. This time, providence was on his side.

"JD, you got a minute?"

"Yeah, just sitting in traffic. You can't go anywhere in this state without getting stuck in traffic."

"Tell me about it, dude…I plan my life around it."

"So what's on your mind?"

"I have a theory about those serial murders."

"Really? Well, let's hear it. Not that it matters anymore, since they have their man."

"Uh…I'm not so sure of that, JD. It's just a hunch, but I'm not so sure Zane Rayne is this creative."

"So you're working for the fucker, too, now, huh?"

"Yeah, he promised me a job after we kick your ass out."

"I'm sure. Everyone else has fucked me. Now it's your turn."

"Ha ha… Seriously, though, remember that book I bought a few months back that I've been reading?"

"Yeah, seventeenth-century France."

"Sixteenth-century England, actually."

"Yeah, right. What of it?"

"I got to the part about the Tudors—Henry VIII, specifically. As I'm sure you know, he had six wives."

"Right, but I don't know much more than that."

"So he had six wives: Catherine of Aragon, Anne Boleyn, Jane Seymour, Anne of Cleves, Kathryn Howard, and Katherine Parr."

"You would have made a great history teacher. Oh, I'm sorry, you already tried that. What are you getting at?"

"What strikes me as very interesting are the names of the victims, both stalked and killed, in Ft. Bryan. They are all, in order as far as I can tell, variations of both Catherine and Anne… and one single Jane."

"Dude, you're reaching, here."

"That's what I thought, until I ran across a series of illustrations in the book. The pictures were of the wives' badges, basically their respective heraldry. Do you follow me?"

"Yeah," Dothan yawned.

"Stick with me on this, JD. All of these badges are symbols."

"That's what Garza called the clues."

"I'm getting your attention at last. Still sitting in traffic?"

"Why would you even ask? Of course. You've got me, dude, keep going."

"I'll go in order. The first, Catherine of Aragon, has red and white Tudor roses and a pomegranate; the second, Anne Boleyn, a falcon; the third, Jane Seymour, a phoenix; the fourth, Anne of Cleves, a carbuncle."

"A what?"

"An eight-pointed star—what they found pinned on Annie Casey's corpse."

"Keep going, Mason."

"Number five, Kathryn Howard, also had the red and white Tudor roses."

"And number six?"

"I'm getting there, JD."

"What the fuck is it?"

"Okay, JD, just chill. The sixth wife of Henry the VIII, Katherine Parr, her patron saint was Saint Catherine of Alexandria, or Saint Catherine of the Wheel."

"What the fuck does that mean? What does it look like?"

"A woman with blonde, flowing hair surrounded by Tudor roses."

"Oh, my God…" Dothan sat in traffic limbo in a state of shock.

"Here's the deal-sealer, in my opinion. JD, are you listening?"

"Yes, yes…what?"

"The beheaded women, Anne Spencer and Katherine Hogan, correspond with and are in order with the symbols, as far as we're aware. Jane Sellers died in labor. Jane Seymour, the third wife of Henry the VIII, died in labor as well."

"Her badge was a phoenix."

"Exactly, JD. What I can't explain is why Annie Casey was killed. Anne of Cleves was retired in wealth, underwritten by Henry. Maybe she got in the way?"

"Yeah, along with Garza and that postal guy."

"I know it's far-fetched, JD, but honestly, it all adds up. Or maybe I'm nuts, too."

"You're a genius, Mason. You should look for a better job.'

Dothan got off the phone and returned to the frustration before him. He could hear Kat's voice in his head: *Every woman secretly wants to be a blonde. Mayor Andy suggested it.* Thoughts raced through his mind—memories of past conversations, that up until now had been forgotten. *Mayor Andy is a film buff…a stage actor, he said…*

"Holy fuck!" he yelled and started hitting the horn to no avail. He felt as if he were in a cage. His truck sat on the incline of an overpass, but he could not see beyond the cars in front of him. He hit the horn again. The guy in front of him flicked him off through his side-view mirror.

Finally, the cars began to move; traffic inched forward and picked up. The exit that led to Kat's apartment was no more than a quarter mile away. When he made it to the overpass, he saw nothing but bands of cars in every direction. He tried calling her. She did not answer. He struggled whether to leave a message. *Maybe she'll think I'm fucking with her?* He did not. *Am I panicking?*

Mayor Andy slathered his neck in cologne and straightened his bow tie. An elegant bouquet of red and white roses sat on the end table near the front door. Next to it was a small burgundy case, which he carefully slipped into his suit coat pocket. As he checked himself one last time in the entryway mirror, one of the only hanging items in his home he had yet to destroy, the door-bell rang. For an instant, he thought it might be his bride, but when he peeped behind the violet curtain, he recognized a car he wished never to see again. The person at the door switched to loud knocking. He opened the door.

"Where have you been? I've been trying to contact you for weeks. You've missed three city council meetings!" Janet Morgan took note of his dress and the bouquet. "Where are you going with those? Are you taking them to Kat? I know you're meeting her. Why?"

"Hello, Janet. I'm off into the past."

"To where?" she asked angrily.

"Into the past, which is the future become the past."

Janet stepped through the doorway. She looked to the side of Andy and saw the den in disarray. "What have you done to this place?" she demanded.

"You are like a scolding mother."

"And you are like a disturbed child," she shot back and stormed past him. "And what are you meeting my daughter for?" She entered the den and was astonished by the damage. The only item in the room that wasn't demolished was his cabinet stereo. She attempted to maneuver through the shards of glass and debris, but she stumbled repeatedly in her high heels. Atop the stereo sat an album cover. She lifted it for inspection. "Rick

Wakeman, *The Six Wives of Henry VIII*," she read. "You've gone and done it haven't you? I knew it was you. I knew it was you all along. Oh, Andy, you shouldn't have told me your fantasies while we were in bed together."

She started to weep. "And now Zane is in custody, charged with crimes he didn't commit, and—" Janet fell to the floor with fragments of glass and rose petals raining down upon her.

Andy looked at his hand and saw a curved slit fill with blood. The blood started pouring from the open wound. He went into the bathroom calmly and turned on the faucet. Thick red coagulated around the oval of the sink. He wound a fresh washcloth around his palm and tightened it with white tape. In the den, he gathered what flowers he could and left.

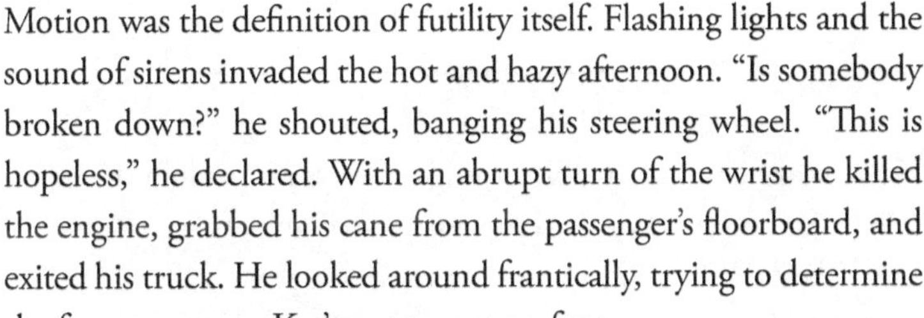

Motion was the definition of futility itself. Flashing lights and the sound of sirens invaded the hot and hazy afternoon. "Is somebody broken down?" he shouted, banging his steering wheel. "This is hopeless," he declared. With an abrupt turn of the wrist he killed the engine, grabbed his cane from the passenger's floorboard, and exited his truck. He looked around frantically, trying to determine the fastest route to Kat's apartment on foot.

The driver directly behind him yelled out his window at Dothan, "Where the fuck are you going, asshole?" The man honked and honked as Dothan made his way down the weed-ridden mound that supported the overpass.

At the bottom, he rapaciously limped between cars that sat on the feeder road. He slid down the shallow but steep ditch that divided interstate from vast shopping center, his cane jabbed into a large crack of dry earth. Momentum jerked his arm back and forced the cane from his sweaty grip. Dothan ate the ground. He stood back up with a sharp pain in his shoulder. He surveyed the layout for the most expeditious route: *Straight through the parking lot.* Cars whizzed by and honked as he crossed street after street. With his heart galloping and labored breath, he paused in the same Home Depot lot where he had met Kat on their first date. He pulled out his cell and called Mason.

"Come on…answer!"

Mason answered. "Mason, listen…"

"Why are you out of breath, dude?"

"Never mind, what happened to Henry VIII's sixth wife?"

"Nothing. They remained married until Henry died."

"Oh, Jesus!"

"What, JD?"

"I need to call Kat again. At least leave a message. I gotta go, Mason!" The phone died before he could hang up.

Kat was at her kitchen table typing on her laptop when she heard a light tap at her door. Giddily she rose to answer it.

"Andy!" she said, swinging the door open.

"Katherine!" Mayor Andy stood with a wad of ragged roses in his fist. The other hand was wrapped in a crimson rag.

"Since when do you call me that? What happened to your hand?"

"Oh, nothing, a sword fight," he answered with a broad smile.

Kat laughed. "Politics! Come on in. Do you need anything for that hand?"

"I'll be fine. By the way, these are for you." Mayor Andy thrust his arm straight out.

"Thank you," Kat said awkwardly, noticing their sorry state. "Would you like a glass of something?"

"Wine?"

"Sure, I have some Cabernet." Kat turned and went into her kitchen, placing the remnants of the bouquet on the counter. Mayor Andy stood apprehensively in the den. "Take a seat, Andy," Kat suggested as she poured.

Dothan was nearing his destination. He paused several times, both due to the cramp in his side and to the fact that he had only been to Kat's apartment a couple of times. He'd never been good with directions in a car, but on foot, he was worse. *If I only knew her address. Maybe I should flag down a car. Of course, I haven't seen one fucking cop.* He debated whether to call 911. *What if I'm wrong? I'll look the fool. Nobody in their right mind would believe this. The Credo of the Day: better I die than embarrass myself by acting responsibly.* Just then, he spotted the Burger King. *I know where I am!*

Janet Morgan licked her dry lips and tasted salty blood. She opened her blurry eyes to disaster. From her worm's-eye view, the cluttered carpet resembled a surreal mountain range. As her vision tightened and her perception cleared, Janet understood she lay prostate on the floor of Mayor Andy's den. She reluctantly sat up and leaned against the stereo cabinet. Her head was killing her. She patted her hair and felt tiny shards of glass. She reached for her phone.

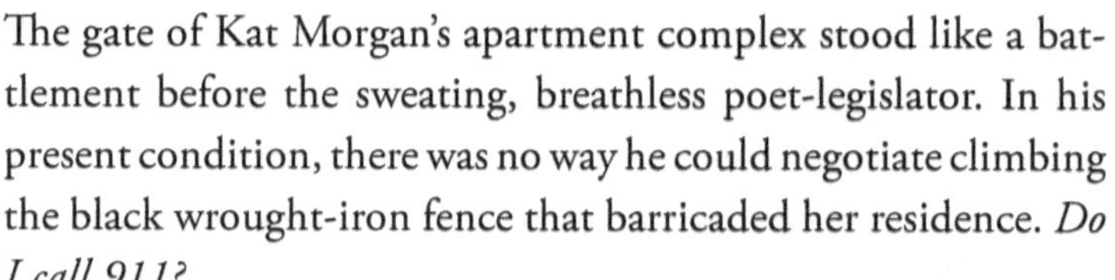

Kat laughed and laughed as Andy told her bizarre stories of his life while they sat together on her sofa. She thought he was being funny.

"Oh, Andy, you have such an imagination! Wouldn't it be great if we could just get rid of the people who get in our way?"

"Oh, but I do, Katherine. I really do!"

The gate of Kat Morgan's apartment complex stood like a battlement before the sweating, breathless poet-legislator. In his present condition, there was no way he could negotiate climbing the black wrought-iron fence that barricaded her residence. *Do I call 911?*

From the street, a car slowed and flashed a blinker to turn in.

"So, why don't you tell me why you wanted to see me at my apartment?" Kat sat up and placed her hands on her knees. "Oh, before I forget, I've had so many compliments on my hair." She cocked her head and pursed her lips in a sultry fashion. Kat heard her phone ring from the kitchen table.

"Are you going to answer that?"

"It can wait. So, what's up, Andy?" Kat wore a huge, expectant smile.

Andy patted his coat. He located the small box and removed it from the inside pocket.

"What's this?" Kat asked, confused. Her shoulders slumped

and her dark, wondrous eyebrows clenched.

"This is for you, Katherine." Mayor Andy lifted the top to reveal a beautiful gold ring with a ruby solitaire.

Kat felt a toxic weirdness take over the cool, pastel blue room. Her shoulders drew up, and her head went back. "It's beautiful, Andy, but what is it for?"

Andy stood up, and then immediately took a knee. He held out the ring in gallant fashion. "I want to spend the rest of my days with you. Will you be my wife, Katherine?"

Kat's phone pinged.

"Uh, is this a joke, Andy? I mean, I thought you were coming over to ask me to run a campaign for you or something."

Kat's phone rang again.

"It's not a joke. I'm in love with you. Oh, and let's forget 'Andy,' shall we? Just call me Henry…Katherine."

Kat got up in haste and went to the kitchen table. "What's with this 'Katherine' thing? I have to tell you, Andy, I'm a little freaked out. I'd like you to leave. Now." She looked at the missed calls. One call was from Dothan and the others were from her mother, as was the text. She tapped the screen and read the message.

Don't meet with Mayor Andy. Leave your apartment NOW!!!!!

Andy stood up from his failed proposal and stalked to the kitchen. "Who is that from?"

"What? Oh, no one. Look, I'm flattered. You really are a gentleman, Andy, but—"

"Call me Henry!" Mayor Andy screeched. Kat's face became fearful. Andy approached slowly with a look of total malevolence.

"I'm asking you to please go." Kat thumbed her phone in panic.

"You stupid women are all the same." He grabbed her

violently, clasped her tightly by the shoulders, and threw her across the kitchen into the den. Kat slammed against the wall and hit the floor. Her cell phone accompanied her. "Just like Annie…I mean, Anne…I mean," Mayor Andy grabbed his temples as if a beast were caged between his ears. "Why can't you love me?" He leaped atop Kat and began choking her.

A knock at the door caused him to loosen his stranglehold.

"Help me! Help me!" Kat's hoarse voice cracked.

Andy backhanded her in the jaw.

The door burst open. It was Dothan.

"You sick motherfucker!"

Andy charged.

Dothan brought his cane up, then brought it down on Andy's neck before the madman's weight and power sent Dothan flying into a corner of the room. The cane fell away. The men were stunned and lay like crumpled paper. Kat, still short of breath and dizzy, ascended. The toe of her shoe crashed into Andy's ribs. Dothan's bad leg was caught under Andy's torso, but his arms were free. With her foot, Kat nudged his cane within reach. Dothan punched the butt into Andy's face again and again and again. Blood spurted from beneath the eye. Mayor Andy was down.

Dothan pulled his leg from underneath him and managed to stand upright. He turned to the woman he thought he had loved… maybe still did. Both were in an indescribable place. Kat began to cry. They embraced. The cane fell to the floor.

It's been said that the strength of a madman is the strength of ten men. Andy, still down, felt the life of Frankenstein's monster in his left arm. Kat and Dothan stood embracing a few inches away. No words passed between them.

Dothan buried his face in her hair. The smell of spring

berries filled his nostrils.

Kat felt a slimy lock on her ankle. With a swift jerk, her leg was yanked back. Her shoulder hit Dothan in the groin as she fell to the floor. Her head thumped on the blue carpet. Dothan dropped to his knees in pain. Rising from the ashes, Andy sat on Kat's pelvis. He gripped her throat. Dothan, climbing out of his private agony, retrieved the cane and began beating Andy wildly. After several blows, Andy slid off Kat and collapsed unconscious.

Dothan fell to Kat's side. He ran his hand through her hair. A discolored ring coiled her beautiful, long neck. Dothan put his ear to her lips and nostrils. Faint warmth was evident. She panted then coughed. Her eyes opened.

"Oh, Jesus, you're alive," Dothan sighed.

Kat's chest heaved up and down dramatically. Her eyes were as big as a blood moon. He ran his arm under her thoracic, helped her up, and dragged her toward the wall. She sat, looking around lost.

"My God," she said.

"Do you think you're okay?"

She only nodded. Dothan found her phone. Thankfully, it was still intact. He dialed 911. After detailing the incident, he was growing impatient with the dispatcher. "No, ma'am, I won't stay on the line. You know what to do." Dothan hung up and got a glass of water for Kat. "Can you drink?"

"Yes, I think." He tilted her head back and brought the cup to her lips. Her swollen Adam's apple flexed.

The police arrived in less than ten minutes. Mayor Andy was still out. EMS arrived as Dothan finished briefing the police.

"Look, I need to get out of here. I left my truck on the Interstate."

"That was you?" an officer asked, accusingly.

"Yeah, sorry. I had a woman's life to save. I imagine you had it towed?"

"Yes." The officer pulled out a card and handed it to him. "Call this number to claim it."

"I just hope your dumbass tow truck driver didn't damage her. She's a classic, you know."

"I'm sure it's fine, sir."

Dothan was leaving when something came to him. He pulled out his wallet and removed a folded piece of paper. "Will you give this to her when she's fully cognizant?"

"What is it?" the officer asked.

"A poem."

"A poem?"

"Yeah, it's a series of ordered words that speak of one's soul."

Twenty-Four

Kat Morgan was sitting with Zane Rayne in her apartment. Kat was displeased by the fact that the cleaning company she'd hired to get the blood out of her carpet had done less than a satisfactory job.

"I mean look at that, Zane. Does that look like the stain was removed?" she complained, pointing to the spot where her attacker had bled profusely some weeks ago.

"You should complain online. Put them out of business."

"I'm not that malicious, Zane. I do think I'll call and insist they come back." Zane sat across from her with a blank look. Kat went to check her laundry that tumbled loudly from the utility. "It's uneven, dammit!" As she adjusted the saturated clump of fabrics, she remarked, "Jail agrees with you, by the way." Kat shut the washer lid and continued, "You've lost a little weight."

"That food is terrible in there," Zane replied. "I'm sure I'll gain it back in no time. House arrest wasn't much better. I had to depend on my dad for food, and he was put out."

Kat returned to her place at the table. "If I were you, I'd keep it off. As your campaign manager, I'm just saying. I'm sorry I didn't come see you after your release, I was just busy in the field."

"Well, let's talk about that. Like we discussed, if you want the job as my chief of staff, it's yours."

"I don't know, Zane. To tell you the truth, I'll have to think about it."

"What, what are you talking about? Don't tell me Kat Morgan has grown a conscience."

"Whatever. Look, I've been through a lot. John David saved my life and has gotten no credit for it. How do you think that makes me feel?"

"You got what you wanted. I got what I wanted. If it took my opponent to exonerate me, then that's fine by me."

"There's an irony or a paradox in that, I think. I'd have to ask your former opponent to clarify which it is. He's so good at that kind of stuff."

"You really fell for him, didn't you?"

"If I did, then he caught me. Just like he said he would."

"Well…" Zane rose to leave. "My offer stands, for now. But the legislature gavels in January. I need to know soon, Kat."

"You haven't learned a thing from all of this, have you?"

"About what?"

"About life and the way things work…right from wrong… Anything?"

"What I have learned is that the system works. An innocent man was set free to live his life."

"The system works if you have money."

"That's JD Dothan talking, Kat."

"Maybe once, but now it's me. I'll let you know."

"I hope they clean this carpet to your satisfaction," Zane sniped as he was leaving. The door boomed closed with definitive clarity. Kat sensed a burned bridge, but it was a bridge she didn't mind burning. There was one she now regretted, though.

Kat went to her bedroom. In her closet, set against a dark corner and veiled by hanging clothes, she had something hidden away. She scooted hangers to the side then bent down into the shadows and emerged with the mended shaft. She had coveted it, both out of vindictiveness and guilt. The two sides tugged at her constantly. It had been repaired the best it could be by one of her admirers, a local craftsman. It was slightly crooked where the two pieces had been screwed together and then glued, and had a sizable chip at the bottom.

She went to her kitchen and lay her trophy down on the table. She grabbed her purse off the back of the chair. From the depths of the fashionable handbag she pulled out a folded piece of paper. Kat slowly and methodically unfolded it, as if it were ancient. She had yet to read it. She just couldn't bring herself to know what it said. But it was time. After all, it was just a poem.

OUR TABLE

Under awning odd but humble,
Just an amble from my office,
Stands the Old Railroad Café.

In those May days that were brighter,
When we began, before the spleen,
Having never been, you wished to.

Against a century-old, orange
Wall high, adorned with Texana,
Together we made our table.

I always knew how to find it,
When we returned, the times we did:
Near the rusted climbing trellis.

It was always so natural
Sharing a meal, the two of us:
You: ordering plain; me picky.

Should you wish again to lunch there…
Rue the day, I know I will…
Should we find our table is taken.

The simplicity and honesty of it struck her. She fixed her large brown eyes on the object across her table. Kat understood that it was she who had shattered it.

Late fall sparkled clean in the platinum sky. Dothan crushed his cigarette out with the sole of his boot and spit on the butt, discarding the remains in the municipal waste basket that cuddled the corner sidewalk. Inside the district office it was nice *not* to hear the rattle of the air conditioner for once. He stared into the hallway and sensed the emptiness. He was not up to it, but there was much work to be done. He set about folding moving box after moving box.

A Man Alone, Frank Sinatra's recordings of the forgotten songwriter-poet, Rod McKuen, filled the DO. It had been a favorite of his late mother's. He had inherited her taste. Dothan began pulling books from the vast library in his office, setting the volumes on his desk so as to organize the safest possible transport. He looked up and noticed Sheriff Neilson and Lieutenant Young loitering at his threshold.

"Hey, fellas, come on in," Dothan offered.

"Sorry to barge in on you, Representative, but we thought we'd come by. We'd heard you were moving out, and we wanted to catch you before—" Neilson was cut off by his reluctant host.

"Before I resign myself to the ashbin of history?"

"I wouldn't say that."

"Then what would you say, Sheriff?"

"I'd say, tomorrow's another day, and who knows?"

"Maybe. How can I help the two of you?"

Neilson flashed a hand toward the available chairs that sat ever-faithful before the desk.

"Sure, y'all take a seat." Dothan remained standing, storing books.

"Representative—" Neilson started, but was interrupted again by Dothan.

"Like I've told you before, Sheriff, call me JD. Besides, as of midnight New Year's Day, that designation will cease to exist."

"Okay, JD. We came by to thank you."

"For what?"

Young spoke up, "Your assistance helped us find the real killer."

"He's innocent until proven guilty, not that anyone believes in due process anymore," Dothan said. "You're welcome, Lieutenant. Look, you didn't have to call in the 'big boys' for help. You're quite the hero now, as I understand. Oh, is what I've heard true? You're thinking of running for mayor?"

"We'll have to see about that. With Andy in the predicament he's in, I've been approached by interested parties."

"You mean people with money."

"Yes, sir."

"Life works its paradoxical circles and its angled ironies, as it has time immemorial."

"That sounds like the sayings of a poet, JD."

"Neilson, you may be the Sherlock Holmes you read about as a boy, after all," Dothan chided. "My actions promoted Young, here, and I demoted myself."

"I understand. I'm sorry about the election, JD."

"It's all right, Sheriff. I did what I came to do, even if it wasn't what I thought I came to do."

"Sounds poetic."

"Or maybe just pretense."

"Thank you, Representative...I mean, JD. We owe you a lot," Young said humbly.

"You're welcome, Lieutenant. Just do me a favor."

"What's that?"

"Don't go insane if the electorate grants you self-affirmation."

Neilson laughed, then added, "I second that."

"Back on topic, any news about Mayor Andy? Has he had a psychological evaluation of any sort?" Dothan asked.

"Funny you ask, JD. We got a white page on him yesterday," Young answered.

"Yeah, it was actually more than a page." Neilson added.

"So what of it?"

"Well, JD, according to the shrinks, Andy Adams suffers from ASPD," Young replied.

"What's that?"

"Anti-Social Personality Disorder."

"Which is the politically correct term for 'psychopath,'" Neilson inserted.

Young continued, "He also suffers from paranoid schizophrenia and multiple personality disorder, or whatever they call it now."

"Interesting," Dothan said.

"Maybe for you, JD, but it fucks up the prosecution for us. We don't think he's capable of standing trial," Young commented.

"Why couldn't he?"

"He's just been released from the hospital—after you worked him over pretty good," Young said.

"Shit, he worked me over pretty good," Dothan interjected.

"Right, but after his release from medical confinement, he's really gone bonkers. I mean, sometimes he'll only answer to 'Henry.' He has complete breaks with reality, and he has no memory now of either personality, be it his or the other," Young said.

"Insane…truly insane… It makes one wonder how something like this happens," Dothan said.

"Probably congenital, to a large degree—something triggered it," Neilson said.

"Any theories?" Dothan asked.

"Andy's an artist, or so I've been told by the shrinks. When he was younger, he was apparently some aspiring theater actor. It never went anywhere. I guess that traumatized him. Who knows?" Young mused.

"Well, as a failed artist myself, that still sounds insane," Dothan replied. "Personally, I think it's a symptom of the times."

"Oh?" Neilson asked.

"Expound," Young seconded.

"Think about it, gentlemen. We live in the age of 'look at me.' Everyone thinks they're a star these days. All they have to do is go on vacation and post it on social media. Shit, now their dinner has celebrity status. Then, here's Andy, and though I've never seen him act, I'll bet he's a genuine actor. So much so, that he got to the point where he became the character he was recreating."

"As a matter of fact, Andy played the lead in Shakespeare's *Henry VIII* in college," Young said.

"There you go," Dothan responded. "It was a passion turned obsession turned neurosis turned psychosis and so on."

"Shit, JD, that's more information than we've gotten from a team of shrinks," Young said.

"I told you, Young. The guy comes in handy!" Neilson exclaimed.

"Y'all are funny. Hey, what about the green truck?" Dothan asked.

"That turned out to be perfectly in line with the whole plot. Rayne Turf Works is apparently in financial trouble, which is why he wants to send his son into the legislature to maybe get a life in politics. Andy was brought in as a silent partner. According to Mike Rayne, Andy specified he wanted access to the barn and the trucks. Mike said he thought it was odd, but figured what the hell," Neilson said.

"Where does Andy get his money? I didn't realize he was that well off."

"He's heir to the Adams fortune over in Houston—real old money. First it was in oil, then they helped start the first major electrical company in the region. When they cashed out a few decades ago, they got even richer," the sheriff explained.

"Well, I'll be damned. This has all been very interesting, if nothing else. All I can say is, Andy may be a monster, but at least he's high culture. With average falling IQ, the next case will be a killer who thinks their Miley Cyrus," Dothan quipped.

"God help us!" Neilson laughed.

"If there is a God, Neilson."

"There is, JD."

"Sometimes, I hope you're right because if there's a God, that means there's the possibility of Hell. And I know a lot of people who…well gentlemen, I will leave it at that."

With law enforcement gone, Dothan returned to the task of packing books. Sinatra continued from the loft. The album was on repeat. Long, troubled thoughts subjugated his mind. The news report indicated that the stellar December day would end in a nasty norther. In the cell of his office, he was exiled from any view of the sky, so he had learned to read the outdoor light via the hallway. From where he stood, it appeared that the late afternoon sky had gone from blue to gray.

Dothan visited the restroom down the hall. When he emerged, he noticed someone lurking in the foyer.

"Hello?" he said as he checked his zipper to make sure it was up. The figure turned from staring out the front doors. "Mitch!"

"What's up, JD? You're not busy, are you?"

"Not for you. Come on back and take a seat. What've you got?"

Mitch Stevens followed Dothan back and grabbed a chair. Dothan did the same.

"I hope I'm not invading your space, JD. I just wanted to see you before you set out."

"How does everyone know I'm out of Dodge tomorrow?"

"I guess word gets around in a small town."

"Not such a small town anymore, Mitch."

"Old soldiers die hard, JD. You should know that."

"I do. I'll tell you truthfully, I'm going to miss this place. I never thought I would, but I already do."

"So, what are you going to do? By the way, I have to tell you, I'm sorry. The best man lost in this instance. I can't believe the electorate voted that brat in."

"Well, your paper didn't help my cause, Mitch. There was nary a word of my finding the true suspect…let alone saving the proverbial damsel in the tower."

"I know, but I just own the paper, JD. Other people make those decisions. You're right, though, they did a shoddy job reporting on your heroics."

"Heroics? That's a laugh."

"Either way, I am sorry. Where to now?"

"I don't know. Maybe I'll try to score a gig with the lobby. It's not like the campaign funds will pour in now that I'm a dead duck. I think the right lobby gig would work—it's just finding the right one. I'm not inclined to whore myself out for human sacrifice like a lot of those guys do. Actually, I'm more concerned about placing my staff, as they're about to be unemployed."

"A lobbyist, huh? I don't know if I can really see that, JD."

"Like my late old man used to say, 'everybody's gotta do something.'"

"Something tells me you'll find a way back into the fight."

"What fight is that? The way I see it, there are two distinct camps, and both don't have a fucking clue. It just doesn't work anymore, Mitch."

"What, in particular?"

"The country. No, I'm burnt out. I don't have anything left to give. I used to think that if I could find a good woman to love, that's all that mattered, but I guess I have a knack for fucking that up, too. You know, Mitch, men are simple—you feed us, you fuck us, treat us with some regard—it's simple. Men's hearts are not that complex, that's reserved for our brains, if we have any. Women…they're an age-old question."

"What do they want?" Mick asked.

"You give them everything they want, and then they decide

they don't want it."

"I've been married for twenty-two years, JD. Is my wife happy? I think so. But I guess you're right…you never know. It's the little things that kill a relationship. The big things are just the symptom, not the disease."

"All I can do is try to just not care. Period. Becoming angry and indifferent simultaneously makes for a potent alchemy. You have to stick with the latter because the former burns you up inside."

"You have every right to be angry about everything," Mitch said. "You got a raw deal. It's kind of tragic, really, but I'm sure you'll make something of it."

"I can't decide if it's a tragedy or a comedy. Sometimes I laugh. It depends on what mood I'm in, I suppose."

"Only sometimes?"

"I don't want to be rude, but I've got work to do Mitch. I want to be packed up by tonight."

"No problem. Like I said, I just wanted to see you off." Mitch rose and had made it as far as the foyer before turning around. "Say, when can I expect another book of poems?"

"Upon my death," Dothan replied, arranging his books.

"That's a bit dramatic, isn't it?"

"Dramatic, yes, but most certainly accurate," Dothan replied with a sly smirk.

"Ha ha, JD. I doubt that. By the way, do you have any plans for Christmas?"

"No, Tryphena and my daughter will be in East Texas. I'll probably visit Rachael Logan's grave," Dothan remarked with simultaneous sarcasm and sincerity.

"I see." Mitch made it to the front door. An impatient wind hit him as he pulled it open. Before leaving, he called out, "Cold front's coming in!"

Kat stepped out onto her second-story patio to check the temperature. It was getting colder. For once, the weatherman was right. A beautiful day would end otherwise. Gray clouds were gathering like buzzards over the yellowing grounds. She smoked a cigarette and went inside to grab her coat and something else from her kitchen table—something that did not belong to her.

With knots in her stomach, she made her way toward the Cultural District; her twisting insides felt similar to when she'd made her virgin trip months ago to the same destination. She would not call him for fear he would not answer. *Besides,* she worried, *what if tells me not to come?*

Dothan had started packing boxes into the cab of his truck. Wind bustled through the streets. Dead leaves, which had piled along the curb sides, were tossed about. At the end of the street, merchants hanging Christmas lights steadied their ladders. Books are heavy, and demand two arms. Without the assistance of his cane, his trips back and forth grew increasingly arduous. The cab would only fit so many boxes, and he was concerned it might rain. *Only room for one more, it looks like.*

The last box was heavier than the others, as it was loaded with antiquarian volumes, his most precious possessions. *I didn't think this through.* His balance was compromised as he headed down the long hall toward the rear entry. The back door was heavy, with no stopper. He placed the weighted cargo carefully on the carpet, pulled open the door, and stopped it with his numbing foot. He turned his head toward the exterior and saw the back end of Kat's car at the stop sign up ahead. She turned onto the cross street and parked catty-corner from his office.

He withdrew his foot and let the door shut. He locked it. Dothan rushed down the hallway quickly toward the foyer. From behind the glass, he spied her exiting her vehicle. The lock clicked, and he slipped into his office, closing the door behind him.

Knocking ensued. He did not rise to answer. It continued. Dothan had left the music playing and he wondered if perhaps she could hear it. The knocking grew louder…then it stopped.

He waited…and then waited a little longer.

After about fifteen minutes, he emerged and went to the foyer. He saw nothing outside but the intruding night. What light was left cast a shadow in the shape of a staff against the glass—a sea monster, not a dragon. He unfastened the door, which supported its length, and it sank into his hand. The Kraken, though compromised, was intact.

He closed up shop and turned off the lights. With renewed equilibrium, he walked the hallway and ascended the loft. Sinatra crooned, "Loves Been Good to Me"—the only reverberation in this, his solitary world.

Coda Act III

SINE
DIE

Other Novels by Matt Minor

The Representative

The District Manager

The Water Lord

A special thanks to...

Fred Hartman of the *Fort Bend Herald* and Harvey Kronberg and Scott Braddock at the *Quorum Report*.